THE
DALLAS
MERCENARY

M.E. Oren

River Lake Press

First published in Great Britain in 2011 by River Lake Press
(UK)

This paperback edition published in 2011

Copyright ©Michael E. Oren 2011

The right of Michael E. Oren to be identified as the author of
the work has been asserted by him in accordance with the
Copyrights, Designs and Patents Act 1988.

A CIP catalogue record for this book is available from the
British Library.

ISBN 978-0-9568870-0-9

This is for my father

PROLOGUE

The smoke immediately over the raging flames was haphazard, random, helter-skelter, dancing here then dancing there in the labyrinth of fluky wind. But in gradual stages further upstream, the smoke streamlined and organized into a series of swirling circular rings, which then intertwined to form a single gigantic mushroom-shaped dark cloud, and billowed up into the skies as one. The night was clear, but the streets, paths and alleyways were empty, and quiet. Only the bright shining full moon was left to police Mathary-Valley from any potential evils of the night, yet the dark smoke-bubble rings still snaked through the atmosphere derisively towards its intense glare. Somewhere near enough to the moon, the dark cloud stopped still, and lingered, as if taking one last snapshot view of The Valley – the miserable dump of makeshift shelters that housed more than a million people in a place no bigger than Manhattan's Central Park.

Beneath the strata of organised and disorganised smoke, the flames were ripping and tearing through anything in their path. And beneath the flames, was the remainder of what had been an old eroding part-brick, part-wooden building. It was a building that for more than five decades, had served this particular area in the East-End of Mathary-Valley as the local shop. And inside the building were people, human beings; a man, a woman and children.

At a safe distance from the blazing fire, and the smoke, eight men formed a ring round the shop. They had sealed off all the possible exits with layers of car tyres. Some tyres had been placed on the roof. The tyres had all been freshly soaked in petrol, with the surplus fuel being sprayed meticulously onto the remaining exposed wooden sections of the building. Finally, a burning log that had been pre-lit from relative safety had been lobbed over onto the target from about ten yards. The union of flame and fuel yielded a thunderous explosion. They heard the initial screams from within, but it was all soon muffled out by the storm of ravaging flames. The chances of escaping from within the shop alive were as good as walking on water, and they all knew that. Yet these men still thought it wise to surround the burning shop and vigilantly keep a watchful eye, just in case.

They were all armed with machetes.

At the time they set the building on fire, they knew the shopkeeper was in there, with his wife and three children. All eight of them knew him well, some of them well enough to call him a friend.

One of them served with the shopkeeper at the treasury of the local benevolent fund organisation. Two of them had sons who walked to and from school every day with the shopkeeper's eldest. A couple of them shared his ardent love of football, and they frequently spent long periods exchanging endless and often banal views on the game. One of them, for a small fee, helped him put away his deliveries every Tuesday. The other two were older, had known him since he was a boy, and had known his father before him.

Yet as they waited to make certain their victims were charred to ashes, none of them, not a single one of them, showed any sign of emotion. There was no regret, no sorrow, no grief, no anguish; not a single tear was shed.

They simply stood stock still, like a band of warriors, and waited for their friend to burn.

BOOK ONE
The Awakening

CHAPTER 1

In the United Kingdom, news of the violent clashes in Kenya initially broke on the BBC, four days after the first signs of trouble. It was a routine Third World war-story piece: there had been a general election, the overwhelming favourite from the opposition party somehow lost, and a lot of unhappy people took to the streets, vandalising anything they believed belonged to the government and their supporters. Individuals were being lynched, the police were clamping down brutally... and so on... and so on.

Howard Symmonds was slouching with both feet up on a glass coffee table on a chilly January Saturday morning when, as he flipped through channels, the news flashed over his plasma screen TV. It was pure chance: Mr. Symmonds was not a news and current affairs man; he had been looking for the latest on the test cricket match between South Africa and England. But when he heard this particular piece, he turned up the volume and sneaked a glance towards the far end of the living room and his daughter, Sally-Anne.

Last time he checked, she had been hurriedly digging a hairbrush through the back of her mane of platinum blonde hair. Her left hand was now swaying with the hairbrush in slow-motion, barely skimming the layers. Her lips automatically broadened into a smile, then parted slightly to let out a mirthless chuckle. It was Sally-Anne's standard gesture of shock. It was also her standard gesture of surprise, confusion, joy, anger, et cetera. She was a young woman blessed with a truly beautiful smile that seemed to have a mind of its own. It was a smile that offered a spontaneous reaction to almost everything, good or bad, and seemed to suppress all other facial expressions. There were variations to her smile, variations that revealed her true underlying emotion; but these were so slight they could not be detected by the naked eye. As a result, most people thought Sally-Anne was always smiling.

Howard Symmonds was not most people; he instantly identified her present expression as shock. And this was confirmed by the lengthy silence that descended upon the room following the news item. Sally-Anne never broke uncomfortable silences. She could sit there with her smile and say nothing all day if that is what it took. So Howard spoke first.

'Guess you won't be travelling to Kenya very soon then.'

A broad smile and a mirthless chuckle formed her automatic reply.

'It's dangerous, Sal, you don't need me to tell you that.'

'I wasn't exactly planning to go very soon, Dad.' After a brief pause, and with a slight shrug, she added, 'I can't afford it anyway.'

'Well, it's dangerous. I would say affordability is now a non-issue,' he muttered, shifting his feet off the coffee table.

'Sometimes the media exaggerates a little, I'm sure it isn't that bad.'

'Really?' he looked at her, then slowly turned back towards the screen, as if trying to pull her gaze in that direction. A lanky black man with dirty blue jeans and long afro hair was bouncing in front of a group of rowdy protestors. He was waving a long gleaming machete at the camera, miming the act of sharpening its blade against the tarmac, followed by a slashing motion around his throat. A loud explosion somewhere in the foreground sent the crowd into a frenzied stampede that was quickly swallowed in the thick dark smoke.

Mr. Symmonds stared back at her daughter. 'I guess you could be right. Maybe it's not that bad.'

This time her chuckle caused a slight heave in her upper body: what appeared to be a smile on her face was in fact a sneer.

'Maybe this is just one big set-up. A conspiracy by the BBC to stop Sally-Anne going to Kenya.' His gaze was once again on the screen. 'Maybe what we are watching is nothing but a group of actors on set down the road in Elstree.'

'You pick your moments to impress with your sarcasm, Dad, you really do,' she said. 'But I suppose it's easier when you are perched comfortably on your leather sofa enjoying a cosy weekend TV in London.'

'It's not my fault, I was born here.'

'Lucky you.'

'Sal, I know you are a bit sensitive about Africa, but you know it's always going to be like this. You went there when things were good, and had a great time, and you should be grateful to God for that. But Africa will always be Africa; it has been proved that none of these countries can sustain a significant period of stability. A lot of well-meaning people have tried to help and failed. This was always coming; it doesn't have to be anyone's fault.'

'Well, now that you explain it so philosophically, I have to say I'm beginning to get it.'

'Perhaps the only solution for these people would be to take away all their uncorrupted babies under the age of one and drop a nuclear bomb on the rest of their tainted population. We could bring the kids up here, teach them our ways and send them back to start a whole new, pure civilisation.'

'Jeez, you are on a roll, Dad. Hitler will be clapping in his grave.'

'I was just saying...' He shrugged. 'It sounds extreme, but it's an idea...'

Sally-Anne's arms went to her hips and she tilted her head towards him with a grim smile that hinted at how close she was to being drawn into a venomous verbal slugfest with her father. But she reined her feelings in at the last moment and decided to walk away, not because she was being the bigger person, but because she was in a rush.

'I've heard enough of this,' she said, raising both palms and holding the hairbrush loosely with her right thumb in mock-surrender. 'I'm out of here.'

She grabbed her handbag from the dinner table, replacing it with the hairbrush, and dashed out of the room and then the house.

*

As Sally-Anne drove her small silver hatch-back through the north London suburbs, the news was still sinking in. Two years before, as part of her Engineering degree, her class had travelled to Nairobi to work on a section of a huge wind-turbine project to aid the electricity supply to a small part of Mathary Valley, one of the biggest slums in Africa. Her dad had been dead against it. His general apprehension towards that part of the world was taken as read, but her going to work in one of the biggest slums in Africa for a whole two weeks was absolutely unthinkable. On the other hand, his daughter viewed it as the opportunity of a lifetime, and was not prepared to miss it for anything. They had words, and then more words, before they began negotiating. He tried to get anyone who was anyone to talk her out of it. She gathered just about everyone who had ever been to any part of Africa to assure her sixty-seven-year-old father that she was not going to be eaten by a lion, or catch

HIV, or get kidnapped, or be sold as a slave... He had been the first to concede ground in the negotiations. After consulting with his so called Africa-experts, he walked into her bedroom one evening, with a small piece of paper in hand, and, as if announcing results a of a crucial contest, he read out:

'OK... South-Africa, yes! Egypt, yes! Tunisia, yes! Zimbabwe, yes! Kenya... No!' He stared at Sally-Anne, who was sprawled on the bed in her nightclothes pretending not to listen. 'Sal, did you know they share a border with Somalia...? Do you know how dangerous the Somalis are?'

'Who is feeding you this crap, Dad? The border with Somalia is thousands of miles away from Nairobi and no one even lives there. And, Zimbabwe, *yes*? *Zi-mba-bwe...*? Are you serious? Do you know how dire that country is? Do you even know what's going on in Zimbabwe right now?'

'They've got a decent cricket team. The England boys tour there regularly.'

'Well, here's the deal, Dad, this is a university project – voluntary, but it would help with my experience. And it's not in South Africa or Egypt or Zimbabwe. It is in *Kenya*.'

In the end it had been the old man who conceded.

Sally-Anne had a great time in Africa. A significant part of the group even ended up extending their stay by an extra two weeks when they discovered the beach holiday resort of Mombasa on the coast. By then, her nightly phone calls back home had done wonders to allay her dad's fears; the mere fact that it was possible to make a phone call from Africa did half the job.

She had a wonderful time. She made some friends, and promised to keep in touch and come back that very summer on a proper, planned holiday. It was the sort of promise people make under the influence of party euphoria. The locals had been kind to them. They taught them their ways, wined and dined them. They attended traditional festivals and parties, and danced and sang along in languages they had never heard before.

Their long train journey to Mombasa gifted them magnificent scenes of vast, raw, uncorrupted jungles and numerous species of wildlife in their natural habitat. They were also very lucky to witness one of the natural world's most spectacular phenomena: an endless herd of animals on the move, the 'Wildebeest Migration', millions of wildebeests, zebras and gazelles all marching as one in remarkable synchronised motion. The students were informed that the animals were migrating north in search of rain, and that this was an annual event. In fact, they were told, The Wildebeest Migration was now considered one of the Seven Wonders of the World.

When they got to the coastal resort, the change of scenery was sudden and dramatic. The place was filled with white tourists lounging around along the beaches sipping coconut juice like they owned the world. If she hadn't known better, Sally-Anne would never have guessed they were still in Africa. It was a country of extremes – and she enjoyed both sides.

In the end, she had to promise to come back. Then she got back to England and her usual high-speed London life soon caught up with her. Her plan to return to Kenya at Christmas was soon rescheduled for the following summer, and then changed again to *maybe* in the short spring break, which soon became the next summer and the summer after that.

Her contacts with her so-called new friends suffered a similar gradual demise; not an unusual fate to befall a twenty-three-year-old girl working hard to make it in London. She still planned to go back, but she had things to do, people to see... the usual.

But now that news was emerging of possible instability in Kenya, she felt a new twinge of guilt for not honouring her promises.

She tried hard not to allow herself to be too worried by the news, as she cruised down a relatively quiet North Circular – the great ring-road that circumvents the inner boroughs of London – to meet two of her friends for lunch. This was not something for her to worry about, just some news that brought back nostalgic memories of a great time. The media always tended to exaggerate the negatives in Africa anyway. They had just had a general election, and it may well just have been a few demonstrations that got heated and led to some chaos here and there. She made a mental note to try and contact one or two of her friends back there some time that weekend. Memories of her friend J'Alex were creeping back into her mind, and they triggered a gleeful smile. She had promised to keep in touch with him, and she did for a while, then she stopped. But she never forgot.

*

The project had been based in the eastern end of Mathary Valley, which the students had been led to understand was in fact the better end of the massive slum, and which most folks never really considered part of Mathary Valley at all. The immediate vicinity of the wind-turbine site was characterised by somewhat modern and well-organised brick houses. But down below, further emphasised by the viewpoint at the top end of the slope, there was no hiding the unkempt sea of mud-walled, tin-roofed structures. They formed the beginning of an abyss of chaotic life endured by almost a third of the population of the seemingly magnificent city.

A group of small boys who appeared to be anything around five to twelve years-old had taken to coming over to the site to watch the white foreigners at work. It happened to be their school holidays and they were around almost every day for the entire two weeks. They would stand around watching and smiling till they got bored, then they would figure out a game to play for a while, thus alternating between watching and playing around the site. They were always happy and giggled a lot during any conversation the white people attempted with them. They giggled timidly when Sally-Anne told them she was from England, and laughed loudly when she revealed her name. She assured them there was nothing wrong with the name Sally-Anne, and that it was indeed quite popular in England.

They laughed. And she laughed with them.

One day at the beginning of their second week, Guy, one of Sally-Anne's project colleagues, got slightly overwhelmed by the heat and had to leave early to go back to their hotel in the city centre. She gave him a goodbye peck on the cheek, which three of the boys who had been lurking around apparently took for a romantic kiss. And they all giggled an exited chorus of "*Uuuh... huuuh.*"

'Your boyfriend?' asked one of them.

'Noooo way,' she answered, shaking her head playfully. 'You are my only boyfriend.' She pointed at the tallest boy in the middle of the group, the one with striking brown eyes who had asked the question.

They laughed.

At which point a text message alert beeped on her mobile phone, and she got it out of her blue overcoat pocket to read a message from her dad back in England.

'What's your phone number?' giggled her new boyfriend.

'Oooh, so you're planning to give me a call later, huh?' she whispered very slowly, punctuating with a playful nod *the* smile, and finally a cheeky wink for the little brown-eyed cutie. Then she went ahead to recite the eleven digits of her phone number to the confused but very happy trio.

'Can you repeat it?' Her new boyfriend seemed to be taking this seriously.

Sally-Anne smiled and repeated the number slowly. 'Do you want me to repeat it again?' She was now addressing her man. 'And you promise you are definitely gonna call me and take me out on a date?'

'Yesss,' they all replied.

'OK, repeat after me...' and she made them recite the eleven digits with her, like a nursery rhyme, before a fourth boy arrived with a homemade football and they all ran off for a kickabout.

The next morning her new boyfriend arrived with two different friends.

'You never called me,' she said.

He giggled coyly.

'What's your name?'

'J'Alex,' he said, then proceeded to elaborate. 'It's one word, letter J with apostrophe and Alex,' and he enunciated articulately: 'Jay Alex.'

The boy seemed very smart, maybe a bit older than she had first presumed. He was slightly taller and broader than his friends, but his facial features were considerably feminine; milk-chocolate skin, high cheekbones, full red lips and milk-white teeth. In direct sunlight, his brown eyes turned hazel. He was a beautiful boy.

'Huh...? Beautiful name, how old are you, J'Alex?'

He said he was *nearly* eleven. Meaning: *I'm ten, but don't let that come between us...*

She proceeded to ask the other two boys the same questions, before they cunningly used the arrival of another friend to make their escape.

At the end of that day, she spotted J'Alex again. 'Are you gonna call me tonight, my boyfriend?' she asked him.

'Yes,' he giggled.

'I will be waiting, don't let me down,' she joked. 'You have my number.'

'Yes,' he said. And then, very excitedly, he went on to recite the eleven digits of her mobile phone number. Accurately.

She stared at him with her broad, slightly-parted-lips smile: amazed. Then she turned to some of the other members of the engineering team who had been listening and were now looking at her quizzically.

'Oh my God can you believe this? That was absolutely spot-on!' she said. 'I jokingly told him my number yesterday, maybe two or three times, and he remembered it.'

They were impressed. He was proud.

'We have to remember a lot of things in school, I was number one in my class.' J'Alex was now addressing the whole group.

The foreigners were still sceptical, so they decided to test him. Guy told him his own number, reciting it only once, but slowly, then asked them to race each other round the block and come back with the memorised number. J'Alex not only won the race, he also delivered the number effortlessly.

Sally-Anne then produced her credit card, handed it to him and gave him not much more than two minutes to study the sixteen-digit number, and then asked him to remember it for the next day.

The following day, J'Alex repeated not only the sixteen-digit number, but every single detail on the card, including her full name, the start and expiry dates, sort code, security code... everything.

The group that had gathered around for this little show cooed in amazement.

Guy made the first comment. 'This kid's a genius.'

'Sal, you do realise he can now go internet shopping on your credit card, don't you?' Thomas, another of the engineers, pointed this out and everyone laughed in agreement. 'Seriously, think about it, he knows all the details you need to use your card. In theory, there's nothing to stop him.' Thomas pressed his point.

But Guy thought there was a flaw in Thomas's theory. 'He would need her address to do that, wouldn't he?' he asked.

'Not necessarily. But at this rate I wouldn't be surprised if he knew Sally-Anne's address before the end of the week anyway.'

'It's alright, J'Alex is a good boy. He wouldn't do anything like that, would you?' she said, patting him on the back.

J'Alex looked a little confused, but shook his head anyway.

It was getting late, and the other boys, apparently unimpressed by J'Alex's exploits, had now disappeared. During the week they had spent at the site, Sally-Anne had learnt that the kids around here enjoyed a level of independence that bordered on sheer negligence. No one appeared to care where they were or how late they stayed out, even the very young ones. So that evening, Sally-Anne decided to probe a little: she wanted to know where J'Alex lived, how he got to the site every day, and whether his parents were ever mad at him for staying out that late.

In reply he reminded her that he was *almost* eleven and left it at that.

She offered to walk him home that evening, and invited the entire crew to tag along, if only to continue marvelling at the little boy's ingenuity. He happened to live no more than a half a mile from the site, near the bottom of the slope at the eastern end of Mathary Valley.

It was the beginning of a great friendship. In the next few days the entire crew of engineering students got to meet J'Alex's family and their friends. At the tender age of ten, the boy was already a man of the people; if you knew J'Alex you knew everyone and everything. He knew the places to go and those to avoid. He knew where all the good parties were, and had an extraordinary ability to make things happen. The ten-year-old genius guided the students to the core of the rich indigenous culture, and they got to enjoy the things they had been in danger of leaving Kenya without ever truly appreciating.

However, thanks in most part to her colleagues, Sally-Anne remained a bit uneasy about the credit card situation. They advised that she change her card: even though the boy seemed so sweet, innocent and harmless, she could never be sure who he might confide in, long after they were back in England.

She spoke to J'Alex about it, explained to him that she trusted him and that if anyone attempted to use her card in Kenya, her bankers in England would check with her first. Not only would it be a fruitless attempt to steal, but she would also know that it was he who had disclosed her details to someone. And she would be very upset. So upset that she might reconsider coming back to take him on a promised visit to England.

That seemed to work – seemed to. And the boy seemed so honest and likeable, she suspected she would lose her faith in humanity if he ever did betray her.

*

In the past two years, the affair had almost slipped her mind. In her heart she knew she had meant all her promises to her new friends in Kenya: to keep in touch, to return soon, to bring gifts, and one day to take J'Alex on a plane to the great place known as the United Kingdom. She had meant it all; it was just taking longer than expected. But now she felt like she had failed a lot of good people miserably. Even her remote fears about J'Alex somehow attempting a scam using her credit card turned into overwhelming guilt; how could she have suspected such an innocent little boy?

The following evening, after prowling the internet and trying to talk to half interested friends and family about what was going on in Kenya, she decided to buy one of the cheap international calling cards she had used before to contact her Kenyan friends. She tried what until then she believed was J'Alex's dad's mobile number. It failed to connect. She tried a few more times before she gave up. It had been a long time, perhaps the number had changed. She looked through the numbers in her old diary again, and zeroed in on the name Josiah.

Josiah was a very friendly man at the Imperial Hotel in Nairobi who had insisted he was the hotel manager even though there happened to be another and more credible hotel manager. She was a bit nervous about talking to Josiah because this was a man who had professed undying love for her. That was before she invented a husband and child back in England and he moved on to her stick-thin former friend Chloe, making the exact same confession of undying love to her.

Josiah's phone rang only three times before his deep rasping voice came blaring through the earpiece. It took him a while to place Sally-Anne, but the line was clear and his voice exuded calm nonchalance. It was not the distressed, static-filled voice of a man fighting for his life from a remote African bunker, and Sally-Anne found this oddly comforting.

'Hey Sal! What a wonderful surprise!' he beamed after Sally-Anne's third attempt to introduce herself. He then got straight to the point. 'Are you coming back to visit us?'

'Well Josiah, I would love to visit soon, but I'm hearing news that there are some problems back there.'

'Oh well... there's been some problems with the general election. But you can still come as long as you stay away from places like Mathary Valley. That's where the serious chaos is.'

'How bad is it? Are people still travelling into the country... are the tourists at your hotel having to leave?'

'Oh, well, some people are still here... few are leaving. But there's been no directive from foreign embassies for their citizens to leave. They are just warning them to avoid certain areas.'

'Josiah, say if I was to tell you now that I'm on my way to Kenya, what advice would you give me?'

'Oh, well... you can come... or maybe I'd say wait a few days and see how it is. You know the world is sending their best here to mediate negotiations between the two leaders, so you could wait and see. But you can come if you want, my hotel is very safe, I have a lot of British tourists here and they are fine. By the way, I'm not at Imperial anymore. I work at Intercontinental now, one of the best hotels in Kenya. If you come here, I can get you good discounts...'

And on and on he went.

In the end she did not feel Josiah had given her anything of much significance. It was just *Oh well, this... oh well, that...* Besides which, who would vouch for the credibility of a man who, in barely ten minutes of conversation, had come up with no fewer than five cunning hints about her leaving her husband, and hadn't once mentioned the baby?

It was nice talking to someone in Kenya, but she would have loved to talk to J'Alex. She tried J'Alex's phone once again with no luck, then checked how much airtime she still had left on the £5 pre-paid card. Fifteen minutes available for a call to Kenya. She tried the number again, promising herself it would be her final try, and again there was no success.

'Oh, well,' she mumbled, mimicking Josiah as she tossed the calling card in the rubbish bin. She had had her moment of nostalgia. Maybe she would write J'Alex a letter or send him a postcard or something. She had figured that whilst she had kept all their contact details, they probably didn't have any of hers anymore. She had been wary about giving them her address, and she had changed her phone number since her time in Kenya. So the onus lay with her to re-establish contact. She would do something.

But even as the thought crossed her mind, she realised that that would probably not happen for a long time.

CHAPTER 2

Just as Sally-Anne thought she had put the 'Kenya issue' back into hibernation, it became apparent that the theme did not want to be shoved aside just yet.

On that Monday morning she was held up in traffic for an extra half hour by a group of demonstrators in Oxford Circus. On closer inspection she saw placards saying 'KIBAKI MUST GO!' Then, as she finally edged past, she noticed that some of them were waving Kenyan flags and that they were protesting outside the Kenyan High Commission.

When she got to her temporary, and vaguely titled, *office junior*'s job in central London, the young unkempt warehouse manager who had come to hand over some admin papers pulled up a chair next to her and said:

'Shame what's happening in Kenya, innit? Good country.'

This was the last person she expected to be aware that a world existed outside England.

Kenya seemed to be following her everywhere. There was the cleaning lady who wondered whether she would have to cancel her safari, the chef at the canteen who she had never known was Kenyan, her father's long time favourite teabags whose packet's smallprint suddenly lit up to reveal their Kenyan origin every time she opened her kitchen cupboard. And then there was the media and their increasingly frequent features on

Kenya. Everything positive about the country they mentioned in the past tense:

... Kenya had been one of the strongest countries in Africa with a healthily growing economy... what is happening in Kenya could affect most of Africa... a country that had been seen as a beacon of hope in Africa... a country that had had a great tourism reputation...

Where were all these people when she was trying to convince her dad the first time round that Kenya was actually a country with people in it? She had spent years preaching the beauties of this place to people she thought wouldn't care less. Now that things had gone wrong, they were all coming out of the woodwork to declare that they had been with her all along on this – until now of course.

The *Kenya issue* was beginning to take more of her attention than she was comfortable with. It was becoming a leech, sucking on her valuable time. Sometimes, just as she would be winding up her work on the computer she'd sneakily look up "Kenya News" online, then end up spending a good couple of hours imagining what it was like up there at that moment in time. She would wonder if J'Alex was alright, that beautiful intelligent boy whose brown eyes bore nothing but innocent sincerity, but who also had a sly, cheeky side. She could imagine him being a very popular person in London. He had dreams of coming to the UK, and she had promised to make them come true one day. She hoped he was alright while trying to shake the whole idea off as a silly game. But of course he was alright: they had said the problem was affecting less than two per cent of the country, and most of it was in the Rift Valley province, hundreds of miles away from Nairobi.

Then again, why was the trouble receiving so much press? she wondered, as she once again quietly resolved to stop this time-wasting habit of dwelling on the *Kenya issue*.

And she did, until Wednesday evening, when the phone call came.

She had just got in from a long, unpleasant day at work. Her dad was picking up the ringing phone as she stepped into the living room and slumped onto the settee. She heard him mention her name, and quickly made an open-hands gesture to ask who it was that wanted to talk to her.

'Sorry, may I ask who this is?' her dad said, then covered the mouth-piece and relayed the answer back to her. It was someone from Barclays Bank. She quickly made another hand gesture indicating that she did not wish to speak to them. She was not interested in the latest competitive mortgage rates, or the new online banking facilities, or their generous overdraft offers.

'I'm afraid she isn't in at the moment,' her dad politely lied. 'May I take a message?'

He listened for a few seconds, then took a deep breath, and – clearly for Sally-Anne's benefit – he repeated what whoever was on the other end was saying:

'... has she travelled to Kenya recently...?'

Her dad was staring straight at her as he hit the speaker button to let her in on the conversion.

Sally-Anne's first reaction was to shift forward to the edge of her seat. Then, staring straight back at her dad, her lips broadened into a smile through which a quick chuckle escaped, and she began to frantically wave her hands for him to pass her the phone.

'Oh... she has just walked in now. Let me hand you over,' he lied again as she snatched the phone from his hands.

'Hi, Miss Symmonds, my name's Murray from Barclays Bank.' Murray had a Scottish accent but was fairly clear and polite. 'We called regarding a couple of suspected fraudulent transactions attempted using your card details in Kenya. First of all may I ask if you have been anywhere near that part of the world recently?'

'No, I haven't.'

'Well, I have in front of me two copies of suspicious-transaction reports sent by two separate internet retailers, and they both involve your card. The person got your card details correctly but seemingly not your address. In fact this appears very strange because they did not try to put on an address at all.

On the address line they have left some kind of message. It almost looks like someone is trying some bizarre kind of communication with you. But of course we have to treat it as a scam, which it probably is. The good news is that nothing has been taken from your account, so we can cancel the card straightaway and issue a–'

'Hold on a minute,' Sally-Anne interrupted. It sounded like Murray was going to go on forever. 'Did you say there's some kind of message on the address line?'

'Yes. We can fax copies of the attempted order sheets to your local branch–'

'What does the note say?' She was getting overwhelmed with anxiety. She saw her dad was on the edge of his seat too, listening on the speaker.

She heard Mr. Murray ruffle through some papers, then softly say:

'Ok... in both cases the address line contains these words: "NOT TRYING TO BUY ANYTHING. PLEASE TELL CARD OWNER IT IS J'ALEX. PLEASE HELP. I HAVE GOT NO ONE."'

Her grip on the phone tightened, and she realised she was shaking. It had been coming all week: there had been something in the air warning her that whatever was going on in Kenya could at any moment stop being merely endless features on TV, and turn real for Sally-Anne Symmonds.

'Hello...? Miss Symmonds, are you still there?'

'Yes, I'm here.'

But she wasn't, she was thousands of miles away in the violent Kenyan streets. And for some reason she was now seeing images of a young, petite, female CNN journalist called Holly, or something similar, who seemed to report from the deadliest of war zones in the Middle East. She had always wondered whether it was really necessary for little Holly and her crew to be standing on the streets of Palestine with rockets and bullets skimming their heads, all just to tell people that there was some *heavy gunfire* in Palestine. Surely, you could tell people about heavy violence in the Middle East from your *kitchen* and they would believe you. But here she now was, imagining herself in the streets of Kenya, just like little Holly, with bombs, rockets and gunfire blasting left right and centre.

Murray's Scottish brogue was still buzzing from somewhere in the background.

'Helloo... Miss Symonds... you there...?'

She mumbled something in reply without breaking her train of thought. She wanted to help J'Alex, but as yet she had no idea how to. Of course it was not possible for her to go to Kenya. Along with the obvious fact that little Holly from CNN was paid to do it, the woman probably also had bodyguards and all kind of protective body-armour around her.

Long after she had profusely thanked a very baffled Murray and assured him that there was no need to cancel her card, she sat on the edge of the settee with the dead phone in her hand and a confused smile playing on her lips.

'Sal, you cannot possibly be thinking about this?' Her dad broke the silence. 'OK, there is a chance that was him, but there's nothing you can do–'

'It *is* him, Dad.' She cut him short and realised from her shaking lips that she was crying.

'There is nothing we can do, Sal, you can't possibly go there to help him.'

Of course not, she thought as she grabbed a tissue, blew her nose and wept a bit more. Of course there was no question of her going to Kenya. But if she did, she knew she would never forgive little Holly from CNN.

CHAPTER 3

Very early the following Tuesday, Sally-Anne landed at Jommo Kenyatta international airport in Nairobi. It had taken her three long days to decide. She had sought advice from everyone: the British foreign office, the Kenya High Commission, the internet, the media, family, friends... even Josiah. In the end, however, the decision was hers. And once she had made it, she had to move quickly. Because she knew that every passing second after that would present an opportunity to reconsider. And suddenly here she was. There was no going back now.

Sally-Anne had arrived with her life savings and a hastily thought-out plan that she fully understood could fall apart at any point. Nonetheless, in the circumstances, it was her best. She was doing her best, and that was all that mattered.

She would stay at the Imperial again. She had found out that the hotel happened to be just a few blocks away from the British High Commission, where she had been promised some help.

The checkout from the airport was surprisingly swift and hassle-free. All her luggage arrived promptly and un-tampered with, and there were no uniformed personnel standing over them with some flimsy inquiry about the contents while secretly soliciting bribes to hasten the process. This had to be a good sign. In a country where everything was supposedly unravelling, she had to appreciate any small thing that went to plan.

The taxi ride to her hotel revealed a heavy police presence on the streets, but she did not witness any demonstrations or burning buildings along the way. The taxi driver was a wiry, middle-aged man with a bushy beard. He wondered if Sally-Anne was a foreign government official and whether she was here because of the crisis. She merely said yes to the latter: her desire to elaborate was lacking.

'It's a shame,' said the taxi man.

'It is indeed.'

'He did not win the election. Everyone knows it.'

She didn't care.

But she kept that to herself, and simply smiled at the man.

*

By the time Sally-Anne got to her hotel, there was barely enough time for a quick shower and change of clothes before she was due for her first appointment at the British High Commission.

She kept the same taxi for the short drive up Upper Hill Road to the High-Commission building, which surmounted the crest of the street. It was a detached building that, even from the peripheries, exuded grandeur; it nestled within green woodlands with a high, stylish marble wall all round, like a mini-stadium. Locals holding files and parcels queued along the perimeter, presumably in search of visas to the UK. She walked straight past them to the main entrance and informed the tired-looking security guard that she had an appointment.

'British?' he asked.

'Yes,' she answered waving her passport.

He took it, flipped through it, then pointed to the entrance of the white building towards which the visa-seeking locals seemed to be heading.

The inside was reminiscent of most government departments in England, with several peevish-looking individuals waiting their turn on long, back-to-back metallic benches – a scene not dissimilar to a typical waiting room in the UK's hospitals, social services or revenue departments. The immigration agents were lined up behind their glass-partitioned booths like bank cashiers. A pale, red-haired woman who had been floating all over the place led Sally-Anne to a cubicle where her contact was waiting.

The lady she was meeting was maybe mid-to-late forties with a long face and short blonde hair. She went by the name of Mariah O'Sullivan and spoke with a slight Irish accent. After listening intently to Sally-Anne's story, she allowed a few seconds of thoughtful silence. Then she began by expressing how touched she was by Sally-Anne's mission, and wished her luck before proceeding to explain how they could help. She kept it simple: as a British citizen in Kenya, they could offer her some guidance on how to go about her business in the country safely and without breaking the law. If she did find the boy, Mrs. O'Sullivan stated that taking him back to the UK with her would be a very complicated issue which probably did not need to be raised just yet – it could wait until she found him.

Sally-Anne thought she detected more than a hint of empathy in the statement, which she considered unnecessary, unless this woman suspected that she might not find the boy. Or maybe she was imagining things: she had just travelled a long way on nothing but a whim... she had done a very stupid thing, and Mrs. O'Sullivan was just being nice.

She offered her some useful contact details for what they deemed essential for her business in the country; she even managed to arrange a same-day appointment with one of the senior officials with the Tourism Police Unit at the Kenya Police headquarters.

*

The same taxi driver threaded her through the afternoon grid-lock of Nairobi traffic to Harambee Avenue where the police base was located in a tightly secured high-rise building, aptly named Vigilance House. There were flags either side of the entrance; on the left was the Kenyan flag, and the other, a plain blue one with a white emblem in the middle, and the words '*Service to all*'. Sally-Anne figured it was the Kenya Police flag. Upon identifying herself, she was swiftly ushered through, bypassing the cumbersome security. They had been expecting her.

It was when she was finally sitting across the desk from a Chief Inspector Kenneth Limo that the monumental gravity of what she had got herself into began to emerge.

'My dear young madam,' said the inspector after carefully listening to her story, 'do you realise you have just travelled to Kenya at a very, very bad time?'

She answered with a smile.

'You have ignored the warnings of both your and my governments and travelled alone to a country on the brink of civil war.'

'I'm aware of the situation sir, but I want to find my friend.'

'OK, let's say we find this boy, what are you going to do with him? Take him out of the country? What is he now, a refugee?' Despite what he was saying, the inspector sounded quite friendly. 'What is the nature of your relationship with him anyway?'

'He is a friend.'

'A friend. Nothing more...?'

'Nothing more, sir. He is twelve.'

'I did not mean that,' he said, returning her smile. 'I meant are you his sponsor or anything like that?'

'No sir, just a friend.'

'Ok. I will take some details from you and we will do what we can,' he said, swivelling round in his leather computer-chair for the pen and notepad that were lying neatly next to the white telephone. Chief Inspector Limo was heavyset with a slight pot-belly, and even though he had not got off his chair she could tell he was of average height. 'But I have to warn you, my dear, that even without the current skirmishes, Mathary Valley is a place we would strongly advise against visiting.'

'I have been there before, sir. It was not that bad.'

'So you say, dear. But you were doing charity work and you were based at the eastern end. Close enough to the real Mathary Valley – within sight and maybe even within smelling distance. But that, my dear, is *not* Mathary Valley. And it would be best if we agreed now that this time you will be staying as far away from there as possible.'

'So how will you manage that? Send your officers over there to bring him to me?'

'Sort of... The thing is, in the current climate, not even my officers are safe in that area. I would be putting their lives at great risk. I can only think of one man right now who could claim to be safe around Mathary Valley. I will use him.'

'How about if I accompany him?' she asked.

'What!'

'I'm just thinking it would be rather inappropriate – and a bit of a shock – for them to barge into the Gitongas' house saying a friend from England wants to see them at her hotel. It would help if I go with them.'

He stared at her in disbelief.

'You want to go to Mathary Valley? My dear, are you out of your mind?'

'You said your man would be safe there, so I should be alright if I accompanied him there, shouldn't I?'

The chief shifted his weight again to recline further back against the comfort of the shiny black leather. His gaze was directed at her, but he was clearly lost in thought, tapping his pen on the edge of the desk as he weighed up his options. He thought for the best part of half a minute; and she could tell he was seeing some sense in her idea.

He neither agreed nor refused her request. As if his handling of the situation was being secretly assessed by some figure of higher authority, he went on to make great play of repudiating himself of all responsibility for any consequences: if Sally-Anne decided to go to Mathary Valley, with or without his men, she would be doing so at her own risk. She had been warned, served the standard official advice, like all tourists. It was very important to Chief Inspector Limo that Sally-Anne understood this, and he repeated it a few times, rephrasing accordingly. For a minute she thought he was going to make her swear an oath and sign an official document. Eventually, though, he promised to send his man over to pick her up from her hotel when they were ready to go to Mathary Valley.

BOOK TWO
Yesterday and Today

CHAPTER 4

Yesterday

A twelve-year-old boy arrived in the city – the streets of the city. He had a small travel suitcase containing a bundle of rags, and not much else. On his young head he carried the pragmatism of a man several decades older. He was not a dreamer. He had hopes, but kept them realistic; he had just arrived with nothing in a city in which he knew no one at all, hundreds of miles from home. Ending up in the streets, at least initially, was something he fully expected. With time he hoped that would change. He would get a job, any job: construction, cleaning, food-service... anything. He was a young man, not scared of breaking his back working. This, he believed, would make the difference between him and other street boys. He had no ambitions further than hotel waiting, but he was not staying in the streets forever. That he promised himself.

He encountered his first hurdle right away, and it was an unexpected one: the streets did not accept him. He was from the remotest of rural villages, an obscure settlement deep in the middle of nowhere, and the street people spotted this immediately when he asked his first questions. They laughed at him, calling him things he could not understand, and when they realised he couldn't understand their slang, they laughed again.

They explained to him that in simple terms they were implying he was from the bush.

And from then on he was known to them as Bushman, or simply B-man.

B-man's second hurdle came with the realisation that street people actually slept the night in the streets. That this was a surprise was a result of a fundamental oversight on his part. He should have known: they were called *street people*, after all. But his naivety had allowed him to assume that, although they might not have anywhere to live, they had somewhere warm to run to when the chilly night descended.

He was wrong. It was just the streets, the plain, open, freezing-cold, dusty, mosquito-infested pavements of the streets. This was where he found himself on his first cold night. And since the other so-called street urchins did not care too much for a clueless country boy, he was also on his own. He removed from his travel suitcase a small, tatty blanket and a loaf of dry, mouldering bread he had found hidden in his grand-dad's barn, then he curled up under the blanket and braced himself for the night. The old rag was too small for him and left a good part of his body exposed to the dangerous chill. He tossed and turned, flipping and tugging at the blanket, hoping that maybe by some miracle it would stretch enough to wrap his entire frame. Before he became convinced that this was simply not possible, four boys appeared from nowhere and snatched the blanket, then the bread.

He knew he was going to freeze to death. And he missed his grand-dad.

Today

The Land Rover was a fine vehicle for the job. Anything grander would have been wasted on the hostile Nairobi potholes, anything lesser would have crumbled under the pressure. The Land Rover was a fair compromise: a grey, dusty, off-road vehicle with tyres broad and firm, bodywork slightly beat-up but sturdy, and adequate upholstery to soak up some of the vibrations whilst allowing just enough to get through to serve as a reminder that you were indeed in Africa. The Land Rover was just fine; fit for purpose.

Sally-Anne was the sole passenger. The man on the driver's seat called himself Biggy.

The sheer swiftness of the events that resulted in her travelling towards Mathary Valley in this Land Rover, with this man, offered Sally-Anne yet another reason to be positive. She had heard the jokes about African timekeeping, the cynical quips that went as far as suggesting that the concept of strict timing, in this part of the world, was observed with such flimsiness that if an African man said he would see you in about an hour, one had to be prepared to free up at least *three* hours. This man, Biggy, had thus far bucked this claim.

He had called on her mobile phone at eight o'clock in the morning, announcing that inspector Ken Limo had assigned him *a job* in Mathary Valley, and that he understood she wanted to come along. She had found herself sleepily mumbling a series of yeses, and before she had time to shake off the sleep, the man with a distinct, deep drawling voice had invited himself round to pick her up from her hotel in an hour.

One hour later, he was waiting in the lobby. He offered the briefest of introductions.

'They call me Biggy.'

And that had been it.

She thought he could have offered a bit more, but decided it was probably not important. One thing he did not need to elaborate on was why they called him Biggy; that much was self-explanatory. He towered over her five-foot-seven frame. He was at the very least a couple of inches north of six foot, and almost as wide as his Land Rover, with well-defined muscles clearly evident even through his oversized blue T-shirt. He looked rather young, and too casual in jeans and T-shirt to be a policeman of any meaningful rank. She assumed he was some low-rank detective, and decided there was no need to pry any further because he was quite happy to be referred to as Biggy.

Other than that, he seemed friendly, and inquired a lot about her journey and her stay so far.

He tried to engage her in various topics of conversation about England and London as he drove through the busy streets of Nairobi. He tried English football – he was a keen follower of Arsenal FC – but that did not get far when he realised he knew more about English football than she did. He tried British politics, and outsmarted her on that too. Then he switched briefly to American politics as they escaped the city centre and the roads began to get bumpier, right on cue, just when she was contemplating falling asleep.

This was indeed a city of extremes. One minute she was convinced a terrible headache was imminent as they dragged through the disorderly part of town, enduring a cacophony of hooting, shouting and old, croaking engines spewing thick, toxic fumes in between the violent quakes of the Land Rover bumping over crater-sized potholes; the next minute, they would be sailing through the fresh breeze along the smooth roads of suburban Nairobi, with huge mansions and manicured lawns that would have put to shame even her stuck-up, spoilt friends from Hampstead.

The man they called Biggy continued to chatter. He was in the most part trying to impress her with his knowledge on matters she believed were of very little significance to him. He reminded her of Josiah, and she took an instant dislike to him on that account. It was something to do with the I'm-not-your-average-African attitude: *I know things, I talk different, I look better, I dress better...* Sally-Anne did not have a lot of patience for such characters, but she did her best to play along and not upset her host. By the time they finally got to the outer ring-road, Biggy had attempted discussions on nearly every topic Sally-Anne could think of, other than the situation that was currently facing his country. Maybe the endless small-talk was a deliberate ploy to avoid the depressing subject. But Sally-Anne suspected that this man was not that clever. He was just a conceited individual wrapped up in his own little fantasy world.

The road was at the crest of Mathary Valley and seemed to form a ring around it. It was not the same route they had used during the wind-turbine project two years before. This one provided a clearer perspective of the cluster of iron-sheet roofs and mud-walled structures.

'In a minute I will be heading round to the East End where the boy lives. I'm just taking this outer ring-road so you can have a clearer view of Mathary Valley,' he announced as if reading her thoughts. 'Most tourists come here just to see this place.'

'I'm not a tourist. I've been here before.'

'You were working at one particular site in the East End, and you probably hardly ever left that site. It's not quite the same.'

She got the feeling that this man, like many others here, was accusing her of something. She had come to this country to work on a voluntary project in one of the biggest slums in Africa, yet no one seemed prepared to give her credit for it.

'Why does it matter where exactly I was in Mathary Valley? Most people only see places like these on TV, whereas this is my second time here.'

'I understand, but maybe you will see a different side this time. I hope you are not in a rush. I sent some of my people over to warn the Gitongas you are coming, and they haven't called me back yet.'

'It's alright, I'm sure they won't mind me turning up unannounced.'

'At times like these it's good to check what's happening in the vicinity. Just a precaution. In the meantime I'll drive you round the real Mathary Valley for a few minutes, you might enjoy the scenery. If my guys still haven't called back in a few minutes, I will call them.'

He stayed silent for a while, his big hands firm on the steering wheel.

'You know, to be honest, that really scorches my guts,' he began again. Sally-Anne didn't know what '*scorches my guts*' meant, and didn't ask. She waited for him to continue, hoping to work out the meaning by placing it in context. They were now stopped at a level crossing, by a railway line that seemed to go right through the middle of the slums. 'I mean, this place has become a global tourist attraction. Can you believe that? Real human suffering, has now become an attraction?' he *tsk-tsked*, shaking his head. 'Things could change in Mathary Valley, but with such perverse fascination from rich, paying tourists, you wonder if they ever will. That really scorches right through my guts!'

'What's that?' she asked.

'It's a train, ma'am.' He was pointing at the long series of old silver carriages that were clanking and screeching through the crossing. 'A goods train. Travels from the port in Mombasa all the way to–'

'I didn't mean that, Biggy. I know what a train looks like.' The clanking and screeching was beginning to drown out her voice, forcing her to shout. 'I meant that phrase about scorching guts. What does it mean?'

'What?' He was also shouting.

'I said, what does scorching...' She gave up mid-sentence. It was not worth the strain. 'Never mind,' she said.

'What?' he tilted his broad shoulders towards her and cupped his ears to trap the sound of her voice.

'I said, never mind.'

'Oh, OK.'

She watched the back of the train disappear into the horizon as they eased past the level crossing and approached Mathary Valley in silence.

*

Sally-Anne began to experience the true nature of the slums, the moment the Land Rover started its bumpy descent into the valley. It started with the smell, then the sound, then the sight. A mild but distinct stench lingered in the air as the morning sunlight found its way in patches through the clusters of makeshift shelters. Biggy was driving the Land Rover through seemingly impossible narrow alleys, making people duck into the mud buildings to make way. There were sounds of people and animals as chickens and goats ran around side by side with half-clothed children. It was not deafeningly loud, but the noise was continuous and annoyingly monotonous as Biggy attempted unthinkable manoeuvres to evade endless obstacles. If it was not the closely clustered rusty buildings, it would be malnourished children or animals. Driving around here was clearly not a great idea. Whatever was left of the narrow alleyways was blocked by all sorts of other things: there was the occasional foodstuff that people had laid in front of their houses, presumably to trade, and rags hanging off zigzagging clothes lines, and children darting in and out from all sides... everything added to the sense of disarray.

Against the backdrop of the mud-walled clutter of somewhat uniform brown colour, the soil seemed a slightly lighter shade of burgundy. But even the sight of this pure soil was a rarity: any space not occupied by the rusty structures was covered by huge piles of rubbish or rivulets of raw sewage. There was not a single hint of green on the ground. Maybe somewhere under this valley there was room for a plant to breathe and even develop some roots, but above the surface they didn't stand a chance against the millions of starved animals and human beings competing for the limited air thickened with all known forms of pollution.

The windows of the Land Rover were getting covered in dust, even at this time of the morning.

'You alright?' asked Biggy, after allowing her enough peace to wallow in this sea of human misery.

Of course she was not alright, she could not breathe.

'Yes, I'm alright,' she answered.

'*This* is Mathary Valley!'

CHAPTER 5

Two months later, B-man had tried every trick he knew to beat the harsh nightly freeze and the mosquitoes. He tried covering himself with whatever rags he had left as he slept on city pavements or in alleyways. He also attempted to shelter in abandoned vehicle wreckage in scrapyards, or sneaked into late-night buses, hoping to hide long enough to get locked up in their garages. He even slept in plastic garbage bins. He explored all the corners a living being might squeeze into, to stay alive in the city. Everything was desolate and excruciating. The sore mosquito bites had turned his skin to sandpaper. Waste food from dumpsites had become his main source of nourishment, sometimes augmented by occasional income from begging. But he was still around: alive, and in one piece. And his dream of becoming a hotel waiter was also still very much alive.

One of the other boys, a deep voiced teenager maybe a few years older, started talking to him. He had skin darker than B-man's, kind of black coffee, and his hair was slightly discoloured and lumped into small, untidy locks, not by design but due to lack of care. One bright Sunday afternoon the boy sat himself next to B-man on a bench near the entrance to Independence Park, and, without looking at him, in a very low relaxed tone, he began:

'I know what you are thinking.' He waited for the startled B-man to recover before he went on. 'You are watching all these people driving big expensive cars and going into these marvellous buildings, and you are thinking: is this fair? Are we the forgotten people of the moral world?'

He was wrong. B-man's only thoughts at that moment were on how he was going to stay alive. But the stranger smiled with satisfaction nonetheless and continued:

'I'm going to tell you something; something Martin said. Think of the moral universe as a very long arc. It is so long you cannot see the end of it, but because it is an arc, you know it bends at the end... right?' Then he lowered his voice to a whisper. 'Well, that arc, my friend, eventually bends towards justice. Our time will come one day.'

B-man was confused. All the indications suggested that the boy was mentally retarded, but he realised it would only be polite to make an effort to contribute to this unprecedented conversation.

'Martin said that? Er... who is Martin?' he asked.

'The great Martin Luther King, my friend.'

He called himself Poppa.

B-man soon realised Poppa was a very informed young man who, for an urchin who spent every hour of day wandering the streets, possessed some truly fascinating knowledge. His speciality was history. Poppa spoke of the great historical figures as if they had once been his close buddies. It was *Martin Luther King this, Nelson Mandela that... Marcus Garvey this, Abraham Lincoln that...*

He loved telling stories of great people who did great things in great times, light-years before he was born.

At first, B-man found it all very disappointing, if Poppa was trying to educate him, he had chosen the wrong subject, for his priority was survival. He would have greatly appreciated it, if this boy told him a trick or two about how they survived here. He soon realised Poppa had absolutely no intention of being friendly. It was simply a relationship of convenience: Poppa had a lot to say, and B-man was a good listener. But he kept his patience and listened anyway; it was better than not having anyone talking to him.

He listened to everything from Vasco da Gama's exact routes on the very first journey round the world, to why Christopher Columbus thought he saw North America before anyone else. Poppa narrated everything with great expertise. He turned out to be a better storyteller than B-man's own grandfather had been. He had the ability to make one *feel* the history. When he set out to deliver a lesson, he turned into a poet, a singer reciting the lines of a beautiful sonnet. He would lean back on a park bench, thread his hands on top of his locks, clear his throat, and talk about the world-changing events of the past. And at such moments, B-man would know that Poppa was lost somewhere far, far away with his friends and family: the great thinkers and revolutionaries of times gone by.

***

When Biggy was convinced that Sally-Anne had had enough time to soak up the atmosphere of Mathary Valley, he resumed his pointless chit-chat. He appeared to speak with a mixture of accents that belonged nowhere near this continent, and she appreciated that he was probably doing this for her benefit. One moment it sounded like a lousy attempt at an American drawl; the next, it was a twang that would not be out of place in the English Midlands. He only stopped when his phone rang. She guessed this was the call he'd been waiting for, his so-called 'people' informing him that it was clear for them to make their way to the Gitongas in the East End. She simply could not wait.

He started conversing in Swahili, with occasional English words, and even in Swahili she could decipher most of the initial pleasantries. Then the conversation began heading beyond her limited Swahili vocabulary and she gave up trying to eavesdrop. She stayed calm until she heard Biggy's baritone voice rise dramatically and he suddenly hit the brake-pedal hard, bringing the car to a screeching halt. What he was saying on the mouthpiece was a very loud whisper:

'Oh my God. Oh my God,' he muttered in English, then repeated what she believed was the same phrase in Swahili.

She guessed this was not a good sign, and felt herself freeze. But she recovered quickly and blamed her paranoia once again. Of course there was nothing to worry about. He could have been talking to anyone about anything; not everyone's world revolved around J'Alex. She sat back and tried to relax.

Then, just as she was beginning to regain her calm, she heard the name Gitonga being mentioned, and her reassuring thoughts were dashed.

This was not good.

She waited anxiously for the news, with a smile firmly in place, as Biggy tucked the phone back into his hip pocket.

'You did say the place is Gitonga's shop in the East End, didn't you?' he asked her.

'Yes. Near the wind-turbine site,' she replied.

'Well, those were the friends I told you about, the guys I sent to warn them we are coming. It seems there is a bit of a problem.'

'What problem?'

'The shop is not there.'

She considered this for a moment. 'You mean they can't find it?'

'No, I'm sorry. I... Er... I don't really know how to say this. They are saying the shop was burnt down about two weeks ago in the middle of the night, with the whole family inside... I'm sorry.'

She waited with the faintest hint of a smile for the chill to travel through her body and the knot to tighten inside her guts, trying to digest Biggy's sentences in small chunks. But her next words still sounded silly.

'Are they... dead?'

He nodded solemnly.

'All of them?'

'I'm so sorry, ma'am. I am so sorry. You have come such a long way.'

For the next few minutes she simply stared blankly at the sorry scenery around her. She was biting hard on her lower lip without knowing whether this was to suppress a smile or to stop herself from crying. Finally, she gathered herself and said, 'Take me there. I need to see for myself.'

*

The rest of the drive was a blur, until they went past the wind-turbine and she spotted the ruins from about fifty yards.

The shop was not there alright.

There was a churning in her stomach as all her senses drained away. And the closer they got to the debris, the sicker she felt.

'I think maybe you should stop here, Biggy. I don't want to go any closer.' She had seen enough.

They were now about thirty yards away from the remains of what had once been the Gitonga shop. Where they had sampled local foods and drinks... where they had listened to local music and swayed to the latest dance craze... a place that had been awash with smiles and laughter. The Gitonga shop was gone. And she had travelled all the way from London to witness it.

'I'm sorry,' Biggy said again.

She propped her elbow over the open window and rested her head on the palm of her left hand. She was still biting her lip.

'Those are my friends over there,' he pointed out at two older-looking men who were standing just outside the area that had been cordoned off with police tape. 'I asked them to meet me here, need to ask them some questions. It's probably best you stay in the car.'

He stepped out of the car and began walking off towards the two men. He had a pronounced swagger to his walk. For some reason, despite her shock, this man was beginning to irritate Sally-Anne: the way he spoke, the way he walked, the way he looked... it was just not right. From the Land Rover, she watched the three of them step over the tapes into the restricted area to survey the ruins. They continued to converse, with a fair number of hand gestures, for about ten minutes; then they all started making their way towards the car. Biggy leant against the driver's door with his arms folded on his chest and continued to listen to the two men, who seemed to be debating something in Swahili.

The name J'Alex came up often.

Biggy then made a phone call to inspector Limo. The conversation alternated between English and Swahili, and at one point, he made what looked like a deliberate move to step away from the group as he spoke. But Sally-Anne still gathered that J'Alex's name was again mentioned at least once. In her time here, she had tried to pick up a few Swahili words, but they had long since deserted her, so all she could do was wait for someone to explain things. When Biggy was finished on the phone he rejoined the two men's debate. Yet again the names Gitonga and J'Alex, and the hand gestures remained prevalent. This carried on for almost another ten minutes before Biggy thanked them, shook their hands and patted their backs rather patronisingly. Then he jumped back into the car as they walked off.

'They were just explaining to me what they know about what happened,' he started.

'What do they know?'

'Not a lot, it happened in the middle of the night. It was very bad I'm afraid, nothing remained, even for burial.'

She suddenly remembered the call from Barclays' Mr. Murray, the call that had kick-started her journey. She found herself wondering exactly when her card had been used.

'Did you say this happened two weeks ago?'

'Happened Friday before last. Twelve days ago.'

The call from Mr. Murray had been Wednesday: exactly one week ago. All sorts of great-escape theories started criss-crossing her mind. She recalled J'Alex once confiding that sometimes at the weekends he would sneak out of the house at night to hang around with his friends in Mathary Valley. At the time she had dismissed it as a childish attempt to boost his street credibility. But it seemed to be turning into a crucial piece of information.

'Was anything said about exactly how many people were inside? Was the entire family indoors when it happened?' she asked, wishing she could speak to Mr. Murray.

'It was in the middle of the night, ma'am. They were all inside, sleeping.'

'But they have just said it was so bad there were hardly any remains, how would they know for sure? I got the call exactly a week ago, *after* this happened.'

Biggy hesitated. Then he said:

'As far as they know, the whole family was killed in there. That's what they have told me. I will check with Inspector Limo if we can get any conclusive confirmation from the crime-scene reports. But you have to understand these are not normal times, I doubt that normal procedures would have been followed. I don't even know if such records would be available.'

She did not believe him. There was something about this man, she was yet to figure out what, but there was something. Maybe it was the way he walked, or the way he spoke, or the way he patronisingly patted the older men's shoulders... Something.

'Could you just give me one minute,' she said, opening the door. 'I think it's a bit rude that I didn't even say hello to those kind gentlemen.'

Without waiting for a response she jumped out and started hurrying towards the two men, shouting to get their attention.

'Excuse me!'

They turned in unison. She introduced herself, and went straight to the point.

'You were talking to Biggy a lot about J'Alex. I just wanted to hear what you were saying.'

The light-skinned one spoke first. 'Gitonga's little boy? They say he was missing for two days before the fire.'

'Really? Is that right?'

'Yes, that's what people are saying.' It was the darker one talking now. 'They say Gitonga had been looking for him. All kind of rumours, but the most popular one is that he wasn't in the fire.'

She spotted Biggy getting out of the car, and thanked the two gentlemen. She turned, and started running back towards the Land Rover.

The drive back was relatively quiet, but every so often Biggy would bring up a topic to test her mood. She could not stop wondering why he had lied about what the two men had told him.

She was beginning to feel uncomfortable with this man.

***

B-man endured almost a week as the sole audience for Poppa's narratives before he gathered enough courage to raise a question. It was a question he had harboured before he met Poppa, and one that had remained pertinent despite his new friend's great stories and legends.

'Poppa, where do the others go at night?'

Poppa had been in the middle of a tale about Mahatma Gandhi's freedom quest, so the question threw him.

'The others?' He snapped out of the depths of early twentieth-century India and shot B-man a puzzled look.

'Yeah, the other Parking-boys... you know... the other homeless people,' he had learnt that the term 'Parking-boys' was the least offensive of the assortment of names which city society used to describe the homeless and their kind. It had something to do with the amount of time the street people spent in the parks.

'Homeless people?' Poppa eyed him like an insolent child, feigning ignorance.

'Yeah, homeless people. You know, like you and me.'

'Speak for yourself, B-man, I'm not homeless. I have got a place!' His tone suggested that this line of conversation was at an end, and he resumed his Gandhi story. '... He managed a four-hundred-kilometre walk for what he believed in, B-man. Four-hundred kilom–'

'What do you mean, *you have got a place*?' B-man cut him short.

'For God's sake, B-man, if your questions are not related to this, will you please ask them some other time? We're talking quality history here.'

'So your place... I mean the one you just said, is somewhere in the streets, isn't it?'

'Do you ever see me sleeping with you on these pavements?' He laughed. 'I'm a very important person, B. You don't know this, but at present I actually live in a house, the House of *Lord's*, in Mathary Valley. And very soon I may be invited into one of the gangs, and I will have my own flat there.'

'And what's all this?'

'The streets do not simply mean *the streets*, B. There is a set-up here. There are homeless people and there are street people. They are not necessarily always the same.' The subject had changed, but he had to remain the teacher and B-man the clueless student. 'Most of the so-called street people you see wandering about here actually come from Dallas, where I come from. They have homes there.'

'Dallas?'

'Yeah Dallas, don't you know Dallas?'

'You mean Dallas in Mathary Valley, the slums?'

'Yeah Mathary Valley.' His earlier impatience was beginning to ease. 'There are two houses in Mathary Valley run by gangsters, most of whom grew up homeless themselves. What they do is identify young homeless kids like you and me, who have the potential to one day join their gangs, and settle them in these houses. Then they try using you in a few *hits*, from which you get a small share of the split. If you land a really big hit and do a great job, you're invited to become a fully fledged member of the gang and earn enough to rent your own place in Dallas.'

'But Mathary Valley is quite far from here, isn't it?'

'Mathary Valley is a world away from here. And Dallas is right in the centre of it. One day, when the time's right, I might take you on a tour down there. Dallas residents include former gangsters, gangsters or would-be gangsters. The would-be gangsters are the homeless, only they're not exactly homeless because they're allowed to live in these two houses and wait for their time to join the gangs.'

'So there are homes available there?'

'No, B, they are not simply *available*. As I've explained, you've got to earn your place; they are much respected places, you see. Places where the gangsters raise their protégés.' He said this with pride; he was, after all, one of the esteemed residents. 'The first of them is called Kappel's Corner, and is just a run-down piece of a relic that was abandoned by the owner because it had an enormous flooding problem. Even now, you'd have to swim your way out in the case of any light rain. It is run by Kappel, who lives in a proper house with the rest of his gang.

'A few years ago there was a scuffle within the original Kappel gang, and a man known as Kane decided to split with a section of the gang. As a result, all the Parking-boys in Kappel's Corner who had been friendly with Kane, or any member of his faction, had to be kicked out.

'This led to the foundation of the second house: the House of Lord's, where I live, and is the better house. Now, let me tell you the history of the House of Lord's, you are going to love this.'

The great teachings of Gandhi were receding into the background as fresh excitement began to boil over about a place far away that was known as the House of Lord's. B-man was disappointed. He had indeed learnt that there were some abandoned houses in this city where the homeless sometimes sought refuge, and he had hoped to find out more from Poppa. But it seemed that Poppa had turned the whole thing into another historical legend.

'Can you tell me about this house, Poppa? Can I go there sometimes–'

'This happened back in the days, B. This is way back in the days–'

'Poppa please, I need to know about the place, it gets very cold out here.'

'I bloody am telling you about the place, so just keep cool and listen. This is the sort of history that will make you proud to be associated with someone living in the House of Lord's.'

Poppa leant back against the wooden bench, threaded his hands behind his head, cleared his throat, and closed his eyes to enter this little-known but hugely significant period in history.

*

'Way back in the days, B-man, a certain prodigal son, one of our own, who had for a long time travelled the vast expanses of oceans and sky to learn the ways of the better worlds, finally came back home. And he brought back with him a soothing breeze of hope that lifted the spirits of Dallas like never before...'

Once again B-man noted this boy's finesse in the art of storytelling, as Poppa's voice adjusted to a fine melodious tone, to capture the mood of a period that was, in all probability, a mere figment of his imagination.

'Thomas Dwyer's life began in an orphanage run by an international charity. He was a smart kid, the smartest at the facility. And when the charity decided to explore better ways of giving aid to a poor country, what better way could there have been than to educate their young ones, and let the future look after itself? So they went ahead and picked the smartest kids, starting with Thomas, and provided them full scholarships to study abroad. Thomas's many years of academic adventures took him from England to the USA where he blazed a trail and draped himself with degrees upon degrees. In England, along with the degrees, he also gained the title *Lord*. It would later emerge that this was a self-awarded title, but hey, the degrees were all genuine, so if he wanted the title that much...

'Lord Thomas Dwyer then went on to spend so many years in the US that he virtually considered it home. But it was yet another big, wealthy NGO in the US that conceived the *Mathary Valley Regeneration Project*. This organisation spent years studying the Mathary Valley slums until finally they came up with a development plan that was to be dubbed a *world-changing idea*. A Nobel Prize-winner, for sure.

'The *jua-kali* business was already thriving in the slums: a basic system of manufacturing where a kid picks up a used oil tin from a rubbish dump, knocks it about a bit, and within minutes has built a kerosene lamp. So the talent and creativity was there. The country was blessed with endless natural resources: wind, solar – a perfect climate... the lot. Add to that mix the million-plus poor and hungry population of Mathary

Valley willing to work for a pittance, and what you have is an endless field of resources. All that was needed was someone to put it all together, to harness this raw energy: the *Mathary Valley Regeneration Project*! They were thinking manufacturing, big production lines, major corporations out-sourcing their construction and assembly requirements to plants right here in these slums. From used oil tin to kerosene lamp to car body panel to aeroplane wing to next generation wind-turbine blades... the possibilities were endless. The face of Mathary Valley would be transformed beyond recognition within a couple of years.

'The NGO drew up a plan. Thomas Dwyer was at this time an academic in America who had written a paper loosely related to a similar topic. Combined with his Kenyan roots, it made him an invaluable part of the plan. He was hand-picked by the NGO from his research degree at MIT, on a name-your-salary deal, to head the operation in Kenya. What better way to give something back to your country of birth? What a homecoming!

'The team landed in Mathary Valley with the good news. Instantly they became gods. Residents were assembled in big rallies in which Lord Thomas Dwyer outlined the vision to electrifying applause. He was one of them, and he would be based right here in the slums with them to see this through.

'They started building him his base right at the centre of the slums; it would serve as an example, the first ever three-storey brick building, with state-of-the-art facilities, in the middle of this dump. Everything would follow from there. In the meantime his backers were already dealing with the legal side of things, talking to the right government officials to get this going.

'The application for clearance with the Ministry of Local Government came with a mandatory non-refundable administration fee. So did those to the Ministry of Lands, the Ministry of Development, the Ministry of Technology, the Ministry of Human Resources, the Ministry of the Underprivileged... and even the Ministry of Future Vision Kenya. Every time an application was made Tom Dwyer would convene another rally and update the residents on progress, keep the fire of hope burning. After he informed them of the application to the fourth ministry, the residents got the point. They already knew. They stopped coming to Tom Dwyer's rallies: *it ain't gonna happen!*

'Meanwhile his backers from the NGO were still relentless in their pursuit of the official clearances. They went through all the ministries and sub-ministries and assistant-ministries and committees and sub-committees, till they got to the spiritual-cleansing department. That slightly knocked them off their stride, *the spiritual-cleansing department?* Yes, such vital project had to be blessed by government-appointed religious and spiritual leaders, the so called spiritual-cleansing department. And yes, that too came with a mandatory non-refundable administration fee. Ha! Now, even to the unsuspecting foreigners, the penny finally drops: *it ain't gonna happen!*'

Poppa paused at this point and changed his tone to give his next line the necessary clout.

'The tragic thing was that poor Lord Thomas Dwyer would be the last to know.'

Then Poppa switched back to his original narrative rhythm, with a deliberate shift to the present continuous tense to add some pace to the story.

'So having worked so hard, the officials from this NGO realise their mistake and decide to pack up and head back home to begin a fresh feasibility study on a slum in India. Even Tom Dwyer's supposed base in the slums is not complete. He has been living in expensive hotels on the NGO's account. When his money runs out, he calls his backers in the US and says: "I need some funds for the Mathary Valley Regeneration Project." Someone riffles through some papers, and, oops! There is no Mathary Valley Regeneration Project!'

Still, Lord Thomas Dwyer refuses to panic. He is a very well-educated man. He can find something else to do in Kenya to make a living and a positive contribution to society. He asks around and they tell him his education counts for little if he doesn't know anyone who knows anyone. Tom was taken away from the country as a young orphan; all the people he knows live in the US. Not good. So he goes back to his former backers: "OK, I've just realised *it ain't gonna happen,* now can I come back to the US?" "Oh, you will need to ask the immigration department that one." Immigration department: "Sorry, sir, you were here to study, and you have got your degrees. Your time here is up. We wish you the best of luck, sir, but not in the USA."

'Within weeks Thomas finds himself right in the centre of the slums, living in the incomplete construction that would have been his base for the Regeneration Project, the only thing he can now call his own. At first the slum dwellers still have great respect for him. When he joins other diners in a restaurant that is constituted entirely of three rows of creaking benches outside Mama Kuka's mud house, they rise and bow to shake his hand. "Eat as much as you want, Lord Dwyer," says Mama Kuka. "And keep your money in your pocket. Your money is no good to us."

'But after a few weeks, people barely nod in his direction as he walks past, and Mama Kuka's now saying, "I love you very much, Lord Dwyer, I wouldn't want to see you go hungry, but I've got mouths to feed..." Tom Dwyer then discovers the local brew and realises it helps the pain a little. He discovers that only the gangsters command lasting respect around the place. He is not built to be a gangster, but he wants the respect: he craves the adulation he received when he first arrived here with his great vision. So he starts hanging out at *Kauzi's chwaka joint.*'

Poppa paused again and looked up at him. 'You know what a *chwaka joint* is, B, don't you?'

'No, not really...'

'A massive pot of the finest local brew in the middle of a hut, men on stools gathered round drinking from the same pot using big long straws...?'

'Oh yeah, I know that. Back in the village we call it–'

'Yeah, so Lord Thomas Dwyer, in search of respect, starts hanging out at Kauzi's *chwaka* joint,' Poppa had not even waited for him to finish; his question had obviously only been a tactic to keep him attentive. But B-man was paying attention alright. He was beginning to enjoy this story even though he could bet his tattered shirt that at least half of it was nothing but a product of this boy's imagination.

'This is where all the gangsters drink,' Poppa went on. 'So Lord Thomas Dwyer gets drunk around them and talks himself big. Tells tales about his exploits when he was in the US – *"I did this... I did that..."* But the hardened gangsters are unimpressed. They've seen it all, they've done it all. "I did cocaine," he says one evening over his drinking straw. This gets some attention. The gangsters raise their heads above their straws. Maybe he knows someone who can supply cocaine, maybe he could help add a new line to their business. But Tom proceeds to tell them how he never once flinched at the needles they used to inject the cocaine. And everyone immediately puts their mouths back round their drinking-straws.

'But that brief moment of attention impresses Tom greatly. For just that short moment, they had taken notice of him; he was Lord Thomas Dwyer once again. He comes out of the joint that night singing, "Cocaine... cocaine... cocaine," and shouting around the slums in an American accent, "I'm a cocaine-head, mutherfuckers! That's who you messin' wit' right here, co-*fuckin*-caine."

'Some people find this funny, some kids are running around the next day doing an impression of his accent. Tom Dwyer, who by now is drunk almost twenty-four hours every day, likes this. He looks for other ways of enticing attention at the joint. "I used to fuck everyone... even men!" This time he's asked to leave Kauzi's *chwaka* joint, and is informed that he is not welcome anymore. But no worries, he finds another *chwaka* joint, they are everywhere in Mathary Valley. He still aims to shock, to get attention. He comes up with a line about AIDS, and that one sticks, becomes his anthem: "I have AIDS, mutherfuckers, and I'm gonna die soon. Yeah, that's right, mutherfuckers, Lord Thomas Dwyer's lived fast and is gonna die young! That's gangster shit right there; live fast, die young! I'm the American VIP with HIV." He sings and sings and sings at the top of his voice every night and people don't even bat an eyelid:

Lived fast, died young,

I'm the VIP, with HIV…

'Only when he is being very disruptive does he get beaten up and carried unconscious to his unfinished building that is now also falling apart. He's now the slum-idiot, his name a joke, the title *Lord* an insult. A kid does something stupid, they call him Lord: "Why are you being such an idiot? What are you, Lord Vincent or something?"

'Then one night, Kane, the gangster who had just split from Kappel's original gang, finds Thomas being beaten senseless by a gang of boys, rescues him from near death, and, when he comes out of hospital, they all invite him back to Kauzi's *chwaka* joint once again. This time they treat him with utmost respect, just like old times, when the dream was still alive. Even Kane, the much revered gangster, addresses Lord Thomas Dwyer with humility, like he's a figure of his and everyone else's inspiration, tells him he is a true legend and that no matter what, the legend of Lord Thomas Dwyer will always live. The drink, of course, is free, just like old times: *"Drink as much as you want, my Lord… your money is no good…"*

'Lord Dwyer likes this. He is now drinking too much and he notices that everyone else is just toying with their straws, not drinking. Maybe it's a sign of respect, he thinks: they don't feel worthy to drink from the same pot as this true legend. He likes this a great deal, loves it in fact. He still has the assured smile of a true legend even when he begins to cough and fit, even as he retches up a stream of alcohol, drops to the ground and closes his eyes for the last time. Then Kane and his people look at each other with slow, knowing nods filled with sorrow, before they cover his body and say a little prayer.

'Kane changes his name to *Lord* Kane, acquires Thomas's incomplete building, calls it the House of Lord's, and gives it to the homeless Parking-boys loyal to him, who have been kicked out of Kappel's Corner. The title *Lord* regains respect, and the legend of Lord Thomas Dwyer lives on.'

'Oh my God! Did they poison him? Did Kane kill him?'

'They put poison in his drink, they did not kill him. Thomas Dwyer had been dead for a long time, B-man.'

'How do you mean, Poppa, because he had AIDS?'

'Thomas Dwyer never had AIDS, B-man.'

'Uh...? I don't understand...'

Poppa scratched a spot at the centre of his miniature dreadlocks. Then he looked up at him with a smile, and said, 'You really are from the bush, aren't you?'

CHAPTER 6

The Imperial Hotel marketed itself as a four-star, and so far Sally-Anne had no reason to dispute this. The entire service team from concierge to management were extremely helpful and full of genuine African smiles. She loved her huge king suite. It had a colour thing going, mainly beige contrasted with some black, white and silver. Everything from the king-size bed to the walk-in closet appeared brand new and smelled nice and fresh. She had some neat leather furniture, a wide plasma screen, a well-equipped workstation with high-speed internet, a gleaming marble and granite bathroom – everything she needed, and more. Even a refrigerated mini-bar stocked with an ample assortment of drinks.

Sally-Anne was talking on her hotel phone whilst her eyes swept the room, taking in its magnificence and wondering if the suffering folks she had witnessed in the slums sometimes dreamed of places like this, barely five miles away from them.

'So you asked him to lie to me?' She was doing her best to stay calm. She had called Inspector Limo straight after bolting from Biggy's Land Rover.

'No, that's not what I said,' the inspector's voice remained controlled. 'I only said I made it clear to him that we wanted to put your mind at rest as quick as possible so you could go back home.'

'I asked him directly what those people were saying, and he gave me a straight answer. He lied, blatantly.'

'I can understand why he would not worry you with something that is a result of a baseless rumour. He knows that area, he knows those people; they are always capable of ridiculous tales.'

'Sorry, sir, but I don't get it. Why would they make something like this up? I told you I think J'Alex sent me the message *after* the Friday of the fire. Now his neighbours are saying this... don't you think there is reason to take the matter seriously?'

'I am taking this seriously, and I'm doing my best under the circumstances. I will try and get to the people who dealt with the crime scene. And I will make sure all relatives are questioned. If he is alive, he'd most probably be with a friend or relative somewhere, or they would at least know something about it.'

'Try hard, please.'

'I will.'

As soon as she hung up she regretted the way she had conducted the conversation. She remembered the country's current state and realised people like Inspector Limo had a lot to deal with at this time. She had to be careful that they did not lose their patience with her. She could not do this on her own. She had already called her dad about finding some details from

Barclays Bank, but it had been too late in the evening. The banks in England were shut and she was faced with an agonising night wondering when exactly those transactions on her card had taken place.

It was early evening on only her second day in the country and she was already feeling exhausted. The scenes of misery in Mathary Valley had taken their toll on her, and the news coming in on the the big flat-screens that were strewn around the hotel was only getting worse. The violence was not letting up. Although they said the worst of it was taking place in the Rift Valley province, at least a hundred miles away from Nairobi, it was of little reassurance to her because they also stressed that in Nairobi the slum areas were experiencing the worst of the tensions.

Once again she called her dad, who reiterated what the inspector, the British High Commission, Biggy and the few Kenyan friends she had contacted by phone seemed to be telling her: *stay indoors!* She felt trapped inside the hotel room and she was yet to decide whether the view from her window was beautiful or scary. She was floating on top of the city. From up here, Nairobi could have been any of the great world cities. Some famous iconic buildings rose above the rest. There was the KICC, the Grand Regency building, the Hotel Ambassador, and, in a direct line from her window, the odd-shaped skyscraper that most people here referred to as the Bell-Bottom.

The Bell-Bottom, as its name suggested, was the shape of tight, flared jeans, which, incidentally, were still considered pretty fashionable locally. Personally, she found it strange that nobody mentioned that the building looked like a giant penis. Every single day, potent young men and women walked past this mammoth building with spheroids bulging at base, under the slanting curve of a dark, rough, baggy scrotum, and the only thing they could think of was a pair of jeans?

Sally-Anne watched vehicles climb up the curve of Tom Mboya Street and disappear within a mass of thick green brush that began at one end of the Bell-Bottom's scrotum and ceased exactly in line with the other end. This made it look like the Bell-Bottom was swallowing the cars from one end of its scrotum and spewing them out at the other. Sally-Anne's perverse side found this very interesting and she found herself making mental calculations of how long it took for different vehicles to emerge from the scrotum. An SUV took four seconds to cross the width of Bell-Bottom's scrotum, so did a small mini-van. A lorry took five. For no reason at all, she started noting down these numbers. Her engineering instinct had taken over from her perversions. She averaged out the times, and within seconds she had figured out that, with certain assumptions about the speeds, she could work out roughly how big the scrotum was. Seventy-one meters was the rounded result from her number-crunching.

A seventy-one-meter-thick scrotum – that was all she was left with for company, in this country that had so much to offer, so much to show her. Right now all she could do was stare at this giant penis and wait for Inspector Limo to give her some news.

She called Biggy. She hated herself for doing it but she felt she needed to go back to Mathary Valley in the morning. She had established, just like inspector Limo had said, that he was the only person who could take her there. She told him she wanted to see her friends up there, but deep down she knew she wanted to be there amongst the rumours because she believed that J'Alex was still alive.

He refused. 'It is dangerous,' he said.

'I have friends up there, Biggy, I need to see them, please.'

'How about you just tell me who they are and where they live. I will go there, find them for you and bring them over to your hotel.'

She refused his offer, she needed to be there. If Biggy was not going to help, she would have to figure something out herself.

**

Poppa made sure B-man had absorbed enough legendary tales about Dallas before he finally agreed to take him on a guided tour. And the true nature of this lyrically hailed 'promised land' disappointed miserably: Mathary Valley was indeed a slum. And Dallas, sitting bang in the centre of the valley, was the direst part of it. Occupying a lower berth of the contoured landscape along the northern outskirts of the city, the name Mathary Valley was no misnomer.

B-man took in a bird's-eye view of the scene before they began sinking into the valley. He felt himself getting dizzy watching the haphazard masses of dark brown and silver lines formed by the ocean of rusting tin roofs, and decided that no stretch of the imagination, even under the hypnosis of Poppa's glorious narratives, could make this a great place.

It was late afternoon and the bright sun was still tossing and turning west through the clear sky. The walk from the city centre had taken the best part of an hour and a half, yet Poppa had not tired of talking. He was keen on pointing out the great landmarks of Dallas, complete with the tales from behind their facades, as they strolled through the bustling jumble of activity.

From one corner appeared a tall dark greasy man pulling a *mkokoteni* – a two wheeled human-drawn cart. On the *mkokoteni*'s wooden back bumper was a big white sticker with bold black slanting letters:

GOD'S ROUTE, NO SHORTCUTS!

The puller was wrestling with the long handlebars at the front end to balance the cart like a see-saw pivoted by the wheels, with the opposing force coming from the two items of cargo lying at the bottom end in a pile, one over the other. The first item was a dark brown sack of charcoal. The second, squashed right at the back end, against the wooden panel, was a man. He was sprawled lifelessly with his feet dangling off the side of the vehicle like branches of a dead plant. His feet flapped about in thick, woolly red socks, but there was no sign of any shoes.

'Just the local drunk getting a ride home,' Poppa explained before B-man could open his mouth.

A group of barefoot children, around six years old, were running after the *mkokoteni*. Ill-fitting tattered shirts barely covering their podgy bellies flapped up and down as they shuffled skinny legs that seemed to be bent one way or another, forming bow-legs and knocked-knees.

'... used to be a highly respected senior diplomat,' Poppa was still explaining of the drunken human cargo, 'speaks no less than seven global languages, worked in five different countries over three continents where he lived in huge mansions and drove big cars. Then he retires, and this is how it all ends.'

When the *mkokoteni* splashed through a puddle of sewage, B-man thought he heard the retired diplomat groan. Then he raised his right hand and feebly attempted to wipe the murky sewage water off his face. The chasing kids stopped and howled with laughter. Then they stretched their odd, thin legs again to overtake the *mkokoteni*-puller and wait a little further ahead, beside another puddle of sewage, for the next episode.

Poppa showed no further interest in the *mkokoteni*. He was back to his story-telling tour-guide persona. And the stories got more ridiculous with B-man's growing indifference, as though he were daring B-man to challenge their authenticity.

'... That is Jesse's house... he's the biggest drug pusher around... he once strangled a killer cobra to death with his bare hands...'

If Poppa was to be believed, the fairer-looking shelters were those belonging to the gangsters. But they were only fairer by comparison. It soon became clear to B-man that nothing in this place was even good enough to be referred to as a house; yet they were shelters nonetheless. They could offer a degree of warmth, they could afford some shield from the rain; they were miles better than the city pavements.

B-man was now desperate to see the two much acclaimed shelters, the House of Lord's and Kappel's Corner. He wanted to ask, but Poppa was busy. He was in the middle of another history, and B-man couldn't afford to piss him off now.

Poppa's account of the Second World War was not up to his usual high standards in terms of his delivery. Tiredness was finally catching up with him. The story soon began to drag, with Poppa taking ever longer pauses to draw in more air. B-man picked this as the ideal opportunity to interject.

He was set to pounce with his unrelated question when Poppa suddenly switched to Nelson Mandela. And to B-man's disappointment, he immediately got back his rhythm and the story picked up pace. B-man was left rueing his missed opportunity as he laboured to walk what he believed were now his last few strides. The foraged remains of food from marketplaces and hotel dumpsites they had been surviving on had become scarce lately. He was yet to have his first proper meal today. He simply could not move his feet a single step further.

When they came to what looked like a wilting oak tree with sparse dry leaves, standing firm in front of the disintegrating structure of what was once a tallish brick building, he caved in and lay on his back under the tree. Poppa continued to breathe over him about Nelson Mandela.

The stench of urine and human excreta from the derelict building eased through his lungs. But his brain refused to register the smell, electing instead to concentrate his thoughts on tonight, when, out on the dusty street pavements, the stinging chill would be adding its contribution to the nightmare.

In the meantime, the passion of the voice buzzing in his ears seemed to have gained fresh momentum. A skewed comparison between the two of them and Nelson Mandela was being drawn.

'You keep telling me your dreams about your nice little job and your nice little flat in a nice little estate out there. It's all good, B, but it does not make you somebody. You are nothing! I teach you quality history about the things that make our world what it is today. I do it for free, seeking neither reward nor recognition. But it still doesn't make me somebody, because ultimately I too am nothing.

'Nelson Mandela allowed himself to be imprisoned for twenty-seven years so his people could be free. *Twenty-seven long years!*' Poppa buried his face in the palms of his hands, showing B-man only the lumpy, unkempt locks in the middle of his head, as if he were haunted by the thought of Mandela's persecution. 'Nelson Mandela *is* somebody, B. You, me and all those suburban middle-class folks that you dream of becoming, we are nothing!'

B-man let this invaluable piece of wisdom skim the surface of his battered senses as he took in the rotting structure drooping in front of them. Two ragged boys had emerged from the very top floor, shouting vulgar abuses at an old man down below, who picked up a small rock and hurled it up at them. Aside from his own discomfort, he wished these boys would find somewhere else to play: the sagging heap looked like it could collapse on them at any minute. Why couldn't the city council demolish these rotting yet unfinished buildings?

B-man suddenly decided enough was enough, the history lessons would have to wait. 'The houses, Poppa. When are you going to show me the houses?'

'Oh yeah!' he exclaimed, pointing at the very structure in front of which the old man was now trying to dodge a steam of urine from one of the two boys he'd hurled the stones at. 'This, B-man, is the House of Lord's,'

So *this* was the House of Lord's, indeed.

Later, they set off to see Kappel's corner. Surely it had to be better, he hoped, with his mind on the freezing night.

Eventually, right at the heart of Dallas, they saw it. And for the sake of comparison, he would have said it was about the same standard as the House of Lord's. What was even more tragic was that, dire as they were, the House of Lord's and Kappel's Corner would not accept him. After that day, he launched into a relentless inquiry about a place and tried to befriend more of the boys. But the friendships seemed to cease at the doors of the House of Lord's.

*

It was the gradual development of his friendship with Poppa that eventually opened the doors for him. After weeks of being used merely as an audience for his frustrated storytelling, the homeless narrator gradually began taking some genuine interest in him. He began to teach him survival tactics on the streets.

He started with the drugs.

He explained to B-man how the glue-sniffing habit was an essential part of street-endurance. 'If you hold those jars to your nose and sniff for long enough, it can take you to a faraway place where you can't feel any pain or hunger or cold,' he was saying as he took B-man on an excursion around the city centre to find discarded glue jars from city cobblers. 'You see, you are already better than the other Parking-boys, B. You have survived so far without the help of the drugs.'

'But Poppa, I've never seen you sniff that stuff either.'

'That's because the first time I tried it, I puked my guts out. Nearly died. It's just not for everyone, B.'

'Why are we collecting them then?'

'We can sell them to others who need them, and use the money to buy things we need.'

'So they're useful to others, but not to you.'

'It depends how you look at it. A few weeks ago a little boy of about ten lands out here, claiming he's escaped the clashes in the north-east. He's got a baby with him, maybe three years old. His baby sister, he says. Everyone else he knows has been killed. But who knows, he could have stolen someone's baby to gain sympathy. Begging can be a tough business.' He was shaking his head as he said this, causing a momentary flutter of his shaggy locks. 'Anyway, this boy arrives here with his three-year-old baby sister. He is trying to fend not only for himself, but also for his toddler sister, on these harsh streets. He is trying his best. He carries her everywhere with him, begging and scavenging for food and searching for shelter. But the baby won't stop crying, she can't sleep at night, she screams till her lungs are sore, then screams some more. Then the boy discovers glue, he introduces his baby sister to this wonder drug and it brings them peace. And then, just the other day, this baby girl, sitting calmly on her brother's lap on a park bench, took a good long drag of the glue, her tiny eyes rolled back, and she went into a deep peaceful sleep from which she will never awake.'

'Oh my God! She died?'

'Peacefully.'

'Why do you sell people stuff that can kill them, Poppa? It is wrong.'

'Good question, B, very good question. Let me ask you this in return: why did our ancestors sell their own people to slavery?'

'Because they needed the money?'

'That might be the correct answer, B. But it's not the *right* answer.'

B-man simply shook his head in bemusement; he knew better than to ask Poppa to explain himself.

'Try again, B-man,' Poppa pushed, 'why did they do it?'

'Is it because they hated each other?'

'OK, you are drifting further from the truth now. So I will tell you.'

He cleared his throat and B-man sighed: he could sense the narrative coming.

'Our ancestors traded slaves because the European empires were strong. They wanted slaves, and they were going to get slaves. So if you weren't selling, there was a good chance *you* were going to be sold.

'If what I'm doing is wrong, try showing me one righteous business establishment. The whole structure of modern society is wrong. But we are within this structure, there's nothing you can do about it. All you can try and do is choose your place and your role within this structure. I have picked my role, B-man. I will be the supplier.'

*

That night, Poppa took him back to Dallas and started him off in the battle to earn the right to sleep in the near-rubble that was the House of Lord's. The drunken boys beat him out of the overcrowded squat, then turned to his host, Poppa, and delivered similar treatment.

'It always starts rough,' Poppa reassured. 'Eventually they will get tired of attacking you, and they will get used to you. Then after that, your only problem will be when Lord Kane's people pop round to check on their boys.'

'What will we do if they come round?'

'You mean what will *you* do? Because if Lord Kane's people catch you in here, I do not know you.'

'What would you suggest I do then?'

'I don't know, B. Survive, just survive.'

At first B-man had to share a seven-by-four-foot space that had been officially allocated to Poppa. It was located in a far corner of the top floor of the disastrously executed two-storey conversion of a building that was originally three-storeys high. The top floor had long ago been knocked down when it started giving way under the stress of constant flooding through the leaking roof. Before that, the walls that separated the various rooms had similarly been knocked down over time, to leave the building as two vast, messy halls, one on the ground floor and the other on the top floor. The top-floor hall was thus left with a twenty-foot-high roof and a second row of windowless window-holes, the only reminder that there had once been another floor above. The missing windows were patched with pieces of multicoloured polythene rags. They flapped towards the outside in the wind, like flags symbolising the supreme dignity of the great of the House of Lord's.

The exterior was still the maroon colour of the bricks that had been used in its construction, while the inside was mostly the colour of cement. Careful inspection would reveal that the building was beginning to lean: a disaster waiting to happen.

*

The mosquitoes inside the House of Lord's did not bite. They hovered and buzzed and crawled under the skin and irritated with their nerve-grating squeak. But they did not bite. Legend was that the thick smell of narcotic compounds within the house disorientated the mosquitoes and turned the blood-sucking vermin into pets.

*

B-man's earliest memories of the House of Lords, and one that would stay with him for a long time, was the late-night laughter downstairs. Every night, a group of boys gathered around a candle on the ground floor and played cards, initially in silence, while sniffing glue, smoking weed and doing anything else available. The roar of laughter would begin rasping through the house around the time B-man started to doze off, curled under his rags upstairs. The laughter would not relent till he was somehow fast asleep. He would later learn that there were never any jokes told at these gatherings. In fact, not much was said at all. The laughs were merely begot from laughter itself. As the smell of smoke and glue thickened, and rolls of weed shortened, someone would giggle, and the next person would find this funny enough to snort a chuckle, which would then gradually boil into laughter. Then maybe there would be silence again. And in that silence, someone would say something mundane like:

Man! I'm so stoned.

And this time the laughter would be thunderous, till voices were sore and the chuckles began to choke and sound like quacking ducks.

*

At his own risk, Poppa continued to accommodate B-man in his little space. Lord Kane's people missed him on the first three occasions on which they made their surprise visits to inspect the flat and scout potential new recruits. The third time had been a very close call, one of the boys whispered a warning to B-man just as the gangsters were stepping inside the front door, and he fled through a back window. But everyone knew he couldn't hide forever.

Four weeks elapsed before the day of reckoning came. Lords Kane's men walked into the squat unannounced one night, found him smoking with a few of the boys on the top floor, and what followed was standard practice. The impostor had to go alright, but not without some punishment for transgressing against Lord Kane. One of the scruffy men whipped B-man ten times on the backside while they were deciding what to do with Poppa. They stressed that the rules were very clear. No room for strangers! The house was already overcrowded. Each and every member of the house had to be approved first. A place in the House of Lord's had to be earned.

This time, however, in a sudden twist following B-man's painful corporal punishment, Lord Kane's lads came up with a very interesting, and whimsical, resolution: if Poppa himself was ready to give up his place in the house permanently, they would be willing let B-man stay.

And without even pausing to think twice, Poppa, amazingly, agreed to do just that.

The stumpy, whip-wielding skinhead with blood-shot eyes asked him a few times just to make sure. 'We will let your friend take your place,' he said. 'That means we will not expect to see your face anywhere near this house, ever. Do you understand?'

Poppa nodded.

The three men looked at each other.

'Do you *really* understand?' the skinhead asked again.

He nodded again, still keeping his mouth shut.

The big boys were touched by this rare act of selflessness. So touched, in fact, that in the end they decided to let them both stay.

Thus, B-man was officially settled in the great House of Lord's. And he knew he might never live to thank Poppa properly.

CHAPTER 7

Biggy's most repulsive trait was his attitude. As far as Sally-Anne was concerned, this man's only claim to greatness was that, for the time being at least, he was the only person she knew capable of taking her to Mathary Valley. And the big man was making this count. He was acting as though he was slum's gatekeeper, and he had resolved that Sally-Anne would not be allowed back: he had slammed the gates shut and tossed the keys into his pockets.

He was willing to help, but only on strict conditions: he would fetch Sally-Anne's friends from the slums and ferry them for a meeting at her hotel, then back. She had had her trip to Mathary Valley, and he was sincerely sorry about J'Alex, but there was no need for her to go back there.

She, on the other hand, was more interested in getting to the centre of the slums and learning more about what really happened to the Gitongas than merely the opportunity to say hi to cursory acquaintances. She decided that she was not going to be bullied by this stranger. She would take the risk and try to find her own way to Mathary Valley.

She had had a few calls to her mobile from Biggy, which she decided to ignore, despite the temptation to try again, to beg him. She knew her pleas would be rejected, and she did not want to give him the pleasure. After all, this was the man who had lied to her just to get her off the case.

She went down to the reception and asked for a taxi. Ten minutes later, a tall man who claimed to be from a reputable cab company whose name Sally-Anne did not catch, turned up. He had a shiny, bald head, flat at the top and protruding at the back like a bare skull. He said his name was something that sounded like *Alloys*, and when Sally-Anne asked if this was *Alloys* as in metals, he seemed confused, so she let it pass. Alloys was not happy to learn that the job involved driving a white foreigner to the notorious slums. And his protests got louder, the more money Sally-Anne offered. But she also noted that Alloys couldn't bring himself to walk away, so she kept offering more money till his resolve cracked. The final compromise was that he would take her right up to the beginning of the East End of Mathary Valley, and no further.

When they eventually got there, despite all the fuss, she did not notice any sign of fresh trouble. The area around the wind-turbine site did not look any different from how it had been the previous day. But Alloys refused to venture beyond that point, and Sally-Anne found herself sitting in silence in the back of the car, not knowing what to do. She had travelled all this way without a plan. She saw a few people walking down the valley, but all in all it was disturbingly quiet. The usual hassle of men and women going about their normal lives, and kids playing in groups, was conspicuously absent.

But she was here now; she had to do something. The obvious plan would be to go out, approach the first person to come her way and ask them what they knew about the Gitongas. She was still contemplating this when her mobile rang. Yet again it was Biggy, and this time, out of sheer frustration at his persistence, she answered.

'Where have you been?' he started. 'I've been trying to get hold of you all day, I was wondering if you still wanted me to find your other friends in Mathary Valley and bring them to your hotel.'

She was just about to answer when she noticed a shadow sweep past her side of the car. A long, sharp, shiny blade eased through the driver's half-open window, momentarily blinding her with the reflection of the sun's full glare. The gleaming silver blade of a samurai sword rested squarely on the driver's throat. Now, a very dark face leaned forward and calmly commanded Alloys to open the passenger's side door, where another tall figure in blue jeans had also suddenly appeared.

Sally-Anne froze, watching the events swing before her wide eyes in slow-motion. The phone slipped from her grasp and fell to the floor. She felt her body begin shaking in horror as the tall figure in blue jeans was let into the front passenger's side. He was only a boy, definitely younger than eighteen, maybe much younger, but he looked rough and menacing all the same. He pulled out a smaller knife and ordered Alloys to open the back door for his accomplice. It was when she realised the darker figure with a samurai sword was climbing in to take his position besides her that she started seriously considering the possibility that she might not leave this place alive. Her instincts took over, and, without thinking, Sally-Anne found herself shouting:

'I am where we were yesterday, in a blue car... same place as yesterday, in a blue car...' The phone on the floor was only partially concealed under the front passenger-seat. She didn't know if Biggy was still on the line, and, if he was, whether he could hear her and work out what was going on. And more importantly, whether there was anything at all he could do about it. She did not want to die.

'Shut up woman! Or I will cut you.' The dark one slapped her gently as he sat next to her. He was also just a boy. 'Now, give me your bag,' he said, indicating the brown Louis-Vuitton bag that was resting on her lap.

She handed over the bag, shaking and pleading for her life.

The tall one in front had taken the driver's wallet and was rummaging through the glove compartment. He asked for his mobile phone, and Alloys fished a Nokia from his hip pocket and threw it at the boy, as if the thing was infested with leprosy and he was glad to be rid of it. For a moment, it looked like that was that. The muggers had got what they wanted, and their lives would be spared.

The dark one next to her started opening the door, but when he saw his friend take the taxi-driver's phone, it prompted him to rifle through Sally-Anne's bag. He raised his head, shooting a stern, probing look her way. 'Where is your phone?' he asked, and placed the sharp blade over her throat when she hesitated. 'Where is your phone white woman?' he was now almost shouting.

'I... I haven't got a phone—' she started saying, but stopped when she saw him lean forward, his eyes glued to the floor. He reached out, grabbed her phone, glanced at the screen, then snapped it shut and turned it off. He had obviously realised that she had had someone on the line. Slowly, he looked back up at her, his face contorting with menace.

'You had someone there? You are trying to get us caught, you stupid white bitch!' he slapped her on the cheeks, this time harder.

Then, in an apparent change of plan, he slammed the door back shut and ordered Alloys to drive. Alloys, who was now shaking with terror, restarted the engine without any questions.

When she was fourteen, Sally-Anne had once got shoved to the ground by a teenage boy making his escape after fruitlessly attempting to break into an alarmed car in Barnet High Street. The chasing vigilantes had given up on the fleeing thug, and the good people of Barnet had gathered and fussed over young Sally-Anne. She had not sustained a single bruise, but it was the closest she had ever come to a violent crime, and the incident left her shaken for weeks. But even the wild nightmares she subsequently had came nowhere close to what was happening now: her body was quaking, her heart was thumping, and her eyes were seeing flashes of the proverbial bright light and the tunnel. She was going to die in the slums of Africa.

She did not hear the crackling roar of a second engine as a grey Land Rover zoomed in from the left and screeched to a halt in front of the taxi.

For an instant, the two young robbers simply watched, dumbfounded; but it took them no more than three seconds to react. They quickly orchestrated a swift, methodical sequence that led to everything they had stolen finding its way back to where it belonged, and their weapons disappearing into their baggy pants.

The Land Rover's door swung open, and Biggy, in jeans, white trainers and an ill-fitting sleeveless denim top, jumped out and hurtled over to the taxi. He flung open the doors, and dragged out the two boys by their shirts. There was no resistance from the robbers.

'You stupid, stupid boys. You got nothing better to do, eh?'

The boys said nothing.

Biggy proceeded to knock their heads together and beat and kick them to the floor without the boys lifting a finger. Nor did they try to run, even though Biggy was not exactly in control of both of them at all times.

Sally-Anne wanted to warn him that they were armed, but it was all happening too fast.

Something appeared wrong with the spectacle: Biggy, in his street attire, looked like a thug beating up a couple of innocent schoolchildren, not a policeman apprehending violent robbers. When he seemed satisfied with the thoroughness of the beating, he shoved them away with their bloodied faces and tattered clothes.

'Now, disappear into the valley, and don't even look back or I'll kill you,' he commanded them.

This, too, appeared wrong: he had subjected them to a severe beating, and now he had just let them go. Wasn't he supposed to handcuff them and take them to the station? Sally-Anne was too shocked to care.

The big man watched his wounded victims vanish down the valley with an expressionless face. Then he rubbed the palm of his hands together and wiped them on his sleeveless denim top before swaggering back to the taxi. 'How much does the lady owe you for the ride?' he asked the driver.

Alloys hesitated. The extortionate sum he had quoted was forgotten. 'I don't know. Pay me anything you've got, I just want to go away from this place.'

Biggy produced two blue notes from his pocket and handed it to the driver. 'I think that should be enough.'

Alloys stuck the money in the glove compartment without even looking at it.

'I will take the lady back to her hotel,' Biggy said, addressing both of them. Then he began helping her out of the taxi and leading her to the Land Rover.

*

Biggy tried to say some comforting words to Sally-Anne on the way back to the hotel, but she couldn't hear him through her hysterical, shoulder-shaking sobs. When she calmed down it was only out of exhaustion, and Biggy had long since given up trying to talk. Thus the air was filled with an uneasy silence, and Sally-Anne did not like it. She did not like this man. She hated the fact that the only thing she wanted now was to go back home, and she knew that that was exactly what many people had been trying to get her to do, including the man now driving her back to the hotel.

She also knew the next words Biggy was going to utter: they would be along the lines of *I told you so*. She could see it in his cocky little face. She could see him planning exactly how to put it to her so as to make him look wise and clever, and make her look stupid. She hated the fact that this weird, persistently irritating man was now going to assume that she owed him for saving her life. She waited in silence for him to say it, as they wound towards the last stretch of the highway to the Imperial Hotel. She rehearsed her reply, and waited. She knew he was probably going to pull up outside the hotel, look over at her with a smirk, and say: *I told you so... you should learn to listen to me... you should have let me deal with this... I know how to... blah... blah... blah!*

And she knew exactly what she would say in reply.

Fuck you, Biggy!

Then she would storm out of the car and run into the hotel.

After all, she was getting on the first plane back to England in the morning.

He finally pulled up outside the hotel, turned and glanced at her. She waited nervously for him to come out with it, so she could hit right back and run. It was a big risk. She did not know this man. He could take great offence, he could get violent. But she wanted to get this off her chest. She was ready.

'Do you know what really, really scorches my guts?' he started calmly.

Sally-Anne had figured out that this phrase probably meant he was pissed off. Maybe worse than pissed off, otherwise he would have just said he was pissed off. This had to be some serious raw anger burning from deep in the pit of his belly: scorching his guts. This was the situation she now faced. Good start.

She was sure the question was rhetorical, so she waited for his next line. That would be the right time to attack. She fiddled with her handbag, rearranged a few things inside, then zipped it back up, waiting, not ready to get out of the car without showcasing her well-prepared piece. She unzipped the bag again and checked her mobile phone, clicked it shut and zipped up the handbag once more. Still nothing from Biggy. It was as if he had forgotten that he had started to say something.

'Thought you were just about to say something,' she was finally forced to prompt him.

'Ah, never mind, it's not important.'

'Something that really, really scorches your guts...?'

'I was going to say something about those kids, but it's a long, boring story.'

'You know those kids?'

'I know many people in Mathary Valley.'

'Oh...'

And that was it: the tirade did not come. Which caught her completely unawares. Surely the cocky, proud and overly keen to impress Biggy was not going to leave without mentioning something about the consequences of not listening to his *wise* words of warning.

But the dreaded lecture did not come. And when she finally conceded that Biggy was not going to say any more, she eased herself out of the Land Rover and started walking, feeling like the gladiator who prepares all his life to conquer his bitterest nemesis, only to be informed on the day of combat that his opponent has been swallowed by a tiger before entering the arena.

Sally-Anne took a few tentative steps towards the entrance, and then, as an afterthought, she stopped and turned round to face Biggy.

'Thanks,' she said, staring blankly at the ground for a few seconds, trying to justify to herself this unforeseen change of tact.

Well, whatever else Biggy was or did or represented, he had indeed saved her life.

'Thank you very much,' she added.

***

With Poppa's guidance, B-man slowly and surely began to grow into the streets. He soon realised how wrong he had been about Poppa when he had assumed that the boy was just another street junkie. Poppa turned out to be an enigma. He was not only worlds apart from the other street boys, but indeed from anyone else B-man had ever met. And it was not just his storytelling expertise. He was many things: an entrepreneur, a historian, a teacher and a philosopher.

He was also as sly as a dozing rabbit. Always one eye open: ever the teetotal *chwaka* brewer.

In the company of the other Parking-boys, Poppa followed the flow. He performed for the team even if it meant indulging in the assortment of drugs they did. When he was safely away from the gang, however, he was a totally different man. He rarely even smoked cigarettes. The occasional drug, mostly glue, in his possession would be purely for business. A business that B-man would soon learn was going nowhere fast.

Poppa remained adamant that he had no other names, and that he didn't even know his real age. B-man did not believe him, but such matters were never dwelt upon, for Poppa's was always an otherwise preoccupied mind. He was a man on a mission to liberate the entire street population through the teaching of history.

If, later, someone were to ask B-man to point out exactly when he overtook his best friend in the ways of streets, he wouldn't have been able to answer. All he knew was that he was suddenly doing more drugs than Poppa and engaging in more criminal activities, or *hits*, as they called them. When the boys went out to mug middle-class working people, B-man found himself working his way closer and closer to the frontline, while Poppa remained the same old jabbering storyteller who had first spoken to him on the park bench. Maybe B-man's natural strength from a childhood of back-breaking work on his grandad's farm gave him the edge. He was always needed for these *hits*, especially because they often got physical.

He began to enjoy the physicality of their good old-fashioned hit-and-run attacks. He was the strong man, and this was his stage, his forte. Then one day he got introduced to a different style of attack, one that they referred to as the *chizi* attack.

And the *chizi* attack immediately went down as his least favourite.

It started when one night in the house he noticed some of the boys shamelessly pulling their pants down, squatting at the far end and defecating in small plastic bags. They were doing this as a group, group shitting, like some sort of ritual. It was not a pleasant sight. There was a pit latrine at the back of the house that served their toilet needs quite effectively, and he did not understand why they were choosing not to use it. His inquiries about this barbaric behaviour were answered with some mutterings about *chizi* attack, a term he did not understand. So he simply held his nose, closed his eyes and tried his best to pretend that this was not happening and to get some sleep.

Very early next morning, one or two of the boys again mentioned the *chizi* word, asking if he was in. And for the first time he admitted that he had no idea what this was. By way of explanation, they invited him to come along to town with them.

And since going into the city was part of their day-to-day life, that, initially, did not give much away.

Everyone was to make their own way to the city centre. Some were friendly enough with the local *matatu* conductors to enjoy the perks of free rides. B-man walked. They reconvened just off the city hall junction on Moi Avenue, a strategic point just a few yards away from the bus station and not far off the Central Business District. In normal circumstances, he would have assumed that they were simply going to pick-pocket working-class people before the poor gentlemen had even started their day. But the mystery and excitement surrounding this particular operation suggested something special.

'Our targets, chaps, are the lower middle-class, you know what I mean...?' announced Jude, the slightly older, well-muscled boy who had always been a prominent figure in the house owing to his loud-mouthed tough talk and tendency to assume leadership whenever the occasion necessitated. 'We want the man who wears cheap suit and a tie and bounces around thinking he's better than everyone else. That's who we want.'

B-man soon found out what the mission was, when a few yards off the busy Kencom Bus Stage, Little Joey, a short, skinny boy no older than ten, cried to one smartly dressed pedestrian: 'Sir, can you spare some change for my breakfast, please?'

The young man had his long hair intricately trimmed and shaped up flat on the sides and the top, with sharp corners, making his head look like a black box. He casually turned his boxy head Joey's way and walked on without breaking stride.

'Spare some change please...' little Joey repeated, hurrying to keep pace.

Box Head was now clearly getting annoyed. He stopped and contorted the smooth face under the box into a grim hard stare.

'Will you please stop following me like that–'

'And are you going to spare some change for a starving homeless, or do you want some of this on your face?' Joey's voice had suddenly changed from pleading to threatening as he produced a plastic bundle filled with a brownish, clay-like substance.

Box Head, refusing to be threatened, walked on without giving the substance as much as a second look.

'I don't get breakfast, you get to work covered in shit, sir,' shouted Joey, opening the bag and scooping a handful of the clay-like stuff. B-man squirmed from a distance. Box Head also caught this movement and stopped.

'What's that?' he asked.

'It's my shit, as you'll probably have noticed if you've got any sense of smell. You give me some change, you don't get shit,' he threatened. 'It's your call, sir.'

Some passers-by realised what was going on. A middle-aged man in a neat navy blue double-breasted suit jumped in to try and grab hold of little Joey from behind, but someone shouted a warning in time for little Joey to slip away. Before the blue suit could make any further moves, someone shouted to him: 'Behind you... they are throwing shit at you!' He ducked just in time for the handful of shit to miss his face, but it got a good patch on the sleeve of his coat.

Suddenly, a gang of no less than a dozen bedraggled, barefoot street boys appeared as though from nowhere. They surrounded both men, Box Head and his blue-suited hero. They were all armed with a bagful of fresh shit.

Jude had taken charge, and he warned the onlookers: 'Do not interfere. No more heroes! Everyone, start walking away now if you'd like to get to your office with some dignity,' he shouted as he scooped a handful, ready for other potential Blue Suits. There was a squeamish chorus of '*Eeeugh...* ' amidst the commotion of people rushing to safety. Jude was true to his word: they didn't interfere, and they would get to work with untarnished respectability. Blue Suit would have been in this esteemed group had he not interfered. Shame.

'Right, you two,' Jude turned to the captives. 'Leave your wallets on the ground and run to work.'

Both men hesitated. Jude didn't. He hurled another handful straight at Box Head. The man dived to the ground, and the missile missed him. He did not raise his head for a long time, but his hands shot up immediately, complete with his brown leather wallet.

'Yes, sir... you can have the wallet... please don't do this.'

It was the first time B-man had heard a teenage Parking-Boy referred to as *sir*. And if Box Head was queasy about shit, then Mister Blue Suit was absolutely terrified of it – probably because of the patch he already had on his sleeve to prove this was real shit. He bowed to his knees, facing down and away, his left arm stretched to the opposite side with all fingers spread out in a poor imitation of a shield, and his right hand frantically waving a black wallet in the air.

'Can I take my documents please... sir...? Just the documents. The money is all yours... please...?'

But when Jude, still holding a handful, looked him in the eye, he quickly put the whole wallet down and said no more.

'It's alright,' Jude compromised, 'you can take your IDs, papers and all that non-sense. But make it fast, I haven't got all day.'

The two men sorted out their documents with shaking hands, and when they were at last set free, Blue Suit found it difficult to turn his back, not knowing what might come from behind.

'I'm sorry... I'm not a bad man... please don't throw any more of that at me,' he pleaded with a shaky voice as he retreated. 'Please... I just wanted... please ... sir–'

But the boys had already grabbed the wallets and disappeared.

*

Later that night, B-man sat next to Poppa on their corner with a cigarette, itching to fill him in on the action he had missed earlier in the day. But as usual he had first to lend Poppa his ears and wait his turn. Poppa's chosen topic tonight was something about slavery and the colonies.

'Why is it that we Africans bore the brunt of the worst of the social injustices in history?' he asked. 'Why were we enslaved and colonised?'

'I'm sure you are going to tell me the answer, Poppa. Just get on with it so I can tell you about the *chizi* attack and–'

'It was the languages, B-man,' he interrupted. 'The thousands of different languages, and tribes. The distinct surnames. Religions. Cultures as varied as the stars in the sky. Elsewhere out there, people utilised everything that brought them together, anything that identified them as one people, to build strong bases for the pillars of their societies. Religions that, although they oppressed one's own mothers and sisters, were still followed unequivocally, with faith as staunch as the rocks of Kit Mikayi. That is the threat the conquerors faced out there. But on this continent, B, they only found things that drew us apart. We were easy pickings, and have always been.'

'Poppa, you know you are my best friend out here, right?'

That took him by surprise, shut him up for while. 'Yes...'

'I want to tell you something that you might find offensive, but is true.' He paused as Poppa eyed him suspiciously. 'I think sometimes... not all the time, just sometimes, you need to stop thinking about history and start thinking of the here and now. All this historical knowledge is great, but it's not very useful here. Because around here it is all about respect. And that respect comes not from what you know but *who* you know. The other boys make fun of you, Poppa. They laugh at you, like they laughed at me when I first got here. Yet you were here way before me. Make a name for yourself the street way, Poppa.'

'Wow! B-man, is this you talking?' he gasped. 'I'm lost for words. You really have grown up, haven't you?'

'I'm adapting, Poppa. I'm trying to gain respect. It took me months to get accepted around here, but now I think I can say I well and truly belong–' he was lighting another cigarette '– I'm getting involved, Poppa, getting stuck in.'

'Ha! Now, the big bushman is making a name for himself in the streets.' He spat out the words sarcastically. 'Who would have thought it, eh? I thought you didn't belong here, B. I thought you were just passing through.'

'This is not about me–'

'What happened to the man who wanted to belong in society, the boy who dreamt of being a waiter?' Poppa spoke very slowly, with deep passion, like it was coming from the pit of his belly. 'Have you given in to a lifetime of this? Is this what you want to be when the end comes, B-man?'

B-man smiled in disbelief. 'I thought you liked this life, Poppa, didn't you say you wanted to join Kane's gang some day?'

'Maybe I did, maybe I didn't. I say a lot of different things to a lot of people. When I'm with other street people I do what's necessary to survive amongst them. But at the end of the day only you know how you want your life to end up. I don't know a lot about you, B. You probably had a decent early education, you probably possess some useful talents, I just can't know for sure. But one thing I know is that when you first arrived here you believed you could do better. All my time in the streets I've harboured dreams that I wouldn't have dared speak aloud for fear of sounding crazy. But you came along with your naïve determination, and I thought I saw something in you that could help propel my stupid dreams. You got here with something pure and special, B-man. But you are failing to hold on to it. The turbulent tides of the streets are threatening to sweep it out of your grasp.'

He stopped, and for a short while B-man thought that that was the end of the lecture.

'I started life in a charity home,' Poppa picked up in full narrative mode. 'Then I was tossed from one foster home to another, and before I knew it I was in the streets. Tough life, B-man, tough life! My choices and chances were reduced to only two: life or death.'

B-man was silent; shocked.

Poppa was thinking, deeply. 'The life expectancy of a Parking-boy is nineteen, B. That's a fact. So you could choose to blame the circumstances that led you here and start counting down your days; or you can go down on your knees and thank God for making you an able-bodied human being, and use those two hands to find your keys out of this misery.

'The many colours we see in life are but an illusion, for there's only black and white. If you resolve to find your way out of these streets, that path will be your white. Within this path you will experience your reds and greens and yellows, and, even if you don't make it, you will have experienced the magic of the rainbow – all the colours that make white: light. The alternative path has got no colour, B. No light, just black. The true magic of life is a loving family, friends, schools... everything those normal people out there are working for as they go about their daily life. Without that, you are in the dark.'

He paused again and swallowed. 'Will we ever have that, B-man? Will we ever experience this magic?'

Poppa kept his eyes focused on a single point on the floor, and stayed silent for maybe a whole minute. Then, as if to himself, he went on:

'I can mend shoes, B-man. I'd like to one day open a cobbler's shop in an estate somewhere, a *shoes-repaired-while-you-wait* sort of thing. And maybe some children will be sent to me by their parents, and while they wait for their shoes I will tell them some stories: history. And one day, when I die, maybe some residents will remember the old cobbler, and maybe only one or two of the children will remember Poppa the storyteller. Who knows, maybe someone will even shed a tear for me. That one person, B-man, who sheds one tear for the old cobbler, will create the magic of white. Validate my existence. Give meaning to my life on this earth. Just that one person, B-man...'

His voice was faltering, and for a brief moment B-man imagined Poppa was going to cry. But when he looked up there was not a trace of a tear.

He was now barely whispering.

'You once told me you wouldn't live on the streets forever, you said you didn't want to suffer forever, you said you were better than that. Now, you are falling apart, yet you still claim you are enjoying it. You are falling apart because you have walked out on a dream. That is the definition of a nightmare, B: a dream that has been abandoned.'

He swallowed a lump once more to keep his voice steady.

'I don't know who you are, B-man, I don't even know your name, but as for me, I chose white. I saw life and death, I chose life, and for the sake of my choice I'll always try to survive...'

He could have gone on, and probably wanted to, but his voice was failing. So he stretched prostrate along his floor-space and put the greasy blanket over his head. B-man was left looking at the dark blanket, laced by a thin stripe of light from a distant flickering candle, in amazement, listening only to the deathly silence of the House of Lord's, and wondering if this was the closest Poppa would ever get to crying.

There was not one hint of a tear, not a sign of weeping. Nothing but the chilling silence.

That night, B-man didn't sleep next to Poppa in the house. With his rags he moved to the ground floor, where one of the boys rolled a joint and offered it half smoked to B-man as he himself dozed off. B-man held the joint for a very long time, then stubbed it out without smoking.

It had taken him only this long to get into the streets. He had expected a job, yet he did not even know where to start. He had since learnt that to get any kind job he would require an address, to prove he was not a criminal or a junkie. A reference, a proper relative, a friend, someone who knew something about him... something... anything! Anything to prove he was a real human being.

Very late that night, before covering himself in a worn-out blanket that had been acquired from a city recycling bin, he looked around the dark, silent squat to make sure everyone was asleep. Then he lay facing the nonexistent ceiling and whispered audibly.

'A job, even as a cleaner, a street cleaner, is all I ask for, God. Or is that too much to ask?'

Then he lit the joint and smoked it anyway.

CHAPTER 8

Violence still dominated the news in Kenya. The two leaders were still trading accusations because the death toll was rising and somebody was to blame. The opposition was pointing an ominous finger at the government because most of the casualties had been shot, in a country where civilians do not own guns. The government was quick to counter this with their own claims that the opposition had fully expected to lose the elections, and had planned this war well in advance by arming their people. Sally-Anne hardly understood politics, let alone African politics. But she knew there was no sign of a resolution here.

As if this was not enough, her dad was also piling pressure on her. She had just given him a tearful account of her ordeal in Mathary Valley and he was livid. The *I-told-you-so* rant she had been steeling herself for had finally come. Howard Symmonds raved loudly and incoherently, and every time he calmed down enough to say something comprehensible, Sally-Anne heard the same old words:

'You have to come back home, Sally-Anne!'

She could not even bring herself to ask him what Barclays Bank had said about the alleged transactions by J'Alex. It was too late now; Sally-Anne's bubble of pipe-dream heroics had been busted. Things were dangerous out here. It was as simple as that. Whatever had happened to J'Alex, there was nothing she could do. She had to accept that. Her remote hope that J'Alex had somehow escaped the fire was a consequence of watching too many movies; such things simply didn't happen in real life. So, yes, it was time to leave, she had done her best. She would pray for them, she would pray for the country and for J'Alex.

'You have to come back home, Sally-Anne,' her father said for the umpteenth time.

She mumbled something like, *Yes, Dad*, but his order was beginning to grate. Why couldn't he just calm down and for once show some sympathy? It was clear that today's events had been the last straw in this doomed mission. He knew she had failed. He knew she was coming back home. So why not just show some sympathy?

'Sally-Anne, I need to know when you are getting on the plane back,' he demanded as she did her best to stay calm. 'The weather's been terrible recently and they are forecasting snow in the next couple of days. We have to move quickly, there may be flight delays.'

Ah, the terrible British weather!

That did it. Something suddenly clicked.

Two years ago, in the rocky field behind the wind-turbine site where she had just been attacked, she had an interesting conversation with J'Alex about the terrible British weather. She had challenged him to a game of *keepy-uppie* with his homemade football during her break. He had been laughing a little too loudly and with a touch of exaggeration at her feeble attempts at ball-juggling when he suddenly stopped and grabbed the ball mid-air. Then he looked up at her, and, with the cool, assured voice of a veteran interrogator, he asked why her eyes were blue. Caught off guard, without any answers she deemed readily digestible for his underdeveloped brain, she had gone on to explain that in England there were long and terrible winters when it sometimes got pitch dark at three o'clock in the afternoon, and she needed her blue eyes to glow in the dark so she could remain visible to other people. Little J'Alex had been transfixed, looking up her, shielding his eyes from the sun with one hand and hugging the football over his thigh with the other. His face had twisted in concentration as he listened. His eyelids had fluttered wildly over his wide brown eyes with what could have been confusion or suspicion, or maybe bemusement, or simply shock. Then, just as she was beginning to fear that she had perhaps caused more damage than intended to this infant soul, J'Alex Gitonga suddenly flicked on his wide, toothy grin and said: 'I am nearly eleven, you know.'

Her dad was still breathing on the other end of the phone, waiting to hear when she'd be getting on that plane.

'I will come home, Dad,' she said. 'But not before I find him.'

The following morning, Jude, the ringleader of the *chizi* attack, was up early again, and asking who wanted in on the next mission. It was an offer B-man quietly declined. He could use the money, but he didn't feel quite prepared for that. Besides, after Poppa's unprecedented lecture the night before, he was finding himself a little confused.

The mission's mastermind, Jude, was someone for whom B-man was increasingly developing respect and even admiration. Despite the grotesque nature of the *shit-point* attack, there was definitely some fine artistry in the way Jude conceived, organised and took control of the operation. Although slightly shorter, Jude was still bigger than B-man overall, owing to his broadness. And most of the street boys who had fallen foul of him attested that not one ounce of his mass was fat. Word had it that he had just been freed from a juvenile detention centre where for six years, since the age of ten, he had been held in connection with an incident that led to someone's death. During his time in prison, he was trained as a junior boxer as a way to vent his prodigious levels of energy and anger. But all that training came to nothing when they released him back into a world that had nothing for him – nothing but the streets.

At the back of the house, Jude kept a set of weights made from pairs of cylindrical metal buckets filled with cement and joined together by a rod through a hole in the centre of the bottom. He lifted them religiously every night, grunting like a wild animal on his own in the dark when everyone else was indoors smoking, drinking, sniffing glue and producing their jokeless laughs while playing cards under the dim candle-light. The results of this unconventional fitness regime were a set of rather incongruous but rock-hard muscles. His left bicep, for instance, was bigger than the right, yet the right shoulder remained prominently broader. Later, after the work-out, when he joined the card game indoors, Jude would be more active than the boys whose brains were fizzing from a cocktail of hard drugs. He'd be laughing and shouting louder than anyone else. Sometimes also kicking and punching at loose objects, walls, and people, indiscriminately, like a mad beast.

If anyone from the house was going to be accepted into Lord Kane's gang in the near future, it had to be Jude. And like everyone else, he knew it. That was the reason he had developed the propensity to assume control of the House of Lord's. It sometimes got very irritating, but Jude was a tough boy, and nobody would stand up to him. This, however, had never raised any concern for B-man. Their paths didn't cross frequently enough for Jude's bossy attitude to be a problem.

However, that same evening, just a day after B-man had watched and greatly admired Jude's raw industry, this young hero would turn all that strength and willpower against him. To put it mildly, their paths did finally cross: Jude, who was accustomed to bullying, saw no reason to treat B-man any differently from the rest, and B-man, more out of naiveté than bravery, attempted to resist.

That evening, the House of Lord's and the entire Mathary Valley saw miracles.

*

It had started downtown around midday. B-man was wandering into the city centre when he encountered Jude and a few of the other boys underneath the Victoria Bridge. He stopped to exchange some good-humoured banter, after which Jude tried to send him to buy some cigarettes from a convenience store that was barely a hundred yards down the road. B-man, who, at that particular moment, was feeling a little tired, stoned and slightly dizzy, innocently suggested that maybe he would be better off sending one of the other boys instead.

Jude laughed. Changed his tone, and repeated the order.

'No!' said B-man. 'I'm tired.'

So Jude turned round, slapped him a few times and kicked him to the ground, and left him heaving in pain under the bridge.

B-man should have learnt his lesson then. But he did not.

He recovered. And when he eventually strutted back to the house very late that night, he carefully tiptoed over the sleeping bodies on the top floor, to the far corner where he knew Jude would be sleeping. Then he knelt down next to the unconscious Jude, tilted his face to one side and punched it as hard as he could.

Jude woke.

Soon the whole house was up and cheering their lungs out, *uuuhing* and *aaahing* as Jude rained blows and kicks on the semi-conscious B-man.

There was a broken nose. There was blood.

When he thought he was finished, with the helpless body slumped on the floor, Jude dragged him up by the nape of his neck and frogmarched him outside, followed by his cheering supporters. Then he hoisted him up as high as his arms could go and let him drop to the hard ground below.

Poppa was not anywhere to be seen that night. One or other of the many nocturnal urchin businesses had kept him out late and spared him the anguish of witnessing what Jude was doing to his friend.

B-man could have easily been killed by the strong ex-boxer. But before Jude disappeared back inside the house, there was an even louder cheer from a few of the kids who were watching his lifeless body. Jude turned to look. And he saw an arm slowly rising above the ground till it was almost vertical, with the middle finger sticking up. Then he heard a deep, crackling voice.

'It ain't over, bastard... I'm still standing. We're gonna dance till the cows come home... you bastard!'

Jude stormed back outside, seething with unbridled rage, and lifted the limp body before it got halfway up. Then, ignoring the feeble punches, he hoisted it off ground and let it drop with a thud. This time he stayed put for a while, waiting for the next sign of life from the body on the ground. There was another attempt to raise a withering right hand, which failed just short of the upright position, and then the left, which only rose a few inches before wilting back into the dust.

Jude was almost satisfied that the job was finished when, right in front of him, B-man's whole body jolted and his full figure shot straight up, as if electrified by some underground force. B-man had flung himself off the ground, and landed on his feet full of life, bouncing, skipping and shadow-boxing the dark midnight air. Then he walked right up to Jude and levelled his bloody, ravaged face inches from his attacker's, with his bloody nose almost touching Jude's forehead, like a pair of boxers in a face-off.

Jude stood frozen to the spot. The shock alone could have knocked him out, but before he could even register the shock, the erect figure in front of him very slowly and spectacularly collapsed back to the ground like a falling tree.

All the cheerleaders got back in the house without any idea whether B-man was unconscious or dead. Jude was smoking a joint to get himself back to sleep when yet another groan was heard from outside.

'Where the fuck are you now, bastard? We ain't done... we're on till the cows come home...!'

Only a few of the spectators followed Jude back outside this time. They were getting bored.

There was more blood, and a broken bone or two. And to finish off, Jude yet again lifted B-man's body high and let it fall. Only to be answered with another cry: 'We're dancing, mother-fucker... till the cows come home.'

*

It was two drunken, elderly residents of Mathary Valley, mere passers-by, who witnessed the finale to the duel in the early hours of the morning. By now, Jude was also stoned, sleepy, exhausted and aching. But he was still managing, with a struggle, to lift B-man's lifeless body and let it fall, all the while trying to ignore the repeated refrain: 'We're dancing, mother-fucker... till the cows come home...'

By the end of it all, the two old men were left looking at not one, but two bodies lying lifeless on the ground in front of the squat. Even in their drunken state, they realised how serious this was. One of them swayed across the path to knock on the *mkokoteni*-puller's door.

The *mkokoteni*-man was the same dark, greasy gentleman B-man had witnessed on his first day in the slums, giving the retired diplomat a ride. On this occasion, the man started mumbling his displeasure at the ungodly hour of this intrusion by two old drunks who had neither the means nor the intention to pay for his services. He was not a charity, he said. But after one look at the two bodies, he bundled them onto *GOD'S ROUTE, NO SHORTCUTS!* and wheeled them half a mile to the *daktari's* house which also served as a pharmacy and a clinic.

*

The *daktari* (doctor) had been an *askari* (security guard) in his previous life. During his time working as an *askari* in a major state hospital, accompanying doctors and nurses to their late-night rounds, the smart and resourceful *askari* very carefully watched and learned. That constituted the full extent of his medical training. In addition, the *askari* had also mastered ways of creatively letting drugs slip through the back doors of the hospital's pharmacy. Thus, the next time the government decided to cut back on healthcare, with his job one of the first on the line, the *askari* had something to fall back on when he was forced to surrender his government-provided house and retreat to the slums.

The pharmacy side of his business was legitimate: he had found people with the right qualifications but who had nothing at all to do with the running of the place, to sign as licensees. But at the back of the pharmacy, the former *askari*, for additional fees, also endeavoured to put his medical knowledge to practice. He would sit there in his white scrubs, a stethoscope round his neck, stabbing thermometers at patients whilst pretending to listen very carefully to their problems. In truth, the *daktari* would only be listening for one key word: temperature. For temperature always came up. He would then proceed to put them on a full course of malaria treatment, regardless of what else the patient or the stethoscope or the thermometer said. And in a few days they would be back to thank him for saving a life.

*

The *daktari* looked at the two nameless bodies that had been brought to him in a *mkokoteni*, and tried to patch them up as well as he could; but he decided that this particular problem was out of his depth. The boys clearly needed a proper hospital. The *mkokoteni*-puller was thus left in a tricky position, stuck with the two bodies; but he decided to do his best, for he was a good man who strongly believed in doing God's work on earth. He wheeled them another two miles to the general hospital and dumped them near the entrance. Someone would find them, and relinquish him of any further responsibility.

As soon as they were discovered, one of the bodies was taken straight to intensive care, where a life-saving operation began immediately. The other woke up in a hospital ward that morning, and before the end of the afternoon he had jumped through the window and escaped.

The final outcome of this duel would capture the imagination of the streets more than the fight itself, and be the making of yet another Dallas legend. When the police descended upon the slums looking for the culprit who had escaped from hospital, the whole of Dallas was left with a mystery of their own. They had all witnessed Jude batter B-man's body to the ground like a sack of potatoes. Jude had beaten the boy to a pulp and left him virtually dead on the ground in front of them, right there in the open for all who cared to see; and for many years there would be various theories and heated *chwaka*-joint debates over the events of that night. But not one of the Dallas denizens would ever be able to explain how it could have possibly turned out that the young man who eventually found himself in intensive care, on the brink of death, was Jude.

***

The phone call from Inspector Limo woke her up at ten to seven in the morning. It was quite a surprise, because Inspector Limo hardly called at all. It had so far been left up to Sally-Anne to initiate the calls. Her immediate assumption was that this would be about the attempted robbery.

'My dear,' he started. She was beginning to get used to being referred to as *my dear*; he probably used that as a standard title for all females. 'I just got the Gitonga shop crime-scene report, and I thought you would want to know.'

The sleep was suddenly shaken from her head. She was now on high alert.

'Right... I'm listening.'

'The forensics combed the place and gathered all traces of human remains. Apparently it was not completely burnt to ashes; the police and fire-fighters may not have got there in time to save any lives, but they did save some remains. Which are beginning to look very significant.'

She held her breath: the inspector sounded excited. And the fact that he was now referring to a case which they had previously showed very little interest in as *our* case was a good sign.

'They have worked out that there was a total of four bodies at the scene. Two of them belonged to a middle-aged couple, the other two were very young children, most probably under the age of ten. One member of the family was missing from the scene, and initial indications suggest it might well be the twelve-year-old.'

She continued listening intently without a word.

'So it looks like you might be on to something after all. We will begin a missing-person inquiry immediately and I will continue to update you.'

She let the inspector fill her in with details of how they were proposing to go about the case in light of the new developments. Inspector Limo was talking fast and enjoying the sound of what he was saying, clearly elated by the new developments. So she let him talk, chipping in here and there to remind him that she was still there. When it was all over she sat on her bed and considered everything from all possible angles.

Yes, she had told her dad that she was not leaving until she found J'Alex. But that was mainly because she had been caught at a sentimental moment, and maybe also partly because her dad's constant pressures had provoked her to rebel. She was supposed to be on her way back home, it was the only reasonable thing to do. But the image of J'Alex's beautiful smiling face had etched itself on her brain and refused to go away. It was beginning to haunt her in her sleep. She had made him a promise. She had vowed to take him to the UK one day, and the poor, innocent boy had clung on to that hope. She could imagine how he must have held on to her card details religiously, his last existing link with her, hoping they would one day help him make his big break to that lovely, faraway land. He had only used them when he'd needed her.

She remembered telling him: *If you try to use my card, my bank back in England will tell me, and I will know it is you...* It was J'Alex's long shot, last ditch attempt to survive.

Inspector Limo had said they were doing something, but in this political climate there were more serious issues for the police to deal with. For how long could they sustain a realistic interest in this case if there was no one representing J'Alex? If he was alive somewhere, he was probably in trouble. He needed help, someone had to be there for him and offer him a shot at survival.

She remembered the message Mr. Murray had read: I HAVE GOT NO ONE!

How could she leave now?

She considered her own childhood. She had had a good childhood, because someone had given her a chance, someone everyone else around her preferred to forget, but someone Sally-Anne would always remember as the person who gave her a chance to live. It was the greatest contribution her mother ever made to her life. It was also the only contribution she ever made.

*

Sally-Anne knew her mother's name was Karen, and that Karen had grown up a very troubled soul. She got out of care at the age of ten and was fostered for six years by the Hamiltons, the family that subsequently offered Sally-Anne a crucial stepping stone towards survival and normality. They were the old couple that nurtured Sally-Anne through early childhood and told her everything she knew about her mother.

At the age of sixteen, due to peer pressure and various minor disagreements, Karen moved out of the Hamiltons' home and declared herself homeless. She moved into a youth hostel, and got herself pregnant almost immediately. She then used the pregnancy a leverage to apply for council support, and they duly offered her a dingy one-bedroom facility at the infamous Grahame Park estate in north London, where no other self-respecting white Londoners wanted to live, even for free.

Everything was wrong with the pregnancy. The father was believed to be one of five males, all of them almost equal in their degree of unsuitability for fatherhood: three of them were boys under the age of sixteen, and the other two were married men older than thirty-five. The mother was an unemployed juvenile delinquent, unfit to even look after herself. Everyone Karen knew in her chaotic life, including the Hamiltons, advised abortion. It was a no-brainer. But Karen was a very opinionated young girl. She believed that she could speak to the unborn life inside her. She said that every night she would explain to it how hard, miserable and cruel this life, into which it was seeking entry, could be. And every time, the baby would say: *Well, I'm here now. I will take my chances.*

Through Ma Hamilton, Sally-Anne had heard Karen's exact words many a time: *The baby is here now, it has gone through a magical process to turn up in my womb, and all it is asking is for me to give it a chance*

So young Karen went on to have the baby. And she had an almighty struggle with childcare. Neighbours were worried by the frequency and loudness of the baby's screams. There were fears that she left the baby unattended for longer than was acceptable. There were visits from social services, but Karen argued her case well, explaining that she had only ever left the baby fast asleep, and for no more than a couple of minutes, to do other household chores. She pointed out that she was a single mother, and claimed that Sally-Anne just happened to be a temperamental baby.

Only Karen herself would know what she was thinking on that fateful Friday evening when she bathed, changed and put her seventeen-month-old baby to sleep with three bottles of milk next to her, then locked the doors and went out. Maybe she had only meant to go round the corner for a few minutes; maybe she'd only meant to have a quick drink with her friends. Whatever the truth, she did not come home that night, or the following day, or the following night. Her baby's constant screams only alerted the neighbours on the Sunday evening. They considered calling the police or social services. But they called Ma' Hamilton first.

Sally-Anne was found sick, emaciated, tired, covered in faeces, urine and vomit, and unable to cry anymore. Ma Hamilton, then just months short of her eightieth birthday, took the baby. And when Karen came back, there were no harsh words, tirades, arguments or threats. The matter was resolved with a silent admission by both parties that Karen was unfit to be a mother. Sally-Anne could have died or been taken to care and ended up on the same life-path as Karen, with Karen herself possibly in prison. But she found her avenue to life through the kind, cultured and well-off Hamilton family.

Karen was free to visit the baby anytime, but when she came back two days later it was only to hand over the details of Sally-Anne's five possible fathers. And within a few days Karen had left town and simply vanished off the face of the earth.

Nonetheless, Sally-Anne had a good childhood. The Hamiltons employed the best to take care of her; she went to private schools and had pretty much everything she would have wanted at her disposal. The Hamiltons never once tried to pretend they were her real parents. They always believed Karen would one day grow up, sort herself out, find peace and direction in her life, and eventually come back for her baby. They told Sally-Anne tales of how her parents had had to go to some faraway place, and that they would come back for her.

By the time she was eight, the Hamiltons were getting old and sickly, and they did not want Sally-Anne to be taken into care. So they began the process of tracing her real dad, in the hope that he could offer something.

He turned out to be the least suitable of all the five candidates. He was a hopeless drunk, an unemployed fifty-three-year-old former London cab-driver, who had been disowned by his two existing families. But he was a man who would rediscover the value of life when he laid eyes on the last of the offspring he had sired, the little girl who would effectively constitute his third family.

Howard Symmonds began his transformation, and the battle to gain custody of his little girl. He went back to cab-driving, and within a year he owned his own taxi company. He did everything for Sally-Anne, and never left her side. Even his estranged families, Sally-Anne's many half brothers and sisters, finally appreciated the change and afforded him another chance. A very large family was reconciled. At the age of eight, Sally-Anne had finally found a sense of belonging, a family, a name, and, more importantly, someone who would always be there for her and love her unconditionally. And she had a very happy and fulfilled childhood.

It had taken her a long time to find it, but the person who gave her that first shot at happiness had been, and would forever remain, Karen, her mother. That is the way she wanted to remember her.

*

Sally-Anne prayed that J'Alex was out there somewhere, alive. What she knew for certain was that if he was, he did not have a family now. No one seemed concerned. No one was out there looking for him. There was plenty going awry in this country, and, to many, J'Alex was just another name among the thousands caught up in the war: fairly insignificant in the grand scheme of things. But this was an idea Sally-Anne could not live with.

Around noon, she picked up the phone and called Inspector Limo back. 'How long do you think this kind of investigation will take, sir?' she wanted to know.

'Well, that depends, if we can't find the boy, and without any evidence that he is dead, the case could stay open for years. On the other hand, if he is alive and wants to be found, we could find him in days. I cannot promise anything.'

She then called her dad, explained the new developments and tried her best to make him understand why she really had to stay.

CHAPTER 9

After the fight, Jude was never again seen in Dallas. There were rumours a few weeks later that he had been spotted, bible in hand, touring the city with a group of street-preachers. Someone at the hospital had enlightened him to the good Lord's word.

Whatever it was about the fight that led to Jude's enlightenment also did something to B-man. As the other Parking-boys put it: *it fucked B-man up in the head.* His recovery from the flesh wounds was swift, but it was the consequent metamorphosis of B-man's personality that remained unfathomable. The smoking habit disappeared miraculously. The smell of alcohol and drugs began to make him sick. Sometimes the smell got so unbearable that he had to leave the house. *They fucked each other up real good...* said the other boys. B-man, however, remained convinced that this had nothing to do with the fight: it was Poppa's long *black-and-white-life-or-death* lecture that had fucked him up.

As expected, Poppa was the only sober head who considered B-man's condition from a rational point of view. Nothing had fucked him up. Whatever this was, it had in fact shone a light on B-man's troubled life, just like it had for Jude.

In the newly transformed B-man, Poppa saw an opportunity. Their relationship took on new dimensions. Now, once again, they had a common bond, shared ambitions: dreams of getting out of the streets.

Poppa encouraged enthusiastically. 'We can do this, B, we definitely can. We are not like the others. We have a dream! And like I said to you before, you never give up on a dream. The moment you throw out a dream, a nightmare lets himself in. When you tussle with a hyena that has captured your lamb, you do not give up, not only because you want it back, but because the moment you let go of the lamb, the hyena begins to realise that you too are made up of but chunky pieces of juicy steak.'

B-man smiled at that. 'And what have you in mind Poppa? Where do we start?'

'We make a small amount of money first, just enough to get a small place away from here. Then we clean up, establish ourselves as normal people, and start looking for proper jobs.'

'And where is the initial money coming from?'

'Er... well, we might have to do something undesirable at first. But once we break into society, we are in. That's it, no coming back. We either belong here or there, B, and I don't want to belong here.'

From then on their talks got more constructive. A grand plan was soon taking shape. There was an immediate need to carry on with the usual street business, but from now on everything was aimed towards the great target. They exploited all their options: the glue business, some muggings and pickpocketing here and there, drug-running, begging... anything, to make that initial break. And this time the money would be saved wisely.

The savings did not grow as fast as they would have wanted. B-man questioned the viability of the grand plan for the umpteenth time; Poppa urged patience. They were nearly there, he reassured, he could almost see it. First they'd rent a flat, Poppa would get the shoe-repair business started straightaway, and B-man would start looking for a job, any job. It could not fail.

A year went past, and the savings were still short of the big-break target. Extreme thrift measures had to be adopted; after the strict no smoking, drinking or drugs policy, they also introduced a no-spending-on-foods measure. Their dietary requirements now had to rely entirely on stolen, donated or scavenged foods.

During the course of all this, B-man also saw the inside of the city jails on two occasions for pickpocketing, and was forced to give up much of his valuable time to unpaid community service as punishment.

Poppa continued to rack his brains for ways of making more money safely, honestly and fast; a notion that left even B-man, naïve as he was, slightly bemused.

Eventually, one night, after giving B-man a short lecture on capitalism, Poppa got round to explaining how such a system would be of use to them. Money-making business in the streets was conducted, by and large, in big groups. This meant the proceeds would be shared somewhat equally amongst the team regardless of the amount of effort contributed. Poppa worked out that B-man was the strong man, while he was the smart and creative one of the group. Thus, he argued, their contribution to the gang was significantly undervalued by the equitable distribution system.

'We have to run our own show, B, just me and you,' he suggested.

'And what would the other boys think about that?'

'You have to stop worrying what others think, B-man. I have been trying to teach you this for a long time: to conduct an orchestra, you have to turn your back on the crowd.'

B-man shook his head and smiled; he was happy to provide the vent for Poppa's wisdom-saturated young mind. But he still wasn't satisfied with the plan.

'What I mean, Poppa, is if we stop working with the others, we could get kicked out of the house.'

'We can do this secretly, on the side.'

'You think?'

'I know.'

And so they began. They would work with the others normally, but late into the night they sneaked out again to mug drunken commoners. The savings started growing tremendously, and Poppa took charge of keeping it all safe.

*

A few months later, B-man was only weeks off his seventeenth birthday, but he didn't know it. What he did know was that it was around this time that their plan began falling into place. They counted the money and decided that enough was enough. They were ready to go, to escape the streets and start a new life in society.

They secretly began looking for a flat, and it took them a while to find a landlord who'd accept them even with their money. Some wouldn't let them anywhere near their offices. Others took one look at them and shook their heads in sympathy, as if to say, *What about the neighbours, sir? We have to think about the people you'll be moving in next to.* A few remained professional: *As long as the money is right, sir.* But they somehow still found a reason for refusing to do business, brandishing the word 'references' for good measure. The duo soon realised that the honest admission that they were just a couple of hardworking homeless boys seeking to move into mainstream life did not go down too well with potential landlords.

When they eventually found one who was accommodating to them, the rent turned out to be at least double what it should have been, and they knew they had to go back and make more money.

B-man would later blame these landlords for forcing him back to Dallas, and leading him to a fateful meeting with Kappel, the notorious gangster.

***

Sally-Anne's initial *I-have-to-find-him* declaration to her dad had been instinctive and sentimental. The case for staying longer was now backed by hard evidence that J'Alex did not die in the fire; but he was still missing, nonetheless, and that meant there were no more doubts about her staying in Kenya for a while.

However, staying a little longer meant just that: staying and waiting. She was incapable of affecting the search for J'Alex. There was absolutely nothing else for her to do but stay holed up in her hotel room staring absently at the Bell-Bottom building outside her window, waiting for a phone call from the police.

The situation in the country meant the hotels were experiencing a very quiet period, but she still ran into a few other guests who were polite enough to exchange more than a couple of pleasantries. The Wilsons were an elderly couple from Surrey, on the outskirts of London. She first encountered them in the hotel lobby where a handful of guests were trying their best to socialise over countless cups of strong Kenyan coffee while watching the various plasma screens plastered all over the hall. Mrs. Dianne Wilson, huddling with her husband Edward at the corner of a comfortable leather sofa, initiated the conversation.

'Terrible isn't it?' she said to Sally-Anne and nodding towards the nearest TV screen.

Sally-Anne knew the crisis was a popular subject among the patrons, but she was lousy at political discussions. So she simply smiled back at the nice old woman and said, 'It is indeed.'

'You are English?' asked the old lady, with a hint of delight.

'Yes, I'm from London.'

The woman turned towards her husband to deliver the good news. 'Darling, this young lady here is from London.'

Her husband was a small and very old man. He had two thin patches of white hair on both sides of his head, separated by a smooth, shiny rift straight through the middle, like a reverse Mohican. He smiled warmly at Sally-Anne, and then, with some effort, got up from the corner of the sofa and moved towards her. Still standing, he extended his hands towards her, and she got to her feet to shake them.

'Very nice to meet you, young lady, very good.' His voice was clear and slightly shrill.

'It's my pleasure, sir.'

The old man, still holding her hands, let out a shrill, hearty laugh as he hoisted the hands up and down one more time, mumbling '*Yes... yes... yes,*' with his eyes glued to her face, as if listening intently. She found him fairly amusing, but it was hard to tell whether the pantomime was intentional, so she suppressed a laugh, and, without thinking, reiterated, 'I'm from London.'

This was followed by an even heartier laugh and another good strong shake of the hands, 'Yes... yes... you are such a pretty young lady.'

She smiled, slightly awkwardly. 'So, how long have you been here?' she asked him.

Another laugh, and yet another handshake, but the answer to her question was still 'Yes... yes...' Then, keeping the firm hand-grip, the old man turned to his wife and said, 'Darling, what is this pretty young lady saying? I can't understand a word.'

This time she couldn't contain the laugh. And when she laughed, he laughed even more.

Ted Wilson swore he had great difficulty understanding Sally-Anne's accent even though they were from just outside London. Even his wife was slightly bemused by this, because Diane herself could not detect any significant differences in their accents. When she pointed this out to her husband, he released another long, shrill laugh, and claimed Sally-Anne spoke too fast. Then he laughed again. It was hard to tell whether he was serious or if this was just his idea of humour, his little party-piece.

Ted Wilson laughed a lot. And Ted Wilson shook hands with almighty vigour.

Sally-Anne liked the Wilsons instantly. They somehow reminded her of the Hamiltons.

Mr. Wilson was a relatively potent eighty-year-old, with a very lovely wife some seven years younger. They had arrived in Kenya about two weeks before, mainly to see the flamingos of Lake Nakuru in the Rift Valley province. But the timing of their holiday proved awful, because the trouble in the country started almost as soon as they arrived. The holiday company immediately cancelled the tour and offered them their money back. They were advised to go back home and to rearrange the holiday for some other time, but the Wilsons were reluctant. They were convinced things were bound to calm down soon, so they could carry on with their bird-watching expeditions in the Rift Valley.

Mr. Wilson's hearty laughs made it difficult to feel sorry for them. They seemed to have not a care in the world, and were utterly convinced their holiday would be salvaged.

When she left them after that first encounter, she was in very high spirits. She went for a swim and a light work-out in the gym, then spent the rest of the day surfing the internet. And still the day would not go quick enough. She wondered how many more days she could spend like this. When the evening eventually came she made a phone call to her dad, watched some TV and retired to bed relatively early.

*

The first thing Sally-Anne did the following morning was make a phone call to the inspector. She was aware it was still too soon for any significant development, so she kept her expectations low.

'As of now, we have only issued alerts with the surrounding police stations where some displaced people have been seeking refuge,' he informed her. 'But we will be pursuing this from all angles. We are checking out family records and we'll be questioning relatives and friends. If we don't get any useful leads, we could also put out missing person announcements in the media.'

'Thanks, sir, could you please keep me informed?'

'We will do, my dear young madam.'

After the call she braced herself for another long day stuck in a hotel with nothing to do. She wandered around the hotel lobby hoping to bump into the Wilsons, but they were nowhere to be seen. She knew their room, and they had made it clear she was welcome to pop in anytime, but she still felt a bit awkward. They needed their space.

On the other hand, Biggy kept calling persistently, even though she was sure it was now clear even to him that she did not want to talk. She was certain the man was more interested in making an impression on her than in finding J'Alex. She was weary of accepting more favours from him, lest he started expecting something in return. By the end of the day she was again having serious doubts about her ability to continue like this.

*

On her fifth day back in the country, Sally-Anne decided to do something similar to what she normally did at home whenever she was bored: call any friend who was available, even if it was her least favourite, and arrange to meet. Except in this case, there was one problem: when she looked through her phonebook for those friends, there wasn't one within several thousand miles.

There was only Biggy.

She called him, and he was waiting at the hotel lobby within an hour of the phone call. He had on a neatly pressed black shirt, light-grey trousers and expensive-looking shiny black shoes. She figured either she had interrupted him in the middle of some serious business, or he really was trying that much to impress her.

The Wilsons also happened to be there, sipping coffee on their usual sofa. Thus she found herself in the ungraceful position of having to do the introductions between a set of characters whose contrast was unsurpassable. The little old man got up with a smile and treated the large young man to his long and vigorous handshake, complete with plenty of laughs and well placed *yeses*. And Biggy gave back as good as he got; the handshake, the laughs and the *yeses*. Within seconds, two extremely dissimilar men, distinguished by several generations and separated by great expanses of ocean, had found common ground, something that they were both passionate about . . .

Arsenal football club!

It was left to Sally-Anne to be the killjoy. 'Could you excuse us for a moment?' she said, prying Biggy away from the old man. 'I just need Biggy to help me with something quickly and I promise I will bring him back to you.'

When they were safely away from the Wilsons, she started by apologising for summoning him at such short notice.

'Did I interrupt your business?' she inquired, openly looking him up and down to indicate that this was an assumption she had only arrived at due to his smart clothes.

'Nah, it's fine,' he said, waving his arms dismissively. 'I've been trying to get in contact with you for a while. You see, the thing is, it finally hit me how much this means to you. You flew thousands of miles to a place like this to help a little boy. I think the least I could do is offer you all the assistance I can while you are here.'

Oh yes... of course, Biggy! And what are you going to expect in return? she thought; but aloud she simply said, 'Thanks.'

'Listen, I have to start by apologising for not being straight with you about what those men told me. I thought I was following Inspector Limo's instructions, but maybe I was wrong. I know you believe there are some answers in Mathary Valley, so I was thinking maybe we start again. I take you round there, we ask a few questions, talk to a few people, listen to the stories and rumours... anything. It might all prove useless, but like you said, it'll beat staying in the hotel the whole day.'

***

Like true fighters, B-man and Poppa took the rejections by city landlords on the chin and vowed to battle on. It was a minor setback, they just needed to make a bit more money and go back with an irresistible offer. So they headed back to the streets to labour for what they believed would be the last time, and make that final push to break the tight boundary between black and white.

As it was, around this time, Kappel, the founder of Kappel's Corner – the rival squat to the House of Lord's – happened to be looking for strong boys for a big robbery he was planning. And someone mentioned B-man as a candidate. Word about his fight with Jude had worked in his favour.

Kappel was Lord Kane's arch rival, and working for him would definitely mean leaving the House of Lord's. But this was a rare offer, this was no petty mugging or pickpocketing; Kappel was personally asking him to team up with his gang for a big robbery, a meticulously planned operation that would yield serious money. It was a sign of respect. After working personally with Kappel, B-man expected that a lot more options would be open to him, so his allegiance to Lord Kane and the House of Lord's went out of the window. This job would not only inject the much needed cash for their grand plan, it would also mean he would leave the streets with the admirable legacy of having worked personally with a gang leader.

The meeting happened at Kappel's house, a modest semi by slum standards. Kappel turned out to be a rather short, stringy, smartly dressed man who could have easily passed for a banker. Nowhere near as big and scary as B-man had imagined. But he had someone with him, a giant creature he introduced as Titto, his right-hand man, who never left his side. This man-beast was huge alright, but that was not the scariest thing about him. The dark skin around his face bore the scars of a seasoned *chwaka*-joint brawler. When Titto opened his mouth, which was a rather frequent occurrence, the weird set of crooked yellow teeth on display alone wielded the potential to halt a grown man's heart. His dental formula was a complete mess. The front incisors were small, numerous, and all over the place, with some mounting over others. Towards the corners of his mouth, some of the smaller teeth were broken, most probably by design, to give a clear view of the cone-shaped canine fangs. They called him Titto 'K9', which he soon learned stood for 'Canine', in respect of his dental peculiarity.

'This job will be very well paying,' Kappel assured him. 'And I'll allow you and your friend to live with my boys in Kappel's Corner before we find you somewhere nicer with your money.'

B-man liked the sound of it. Poppa was vehemently opposed from the start. He begged B-man not to do it, arguing that they had enough money to run from the streets. Why did he need to risk going to prison, or even dying?

'I've got a very bad feeling about this, B, don't do it! Let's run.'

'You know we still need the money, Poppa. And Kappel is asking a personal favour. Even though we are going away from all this, don't you like the sound of that? Kappel, asking me, personally, for a favour?'

'I've got a feeling this will lead to a disaster, B, after all our struggles. Is it really worth it?'

'Don't be paranoid, just this last one and we'll be free. You have to think money. Eyes on the prize, Poppa, it's all about the money.'

So the robbery went ahead.

The plan was straightforward. Two men would be driving out of the local bakery that evening, heading towards the bank to deposit the weekend's cash. All they had to do was transfer the cash to themselves before the men could get inside the car. B-man and two other men from Kappel's gang would accost them at the car park and grab the package containing the cash. Violence, he was assured, would be a possibility but not a probability, and the two samurai swords his two accomplices were armed with were meant to act as deterrent only. The bakery was small and security, if any, would be minimal. Kappel and Titto, who would be watching from a distance, would catch up with them after the robbery and take charge.

The robbery was nearly through, and B-man was making away with the large envelope when their assessment of the bakers' security was proved wrong. He first heard a few gunshots, then a loud voice.

'Stop or I'll shoot!'

Everybody froze. The voice continued shouting more orders that B-man did not hear because his mind was occupied with wild thoughts. He was facing the barrel of a gun on the very day they were supposed to be making their big break. He was looking head-on at the prospect of either a bullet in the head or prison, neither of which was part of his and Poppa's dreams. They had come so close: so close to getting away with this robbery, so close to living a life in a house, so close to that waiting job. Was this how it was going to end?

There was no time to think. So, with the parcel still in his hands, he broke into a run of death, expecting a bullet to blast his head off at any second. He didn't care, he ran like he'd never ran before, not listening to the shouting voice and the gunshots. Two bullets missed his head by an inch or so, but he kept running, and disappeared in the tumbling masses of old shanties. He continued to run, long after the gunshots had stopped; and when he stopped, it was because he could move no more. He sat down with his back resting against a wall at the end of a cul-de-sac of wooden shacks, threw the parcel containing the cash between his outstretched legs, and waited for his pursuers to catch up with him.

One of them did catch up with him; his name was Kappel.

'Good work, chap,' he said when B-man looked up. 'My boys got caught, you got away. Says a lot about my choice of recruits, doesn't it?' He was smiling as he hunkered down to pick up the parcel.

'Just give me my share and let me go away,' was all B-man said.

'Listen I'll reward you with much more than that. How would you like joining my gang?'

After today, the idea of gangster life, B-man vowed, would forever be consigned to the movies. 'Just the money, Kappel, I don't think I'm ready to be in your gang. Just the money, for now.'

He was already planning how the money would be used to bring an end to this lifestyle. He was going straight to Poppa, they would count their total savings, add the amount from this hit, and head away from Dallas and Mathary Valley and the ghetto and the streets. They were ready; there was nothing more Dallas could offer them.

Kappel was still talking; he had ignored everything B-man had just said.

'I'll arrange for you to move in with the rest of my boys, not the homeless ones, I mean my gang. Straightaway.' Then, opening the parcel a crack to check the contents, he continued with a smug grin. 'Let me take this money to the others. Meet me outside Kappel's Corner in an hour.' And he started to walk away.

B-man suddenly shot up and held him by his arms.

'I want my share.' He surprised even himself when he heard his own voice, raised enough to amount to a threat. And the man on the receiving end was none other than Kappel, the lethal gangster. 'I don't want to join your gang!'

'Sorry, then the money belongs to the gang.' He freed himself from B-man's grip and started walking away. 'I'll let you off with holding me in that manner, but I've withdrawn my offer of letting you into the gang. Have a nice day.'

It was at that point that a part of B-man's brain switched, and he found himself swinging through a mysterious external force outside his control, his clenched fists connecting violently with Kappel's chin. Kappel wobbled under the impact, his head slacking slightly off his neck, but he managed to stay on his feet. Then he straightened back up and stepped a yard away from B-man, shaking off the daze. He started reaching for his coat pocket, and B-man realised he only had a fraction of a second before a gun emerged from that black coat and a bullet tore through him at point-blank range. But his brain was working well with his body, and Kappel's hand was barely inside his pocket when the second blow landed squarely over his nose and sent him well on his way to the ground. Just to make sure, B-man threw another right hook which left a deep impact on the side of Kappel's neck just under his left ear.

As Kappel lay bleeding on the ground, he noticed a small crowd beginning to gather. Considering other people were possibly still chasing him, he knew the consequences of drawing any further public attention could be dire, so he once again broke into a run. One or two people shouted and threatened behind him, but their attempts to give chase were half-hearted, with most of the crowd interested in his victim's wellbeing.

He headed towards the House of Lord's to pick up Poppa so they could get out of this mess once and for all. He only figured out now, that, by hitting Kappel, the damage had been done with regard to his safety. He would forever be a fugitive in Dallas. A substantial prize would be placed on his head. So why hadn't he just gone ahead and taken the envelope full of money from the unconscious Kappel anyway? It wouldn't have put him in any more danger than he was already in. They could only kill him once. He quietly cursed the missed opportunity, but this was not the time to fret on such issues. They had some money, they could find somewhere. Maybe they would be forced to lower their expectations and start off somewhere cheaper. There were several run-down quasi-slum estates out there, that were nonetheless a considerable upgrade from Dallas, which they could manage. The crucial thing was to get set, anywhere, off the streets. They were hard workers; success would come.

*

When he got to the house, B-man leaned against the back wall, then slumped to the ground to regain his breath. Then he remembered that he had just been involved in Kappel's mission, yet here he was, standing outside the House of Lord's. If word had got out about his work with Kappel, he was now an enemy of both gangs. It couldn't get any worse. It was definitely time to leave Dallas.

He climbed into the house through the back window, praying that none of the boys indoors knew about his involvement with Kappel. All he wanted was to find Poppa, get the stash of cash that was buried under a tree at the back, and run as far as they could away from this place. He even began to giddy with excitement as he jumped in and went to the corner he shared with Poppa.

And in their corner, he was met head-on with the blood-curdling teeth of Titto 'K9'.

The man-beast was swinging a giant pair of pliers, opening and closing them slowly, with his generous and horrifying grin on full display. Poppa was lying on the floor with hands and feet bound together. There were four other men, two on either side of Titto. The first pair pounced on B-man, pinned him to the ground, and tied him up in a matter of seconds.

'We got ourselves a hero here, chaps,' announced Titto, inching his huge pliers lower towards B-man's legs. 'Now let's make sure he doesn't give birth to any more troublesome heroes in future.'

B-man tried to wriggle along the ground in an effort to roll away from the greasy hands that were reaching for the fly of his trousers.

'Don't...please...Oh no! Please...' he wailed, and got a good, stinging slap for it, as Titto tore away the trousers all together. 'Forgive me please... I beg you. You can't do this... please... I got carried away... I almost got killed at the bakery... he refused to give me any money... please understand...'

No one was listening. Instead, the remaining two men moved in to help pin him to the ground. His underwear was ripped and he felt a cold rough finger on his limp organ. It was at that crucial moment, while writhing on the ground like a live fish in a frying pan, that he shouted something – something either very stupid or very clever, and most probably just a reflex response from that part of the brain that smells death.

'Please... forgive me... I got him a bag full of money... I got you the money... please don't do this...'

When he felt cold metal on his organ, he closed his eyes and screamed at the top of his voice.

He didn't feel the pain for a few seconds, but he felt a set of cold, hard, rough fingers lightly squeeze his throat. Then he heard a voice whispering something he could not hear above his own screams. The fingers squeezed a bit harder and the voice shouted, 'Shut up!'

That made him stop, then the man-beast whispered again. 'Shut up. Open your eyes. And repeat what you just said.'

B-man slowly opened his eyes and realised he had not been castrated. Not yet. He felt his heart sink as he asked, 'What? Repeat what?'

'You said a *bag* full of money. You mean an envelope full of money, don't you?'

B-man considered the implications for just one second. This was all he had. 'No, it was a bag... a black tennis bag...and I checked it, it was full of money.'

'You sure? Absolutely certain?'

'Yes, I am.'

Titto and the other boys looked at each other, the same thought going through their minds: their leader had played them, betrayed his loyal followers.

B closed his eyes again and said a little prayer. He did not want to die here. Not now.

'He transferred a small amount into an envelope and kept the rest for himself,' he heard Titto breathe just above whisper. The other men agreed with cautious nods. 'Oh Kappel, Kappel, Kappel... he has done it again.' He was talking to himself. 'We've always been loyal, how could you do this to us?'

Titto 'K9' called his friends to one side and they discussed something in low tones for a few minutes; then he walked back to the pair. They were both still on the ground, hands and legs tightly bound.

'We want to talk to Lord Kane, the owner of this place. Do you know where he lives?'

Poppa, who must have died on that floor momentarily, came back to life.

'Yes, I know... I know where his house is,' he proclaimed, attempting an awkward wriggle like a worm. 'I can take you there.'

Titto ordered the others to untie them and said to Poppa, 'You run to Lord Kane's house and tell him Titto has sent you. Tell him Titto and four of Kappel's boys would like to talk to him. Tell him I said it is very important. Are you listening? I want this message delivered accurately.'

Poppa nodded. 'Yes, I'm listening.'

'In fact just tell him that we are willing to help him get his long-awaited revenge against Kappel, and a bag full of cash on top.'

After Poppa had left, he looked down at B-man and smiled. 'You have got some balls, kid. I've got to give you that.'

In the light of recent events, B-man wasn't sure exactly what *balls* he was referring to, until Titto smiled again and added, 'We are going to need every ounce of those balls now, because we have got ourselves a war. And you are on our side.'

CHAPTER 10

Somehow, yet again, Sally-Anne found herself in the same old Land Rover with Biggy, squeezing their way through the narrow alleyways of Mathary Valley. His driving was aggressive, with little consideration for pedestrians or any of the host of miscellaneous items that claimed the dusty pathways. When he stopped the car, it was right in the middle of a passage, almost completely blocking it and causing an unnecessary jam for the locals going about their business on foot. They were being forced to squeeze through a bottleneck either side of the Land Rover, but Biggy did not seem to care.

'Can you wait in the car? I need to see someone,' he announced.

'Are you leaving me here on my own?' She was not happy with this; how could he? There were all sorts of people milling around the car and it was too hot to keep the windows shut.

He stood outside the open door for a moment to think, holding up the pedestrian traffic in the passage. 'OK then, come with me,' he said.

He walked round to help her out of the passenger door. Everyone seemed to be smiling at him and muttering kind greetings, calling him by name. They were clearly not fussed by the disruption he was causing, and were obviously aware he was a policeman, despite the plainclothes. Sally-Anne walked with him along the block of mud-houses till he stopped at an end-of-cul-de-sac house which had a set of large wooden double windows strategically designed to front a small convenience store. He showed no interest in buying anything as he launched into a brief chitchat with the storekeeper, which concluded with the woman producing a small wad of notes from underneath her counter and handing it to him. Then he beckoned Sally-Anne to follow him back to the car.

'What was that all about? Did the woman owe you money?' She was concerned. In this part of the world someone handing over money to a police officer almost always meant a bribe, a good old-fashioned backhander to blind the policeman to some illegal activity.

Biggy nodded without showing much interest.

'What does she owe you for?'

'Well, it's a bit complicated. I do some work for them and they pay me.'

'What work?' she pressed as he opened the passenger door and helped her back in the car.

He waited till he was settled behind the wheels before answering. 'Well, as you might have guessed there is not much in terms of rule of law in Mathary Valley. So these people's businesses are always under threat. I offer them some kind of security and they pay me.'

So on top of everything else he was also shamelessly corrupt, she thought, but decided not to push it any further for now.

She soon realised that despite what he was, this man was very popular in these slums. Everyone appeared to want to wave and smile. The responses to all his actions, which were mostly careless, seemed friendly and respectful.

'This is the place they popularly refer to as Dallas. It's the roughest part of Mathary Valley, which makes it the roughest part of the country,' he announced, sounding yet again like a tour-guide as the Land Rover waded though a sewage flooded path. 'Everyone here is extremely poor.'

She toyed with the idea of responding to this with a sarcastic: *You don't say, Biggy!*

She didn't, but the thought made her smile. And the smile was either missed or ignored by Biggy as he allowed her time to absorb the wretched scenes around them once more before continuing:

'Dallas is the centre of Mathary Valley. And Mathary Valley is a place that almost mirrors the tribal demographic pattern of the whole country. The West End of Mathary Valley is predominantly home to the Kikuyus; the East End, the Luos – the two biggest tribes in the country. Dallas is the melting pot where all the tribes have mixed, and are strongly united only by the fact that they are equals in their tribulations. Nobody round here knows what tribe anyone belongs to anymore, they just know they face the same hardships. It's incredible, considering that just off their backyard towards the east or west people are still very deeply divided. The Gitongas happened to be Kikuyus who lived in the East End with the Luos. It happens; you get the odd Luos amongst Kikuyus in the West End, and vice versa.

'So, when a Luo stood against a Kikuyu in the general elections, some of those in the minorities anticipated trouble, and they moved back to be amongst their people. The few who were either too optimistic or stupidly brave were then evicted or killed as soon as the disputes started over the winner of the presidential elections.

'The Gitongas' case is quite unique. They were Kikuyus by decent but they had lived in the East End for generations. Everyone virtually considered them Luos. When they started burning down Kikuyu properties in the East End, the locals would gather around Gitonga's shop in the evenings to relive the day's events and even plan their next moves in this tribal war. They schemed right in front of his shop, not once considering him an outsider. Then the attacks started descending into revenge attacks whereby, if the Luos heard news of one of them killed anywhere in the country, they would go around and find at least five Kikuyus to kill in retaliation. People were waving placards on TV saying 'For every Luo dead, we will kill at least five Kikuyus'.

'Then one day news arrived that somewhere in the Rift Valley province, the Kikuyus had burnt down a church inside which some Luos had sought refuge. The East End went out in murderous rage looking for Kikuyus, but they couldn't find any. They had all either moved or been killed. They looked left, right and centre, and there were no Kikuyus in sight. It was probably at that point that someone decided that the Gitongas *were* Kikuyu after all.'

He took another breath, and then concluded. 'They killed the Gitongas simply because they had run out of Kikuyus to kill.'

'Jesus...' was all Sally-Anne could mutter.

She didn't know whether she was more astounded by the subject matter, or the fact that this corrupt, self-obsessed, show-off rogue of a policeman did, after all, have an understanding of his country.

She allowed another bout of silence before saying, 'I don't understand politics Biggy, I don't know the difference between Luo and Kikuyu, I don't know the good guy or the bad guy. But the funny thing is, I don't think J'Alex does either. He is twelve years old, Biggy.'

But deep down she was cursing Biggy. She knew he had sowed another seed of political dogma within her, and that it would sprout up sooner or later. She could almost see herself over her computer, looking up the Luo and Kikuyu, trying to find out who the bad guy really was. She did not need this. It was none of her business; the matter at hand required that such political side-issues remain abstract to her. It was neither the time nor place...

Fuck you Biggy...

***

Lord Kane did accept Titto and his lot, and he was willing to help them get their money back. But the war that ensued turned out to be more than any of them had bargained for.

Lord Kane was a tall, light-skinned man with a smartly trimmed beard and long, neat, jet-black dreadlocks which on this occasion were tied in a bunch at the back of his head. If this was the kind of look Poppa, with his shaggy lumps of hair, was aiming for, then he was way off the mark.

Upon receiving Titto's message from Poppa, it took Lord Kane less than ten minutes to hatch a plan. He collected some of his men, and together with Titto and his new recruits they set off to find Kappel. It was going to be an ambush: the money or you die. Kappel would be outnumbered, he wouldn't stand a chance.

They tried his house first, but he wasn't in; they were told he was at Kappel's Corner, where he had decided to run his mobile casino on that particular day. So they followed him there.

The mobile casino was in essence a huge gambling festival that drew most of its punters from Mathary Valley, and some from outside. It involved a lot of drinking, a lot of drug-taking, and some gambling, usually at a prearrranged spot within Dallas. Kappel was staging this one behind the run-down Kappel's Corner because the mobile casino was, of course, illegal and discretion was paramount. Kappel's Corner was an ideal location. It was hard enough to notice the run-down squat, let alone imagine that just behind it a serious gambling and drinking party was underway. Two of Kappel's men were on the lookout, and when they spotted Titto coming on his own, one of them leaned over the window and mentioned it to Kappel. It was information that they would otherwise have considered insignificant: until that point, as far as they were aware, Titto was one of them.

Kappel acknowledged the news of Titto's arrival with a nod and started walking round the front to meet his right-hand man. Titto may have been striding somewhat gingerly towards him, but that would have been no cause for alarm in any other circumstances. Either Kappel had been forewarned somehow, or he possessed one hell of an instinct: as the man who until now was supposed to be his closest ally approached, he instinctively drew a .45 revolver pistol.

'What's it, Titto?' he asked, pointing the gun at him. 'You stop right there and talk to me.'

Titto had no gun on him, but he knew there was a neat set-up behind him. Lord Kane was lying on a nearby roof, with his own gun aimed at Kappel. They would wait for Kappel to make the first move, and shoot only if they sensed real danger. Otherwise Titto's job was to simply inform him that he was surrounded and that all he could do to save his life was to hand over the money.

'Where is the money, Kappel?' Titto asked without breaking stride.

'What money? Stop right there, Titto, and talk, or I'll blow your head off, I swear.'

'You are one ungrateful, lying, scam-bug, Kappel. You kept all the money to yourself, you fucking Judas. After all we have done for you. How long have you been doing this, eh?' He was still walking towards him.

The subsequent events occurred in a flash. There was a click of Kappel's pistol as he cocked it, but before he fired, a loud bang came from a nearby rooftop, and Kappel watched his .45 go flying up in the air as his hands went limp, oozing blood.

*

Three police officers had been doing their weekly rounds in the slums, collecting money from the *chwaka* joints. The money was always collected on the same day every week, and a few of the less-well-informed *chwaka* dealers even believed this money to be some kind of tax. The money was of course a bribe, because all *chwaka* was illegal. This was just their way of enforcing the law. It was three of these policemen-collectors who heard the sound of Kane's gunshot and decided to move in.

And that's when the real war began.

*

As soon as the cops got involved, the rivalry between Kane and Kappel was forgotten, and so was the bag of money. They had to deal with the common enemy first. At the outset it looked like a war between three armed cops against two different gangs now united by the common foe. But there was the added factor that this was happening right in front of a squat crowded with homeless boys, on a day when they were hosting a big party of gambling rogues in their backyard. The policemen were massively outnumbered, but they were not to know; they did not even notice the old, disintegrating house.

They gathered everyone in sight, including Kappel who was already disadvantaged by the gunshot wound, and Titto who was unarmed. But they didn't get Kane because they couldn't see him. While all this was going on, he had jumped inside Kappel's Corner through a back window to rally the boys in the house and the gamblers behind.

'We are going to get as many as we can fit out of the door at the same time. Let's surprise them. You lot,' he pointed at the gamblers on the outside, 'you jump in through the window as soon as there is space and continue the march out of the front door. We keep the flow, keep going at them, no break. We move in as one and surround the patrol car. Do nothing. Just surround the patrol car, chanting. They won't shoot if we stay together, they won't know what to do... I repeat, we stay together and the pigs won't leave this place with our people,' he shouted. 'Right, one... two...three go!'

The cops were bundling their captives into the police car when, from an old building they had not even noticed, a massive group of dishevelled men and boys started charging right towards them like angry bulls.

From what the cops could see, it was not a big house, yet the loudly chanting men kept spilling out. They came in pairs, in dozens, in hundreds... and they still kept coming as the cops looked on in horror. They were witnessing a miracle: an endless stream of chanting people storming through the door in torrents. The squat was raining men.

One of the cops died at the scene. His body was found mangled and deformed; but he had already been dead before the rioters got near him. It was the shock that killed him. The other two ended up in hospital with severe injuries from the stampede. So did seven street boys. One man was caught in the head by a bullet and died instantly. A further eight street boys were hospitalised with bullet wounds. Three of them later died.

*

The next day, even though it was a Saturday, some government departments and local authorities held emergency meetings. And very early on Monday morning, a bulldozer, surrounded with armed police officers, was sent round to the then deserted Kappel's Corner. By noon they had completed the demolition job.

Kappel's Corner was no more.

The House of Lord's was earmarked to follow suit on the following day.

Very early that Tuesday morning, though, the bulldozer-driver was lying next to a big chalk-written advertising board outside a local bar. He was naked. There was a thin, limp, two-inch piece of meat hanging off the side of his lips, as if it were a cigarette. He also had a matching two-inch piece of flesh missing from between his legs. The words on the board were:

ASSIST THE DEMOLISHON MAN WITH A LIGHT

He was, of course, dead. And the House of Lord's was not demolished that Tuesday.

CHAPTER 11

The choice of attire Sally-Anne had picked for this trip to the slums proved wildly inappropriate. The knee-length skirt was fairly modest, but the calf boots over her thick leggings were vintage suede, unnecessarily exuberant and extremely uncomfortable in the hot dusty pathways of Mathary Valley. Jogging bottoms and trainers would have sufficed; it was not as if there was a chance of bumping into any ex-boyfriends here. Biggy's unprecedented arrival at short notice that morning in fresh casual gear had influenced her choice. But so far today she had survived these harsh conditions, in unsuitable clothing, with a man she could not stand, fuelled only by the packs of bottled water they had loaded into his Land Rover somewhere along the way.

A loose pattern had started emerging from the people they had questioned about the J'Alex rumour. Although from the East End, J'Alex had started making a name for himself in Dallas by hanging around with some of the Dallas bad boys. It was believed that he and some of his close friends had in fact gone missing a few days before the fire. That seemed to form the backbone of the hearsay. Everything else – for instance, *why* they went missing and where they could possibly have gone – yielded a wide variety of theories.

The process of information-hunting soon began to head towards frustration, especially after Biggy decided to take charge of all the questioning. He would cunningly switch the questioning from English to Swahili at crucial moments, leaving Sally-Anne the impression that there was some information that Biggy was not happy for her to receive first-hand. She once again found herself thinking of other ways of doing this without Biggy: these folks seemed to be saying a lot, and she was convinced that what she was receiving was only the half of it.

The first opportunity arose late in the sweltering afternoon, when Biggy, who had stopped to talk to a temporary female stall owner, stepped away to answer one of his secretive phone calls. Sally-Anne checked that the big man was safely out of earshot and fully engrossed in his phone conversation before she began conducting her own version of the investigations. She started with a quick but cordial introduction, something Biggy had unsurprisingly chosen to skip. The young stallholder had her hair braided in neat rows, and her dark skin appeared to shimmer in the sun. She said her name was Nyarsakwa, and Sally-Anne did not query what tribe that name belonged to. Nyarsakwa seemed timid but friendly, and she confirmed the key parts of the rumours.

'I don't know much about J'Alex, what I know is these boys haven't got any proper stable families to speak of, so they are always here and there. It'd be hard to tell whether they have really disappeared,' she explained, and then added, 'But one of the missing boys has a mother and I spoke to her yesterday. She believes her little boy was with J'Alex and two others, and that they went missing before the fire.'

'Is there any chance I can talk to her myself?' Sally-Anne asked her. 'Where does she live?'

'Sure, just walk up to the end of this path and turn right. Ask anyone around there for Koli's mother, they will know.'

Then Biggy reappeared, and Nyarsakwa became suddenly reluctant to continue on the subject. Sally-Anne realised it probably was not the same thing, talking to a stranger about a rumour, as talking to the police, so she understood. Nyarsakwa exchanged a few more words with Biggy, after which she produced some money and handed it over to him. And once again Sally-Anne found herself loathing this blatant act of corruption. This time, when they got back in the car, she decided to confront him.

'Are you taking bribes from these people, Biggy?'

'Excuse me?' he sounded genuinely shocked.

'You say they give you money and you offer them security. Isn't that supposed to be your job anyway as a policeman?'

'Policeman?'

'Yeah, you are paid by the government to keep law and order and provide a secure environment for everyone, so why are you making these poor people pay you for it?'

'Wait,' he raised his left hand to stop her. 'Who told you I'm a policeman?'

'Aren't you?'

'No.'

'What are you then?'

'I am Biggy. I'm just another man. I certainly am no cop.'

Another silence descended as this sank in. Sally-Anne knew immediately that this was not a joke; but as if to reaffirm what he had said, he continued.

'I just happen to have a few connections and command some kind of respect around here. This is a neglected place. This is a society that everyone else assumes does not exist. The closest this place could come to some order or rule of law is me. If someone's getting treated unfairly, they come to me and I try and sort it out. If they are in some kind of trouble, they come to me for help. And in return we develop an understanding that they owe me. So next time I could count on their help if need be; a favour here, a job there... or they could just donate something as a token of their appreciation.'

'What? Are you serious? You do all that on your own?'

'No, I don't work entirely alone. I've got a small group of friends working with me, a close-knit community of like-minded people who understand this place.'

She looked at him again and realised just how serious he was. Then it all started falling into place. All the suspicious-looking young men they had dropped in to see throughout Mathary Valley; everyone according him the highest respect; the secretive phone calls...

Biggy was a mafia-style gang leader.

The air between them thinned in the ensuing silence. She looked away from him and out through the open window, at the sea of rusting tin roofs drifting away from the moving car.

'I don't understand.' She was speaking to herself. 'Inspector Limo sent me to you... How could he?'

'Because he knows that around here you are safe with me. It might not be strictly within the law, but what I do here achieves a purpose and benefits a good majority of people. It is an understanding within a community faced with shared problems: an informal respect for a figure of authority... Call it whatever you want, around here it works.

'Take the boys who tried to rob you, for instance. I knew they were armed, but I beat the crap out of them and sent them off with a good lesson learnt. And even with their guns, or whatever they had, they did nothing. Why? It's all down to respect. If it's anyone else, they kill him without thinking twice; no one misses anyone around here too much if they disappear. But they know I've got a lot of friends, connections everywhere. I do many people favours, so I would surely be missed. Of course I do make some enemies as well; it is inevitable in what I do. But I am still standing, walking the streets freely. So, for now, I can assume I have not pissed anyone off that much.'

She tried to speak, but could not quite open her mouth. She did not know whether she was scared or just shocked. How had this happened? Sally-Anne Symmonds, a twenty-three-year-old white British girl, in the most dangerous part of one of the roughest slums in the world, riding in a Land Rover with a mafia Lord!

When she finally managed to summon up the courage, she said: 'Can you take me back to my Hotel please?'

***

No: the House of Lord's was not demolished that Tuesday. But it was demolished in the end all the same.

First the local police cited the delay in the demolition as a tribute to the late bulldozer-driver, claiming it was only right that they wait till he was buried. But they were fooling no one. The truth was that they were struggling to find someone with enough balls to drive the thing. The simple task of demolishing a decaying squat had turned into a war-zone operation. However, after a week of working out an impeccable protection plan for all involved, they finally got enough officers ready to work.

The House of Lord's was brought down the following Monday, a week behind schedule.

What remained was to hunt down the criminals. Every one of the so called Parking-boys was a suspect. The list of crimes was long. All the police had to do was pick up a Parking-Boy, and decide what crime to allocate them. They were all guilty until *proven* guilty.

The punishments for their crimes were left in the hands of the police. They would spot a suspected street boy, make an impromptu decision as to their level of guilt, and do what they had to do. Shooting on sight was the preferred choice for many. This was more than just a hunt for Parking-boys, it was extermination.

Mathary Valley became a battlefield. All who claimed to live there had to own a decent shack, and those deemed to be vagrants faced brutal police action. Searches were conducted in many households in and around the area, and they yielded some interesting illegal finds, but Lord Kane remained top of the most-wanted list.

For the homeless former inhabitants of the House of Lord's and Kappel's Corner, it was a game of hide and seek with the cops, the only question being how long one could hide. B-man and Poppa knew they would be arrested eventually. All their hopes of ever renting a flat had gone. There was a good chance that their stash of savings was still buried somewhere in the rubble of the House of Lord's, but they both knew that that path was now permanently closed.

As usual, Poppa found some solace in history. 'Was Idi Amin a great leader, B?' he asked as they sat on top of a wrecked van outside a garage in the city centre, one hot afternoon. They had temporarily taken to performing unpaid errands for the garage owner who in turn promised to stick up for them and say they were his employees if the cops turned up.

B-man smiled. 'Idi Amin was a madman, Poppa. He ate people.'

'A psychopathic dictator, you might say. However, during his time the people of Uganda had jobs, good food and clean streets. Only the small minority who opposed him got eaten – and what system of government allows you to care about the minority anyway? They lived in fear, but they lived! Now, in the name of democracy, they feel empowered, but they are dying. In Africa, B, democracy is a friend who admits that you have the bigger penis, but still continues to sleep with your wife. What a joke!

'This system conned us all. They promise us the power to choose, then they steal our money to beat off the potential opposition so they can stay in power and steal more money. What a joke!'

'Poppa, I think we–'

'What a *joke*, B-man.' Poppa was in full flow and nothing was going to stop him. 'And look at the result of this joke system. Poverty, illiteracy, disease; Dallas, you, me...'

B-man stayed silent and listened to him explain how the *joke system* that had given birth to them now wanted to pretend that they did not exist. Poppa had a way of putting all these skewed ideas together in a way that eventually made sense, if you allowed enough time to ponder. Right now B-man was having difficulty understanding him, but he desperately wanted to believe.

He wanted to believe Poppa because his own way of thinking was simple. The government had always been aware of Dallas, but they left them alone on the assumption that those misfits would eventually slaughter or drug themselves to extinction. Thus, this whole misfortune had been triggered by a series of events initiated by *him*: it all started with B-man getting involved in an unnecessary robbery, attacking a gang leader, lying about the bag of money, and getting a policeman killed. Without these events, the police would not have been provoked to move into the slums and whip them into shape.

This point of view suggested that B-man alone was to blame for this senseless loss of lives. But if taken back again to the grip of Titto's giant pliers, equipped with the benefit of hindsight, would he do the same thing? Well, it was in Poppa's own words: *Survive, B. Just survive!*

People were dying as a direct result of his actions, but he was still alive. It was a simple matter of survival.

'Do you think it could still happen, B? Our plans to move out of the streets?' Poppa shifted to his side on the rusty roof of the wrecked vehicle.

'I don't see why not, Poppa. We never dreamt of going on a holiday to the moon, we simply want to get out of the streets, and that is achievable.'

'How come you're never scared, B? All the dreams and hopes I've dared to have in these streets were inspired by you, you know. I think you inspired Jude, too, believe it or not. His life transformed completely after that life-saving operation. I've never asked you this; we all know being hoisted six feet into the air and dropped to the ground by Jude can't be nice, but what the hell did you do to that boy, and how in God's name did you do it?'

Still lying facing the sun, B-man threaded his hands round the back of his head, rested his right foot over his left thigh, and said nothing.

'Come on, B. What happened that night?'

'Let me ask you something, Poppa,' he started, 'do you know anything about farming?'

Poppa's chosen expression of surprise was a frown. 'No,' he answered.

'Then you won't know anything about a poor country farmer either. A poor farmer will borrow a mule to till his land, and he'd probably be given a scrawny sick one, on loan, from a much richer farmer. To the poor farmer, though, this is not just a mule, it is hope. As he watches the mule struggle with the cultivators, he's already thinking of harvest time. Who knows what this harvest could bring? Maybe enough to buy his own mule, maybe two mules... who knows?

'Now let's just stop this mule business for a minute. Let me ask you another question: ever heard of El Nino?'

Poppa shook his head, secretly impressed. His brother had definitely picked up some storytelling skills.

'El Nino is a vicious torrential rain that comes with the mightiest of winds. Hailstones break into the house through roofs, windows and doors. For the poor farmer, though, his first thoughts and worries are of the crops in the field outside, and of his sick mule. El-Nino can sweep away not only hopes and dreams of harvest time, but also those of all other harvest times to come. That is what El-Nino can do, Poppa.

'Yes, I was hoisted up six feet and dropped to the ground by Jude. And no, it was not nice. El Nino is a lot worse though, because El Nino you can do nothing about. But Jude is *not* El Nino.'

There was no change in his emotions as he jumped off the ruin of the van and straightened his shirt.

'I'm sorry, B,' Poppa said bitterly.

'What the hell are you sorry for?' B-man remained straight-faced. 'Listen, I'm going for a little walk, I need to clear my head. You can stay and sunbathe on this van if you want. I'll catch up with you later.'

Poppa rolled back and lay facing the sun with an unlit cigarette dangling off his lips as B-man disappeared round the corner. The seemingly meaningless El Nino story had dug far deeper inside him than B-man could have imagined.

*

B-man was beginning to turn the corner into the main street when a police car sped across heading the opposite way. He turned round and saw it screech to a stop, inches short of slamming into the already wrecked van, on top of which Poppa was relaxing. He dashed round the corner just in time to see one cop stick a pistol out of the window and command Poppa not to move, as the other cop stepped out of the car waving another gun. The garage owner was watching from a distance, his mouth wide open.

'Kane, stay right where you are,' shouted one of the cops, 'and keep your hands where we can see them.'

'Hey...I'm not Kane...what's going on –?'

'You are under arrest, Kane. Do you understand?'

Lord Kane was a head taller and a few shades lighter than Poppa. He was also several years older, and kept a neatly trimmed beard, while Poppa's facial hair was hardly visible. Lord Kane had some money, and anyone with the slightest sense would have expected him to dress smarter than the greasy rags Poppa was currently donning. The colossal mistake these policemen were making was inexcusable. However, a quick assessment of the situation from his hiding place behind a brick wall convinced B-man that there was only one explanation for this mistake. Lord Kane's hair was some twelve-inch long neat, jet-black dreadlocks. Poppa's locks were small, shaggy, loosely lumped and discoloured, and were barely two-inches long. Their hairstyles were about as similar as a spade and a spoon. But it was the hair that led these cops to Poppa.

'I am not Kane, sir. Oh my God... what's going on? *I'm* not Kane–'

'Do not move, stay right where you are.'

From the corner where he was hiding, B-man saw his brother's hands, which had been held up high as per the policeman's orders, move fractionally, in a pleading gesture.

It was this gesture that ended Poppa's life. One of the cops must have assumed he was going for a weapon. So he fired. And fired again... And again: three shots.

B-man saw it all in slow-motion. The only brother he had ever had, with head and chest sputtering blood, crouched on top of the van in pain, then slumped with a thud and began to slide down the vehicle's roof. He dangled upside down off the edge for a couple of seconds, as if his legs were caught in something, before finally hitting the tarmac below headfirst.

B-man held very tightly onto the brick wall that concealed him from the policemen. For the first time since leaving home, faint images appeared of his father, struggling with crops and livestock, and then struggling again when the farm refused to yield. Promising that things would get better, he struggled for a son who had never set eyes on his mother, for a mother who never lived to see her son. His father had struggled, and lived to expect the struggle and relish the struggle, until even the struggle was taken away from him.

When the images faded, he stared blankly once more at the scene in which his street-brother had just departed. Poppa had gone without a shoe-repair shop, without kids to tell stories to, without anyone even knowing his real name.

The nature of his whole relationship with Poppa flashed through his mind in that brief moment. They had considered each other best friends, family in fact. Told stories, joked, laughed, worked and dreamed together. Together they had carved themselves a path of hope, and had dared to dream of treading it and marching all the way to glory.

But now, watching his blood seeping between the cracks and craters of the old patches of tarmac, he realised that deep down, he never really knew Poppa.

He wanted to cry for him but nothing came, only a fresh chill washing over him, his emotions waning, his feelings ebbing away towards nothingness.

BOOK THREE
A New Light at Dusk

CHAPTER 12

As twilight engulfed the city to usher in nightfall, and dark clouds captured the sky to welcome a storm, B-man joined a group of boys and girls who had claimed a small segment of Central Park near the University Way junction. They had made a fire to keep themselves warm, and they were all having fun. They were having fun even though they knew it would be just a matter of time before they were picked up, jailed and tortured, or, if very lucky, shot dead instantly.

Someone offered him a bit of speed, which he accepted gratefully. Then a big roll of weed went round the group huddled together round the fire. Someone started singing, and they all joined in. B-man held the roll between his fingers when it got to him, climbed on top of a bench, and started a dance, singing at the top of his voice and waving his arms in the air. Everyone cheered him on; they were shouting his name in rhythm with the song. '*B-man...B-man...B-man...*'

'Yo... yo... hear me out for a second,' he announced from his stage on top of the bench, waving his arms around in an attempt to bring the boisterous crowd to order.

'You are all my brothers...' he started, and everyone cheered, which spurred him to launch into an all-out speech.

'My brothers, we are facing a crisis. We are facing a crisis because for people like us, justice comes the hard way. Now, I know one thing about justice. And, I will tell you this: the arc of the moral universe is long, but it bends towards justice.'

The cheers this time were somewhat subdued. He had not expected them to understand any of this anyway. This rant was for his benefit. These thoughts had played in his mind in varying forms since Poppa's death, and speaking them aloud felt great.

'Er... Well, I don't know what that means either, but my brother told me that.'

This received a roar of laughter and once again he had wave them to silence.

'The brother who told me that is now dead. Shot down in cold blood right in front of my eyes, and no one gave a shit. We are the people they want to forget... we are of no use to them... they wish the ground would just swallow us... they wish we were just a bad dream. But we are here, we are real, and we are many. I have nothing. But I have a million brothers and sisters. And that feels good.'

Another thunderous round of applause followed. He was beginning to enjoy this.

He remembered the days when they had called him Bush-man. He was now seventeen. He had been around here barely five years, and now very few of them even knew what the B in B-man stood for. He realised the streets were good. The streets had always been good, they should never have dreamt of getting away. The streets had always been just fine before the cops started following them, before he single-handedly started all this mess. Yes, the streets were good, the House of Lord's had been good. Kappel's Corner had been good.

His speech was simply rolling off his lips. 'Having a million brothers feels so damn good. Because I know they will never bring the family down. They won't bring us down. They have never seen anything like us. They made us all hopeless, but in doing so, they gave us a unique and very special bond. We are united! Never in this country have so many people, from such varied backgrounds, been so united.

'Our plight will be our strength! And we are going to use this to beat them. They may have guns, but we have something they cannot shoot... something they cannot fight. We have what it takes to make the bravest warriors on this earth: we know no fear. We know no fear! We know no fear, because we have nothing to lose–'

A police car screeched to a stop next to their gathering, and everyone dispersed.

***

On the ride back to the hotel, Biggy stopped the Land Rover at the top of the valley, just before the outer ring-road, facing the slum. He sat back and said nothing.

Sally-Anne was terrified.

'This is all just one big rubbish dump, Sally-Anne,' he started, sweeping a hand through the air to indicate the pathetic clutter of shacks in the valley. 'Since the dawn of multi-party politics in this country, if you are not in any business that is going to help the government cling on to power, then you are just not in business full stop! They completely cut out of the government budget anything that wouldn't help directly or indirectly their bid to continue ruling. They made a lot of people jobless and homeless, and this is the result, Sally-Anne.' He was vigorously pointing at an area in the middle of Mathary Valley. '*This* is how much someone wanted to stay in power.'

Sally-Anne stayed silent. She was alone with a mafia don in the middle of nowhere, and that was bad enough. She prayed that this man was not losing his mind as well.

He was still slouched back, droning unpretentiously. 'Do you know what a land-fill site looks like?' he asked. 'Well, this valley is it, Sally-Anne. Literally! This entire valley was originally intended to be a land-fill site. And that makes all the people you see here the rubbish of this city. This is the place where all the people who had been made jobless, homeless and hopeless could come and erect their shacks with no questions asked, because it got them away from the pavements of our lovely city. This is where they dumped the waste people!

'More than a million people call this their home, and do you think anyone outside of here cares?'

Sally-Anne said nothing.

He continued. 'You've come a long way, you came in good faith for a good cause, and for that you have all my respect, and that is why I try to help. But please, do not judge me.'

Another brief, uncomfortable silence preceded Sally-Anne's attempt to muster some words. When the words eventually came, her plea was the same: 'Can you take me back to my hotel please?'

It was his turn to say nothing. He sat back and stared deep into the valley for about a minute before he started the car and pulled onto the road.

All the way back he tried everything to justify himself and his business. '*What we do is necessary...it serves a purpose... we do more people good than bad... I am not a bad person... we are the good guys...*' But Sally-Anne was not listening. She just wanted to get back to her hotel safely.

*

She was on the phone to Inspector Limo as soon as she got into her room.

'I have been walking along the streets of Mathary Valley with him, thinking he's from the police when he's a gangster?'

'I never said he's with us, but I said he is best placed to do that kind of job in Mathary Valley. We do use him every now and then—'

'But he's a gangster.'

'I don't know what he is. I don't know what he does. But I know those people respect him more than they respect any policeman.'

'What if something happens to me, sir? What would you say then? That I just went off to Mathary Valley with some man who turned out to be a crook?'

'Listen, my dear, the fact that you went to Mathary Valley in the first place is something I can't officially vouch for. Even in normal circumstances we issue a very clear directive to our foreign visitors to avoid these areas. You should not have come to the country at this time, but you are here now and my job is to offer you security while you are here. I cannot offer you that in Mathary Valley. In fact I cannot guarantee anyone's security in that area, my dear. So I think our best bet is for you to stay away from Mathary Valley altogether. We have initiated a search and we are very hopeful we can find your friend.'

Before he ended the call, she remembered the conversation with the female stallholder in Dallas.

'By the way, we learnt a few things today that you may find useful. Apparently there are other boys missing from the area as well. And they were very good friends with J'Alex, so there could be a link.'

'Really? Did you get any names? Anyone we can talk to?'

She got up to grab her bag from the table and found the piece of paper on which she had scribbled the name.

'Yeah, Jon Koli is one of them. He comes from the Dallas area. Everyone calls him Koli, and apparently if you ask around near the temporary market stalls, they will know.'

'OK, my dear. Thank you very much. I will pass this on and make sure we follow it up.'

That night when she spoke to her dad, she mentioned Biggy, but tried to keep it casual. She didn't want to worry him. She merely hinted that there was a man out there helping her around the slums, and that he was a slightly strange character: *a bit mysterious*, is how she put it. And she added that she was also concerned that this man might be expecting something in return for his troubles.

'What do you mean, Sal? Do you think he'll be expecting to be paid? I think maybe we should pay him something.'

'No, Dad, that's not what I meant. But it is fine, everything will be alright.'

'Sal, I think maybe you should let the police deal with this. It'd be easier if you just stay in your hotel and wait.'

'Yeah, I agree. Maybe I should do that.'

She decided to sleep on the idea that night and have a clearer plan when she woke up, but after a quick shower just before getting into her nightclothes, she was interrupted by the loud ringing of her hotel phone.

The Wilsons were having dinner downstairs in the restaurant and wondered if she wanted to join them. Of course she wanted to join them. She had decided that if she took nothing else away from this journey, she was taking good old Ted Wilson's laughter. The old couple had a way of lightening everything up.

At dinner she again expressed her concerns about them and their safety, with the country's status quo not showing any signs of stabilizing. But the Wilsons were not budging on their decision to stay put till they had seen the flamingos.

Apparently, Ted Wilson had been born in Kenya and he spent the first eight years of his life here. His father had owned a big ranch in the Rift Valley, overlooking Lake Nakuru, till the first of the local resistance movements against the British colonialists began emerging. Mr. Wilson Snr. sensed independence, and thus trouble for the white occupiers, some two decades before it happened. So he packed up, sold the ranch and went back to England.

Other than the fact that the move later proved to have been unnecessary in the first place (even to date, there are still some very rich white settlers with big ranches living happily in Kenya), also unknown to Mr. Wilson Snr. at the time was that he was leaving behind the best days of his life. From then on, everything about his life took a downward turn and never changed direction till his death. Back in England, he lost his connections, couldn't hold a decent job, descended to drink, lost his wife... But he never stopped telling his only son about the good old days in Kenya, about the ranch and the mansion overlooking Lake Nakuru. He never stopped talking about the flamingos. He never stopped dreaming about going back one day to have one last view of the magnificent lake and the flamingos, a dream that his son would one day inherit. The recurring dreams of riding an open safari jeep along the shores of Lake Nakuru, watching and listening to the sounds of the flamingos, somehow channelled down to Ted after his father's death. And they had stayed with him throughout his seemingly happy life.

Yet now, after achieving so much in their lives – sustaining a great marriage, bringing up two decent kids, and watching them grow up and have children of their own, then watching the grandchildren grow up – Ted and Dianne Wilson still believed that all that would count for little if he didn't live to see the flamingos of Lake Nakuru.

'If I knew my way, I would hire a car and drive up there myself,' he declared. 'These folks are fighting their wars, and I have neither the ability nor desire to interfere. If they capture me, I will tell them my story and just hope they can let me fulfil the dreams of my father.'

This was a sentiment that Sally-Anne considered dignified, but maybe also rather trivial if considered from a different perspective. Here was a couple who had lived a long and happy life – there are many that don't live to see that age, and there are some that do get there, but not via the same tranquil path; and yet the Wilsons, so late in their lives, were choosing to dwell on a sentiment that was bound to set them and their loved ones up for a major disappointment. Realistically, it was very unlikely that Ted Wilson was going to see the flamingos on this visit and maybe ever. But was all this necessary? Well, she was only twenty-three years old; her whole life was still ahead of her, how could she judge?

When they finally left the restaurant and headed for their rooms, it was past midnight. And once in bed, her mind drifted back to the events earlier in the day in Mathary Valley, and she spent some time pondering the 'Biggy situation' till she fell asleep.

*

By the time she woke up the following morning, she had made her mind up about him.

Biggy was some kind of mafia don who had helped her immensely. That, in her limited understanding of mafia folklore, meant that *she* already owed *him*. It was too late to sever links with him now because she would be, by this time, considered one of his debtors. If he wanted something in return, he would almost certainly get it. Mafia kings tend to get what they want, and there was nothing she could do about that. If there was trouble, she was already deep in it. So why stop now? There were a lot of rumours circulating in Mathary Valley.

Some of which sounded very credible. The answers lay somewhere in the slums, and she could not rest knowing the police were probably never going to get to the bottom of it. She needed to talk to Jon Koli's mother, and she could not do it without Biggy.

Within an instant of making this decision, she grabbed the phone and called him. If she did indeed owe him, she might as well make him work for his quid pro quo.

It took Biggy under an hour to make his way to the hotel. She found him sitting at the bar on the ground floor sharing some friendly banter with old Mr. Wilson. And somehow Mr. Wilson did not seem to have any problems whatsoever understanding his bizarre variety of accents. It was incredible how well Biggy seemed to get on with other people. This was all an act, no doubt. She hoped he wouldn't try to con the elderly couple or harm them in any way.

They were back in Dallas within the hour. Jon Koli's mother turned out to be a rather frail woman whose age seemed indeterminable, due to a very harsh life. She made her living making some kind of pancake-like local dish and selling the pancakes outside her mud house. Before they got talking, she offered both of them tea and pancake in her small, simple living room, which doubled up as the bedroom. A pair of worn and faded blue curtains partitioned the bed from the sitting area, which constituted a ring of four stools with an ancient and remarkably mismatched table in the middle. The table, which seemed too high for the stools, kept swinging up and down at the ends due to a combination of its lopsided legs and the seriously uneven floor. The floor was the same as the ground outside, only slightly firmer, with less loose dust. The mud walls were heavily cracked, revealing the crooked timbers that held the structure up.

'Jon said when he comes back he will have some money for me,' the old woman said. 'I'm sure all the missing boys went away together.'

'Did he say where they were going?' asked Biggy.

'No, they never do.'

'But you are not worried?'

'No, not at all, I'm an old woman now. Koli does the worrying for me. Besides he's done this before and has come back just fine.'

'You mean he's disappeared before?' Sally-Anne got in on the questioning.

'Yeah, they come and go all the time. Sometimes they go for too long. They are just young boys with nothing to do. I'm sure they are around Mathary Valley somewhere; probably got themselves in some kind of trouble and are just keeping their heads low for a while.'

Further details were vague, and the weary woman seemed to get uncomfortable with the questions as they wore on. Sally-Anne decided to wrap things up.

'Do you know any of the other boys who are missing?'

'Yes, Ozzy and Ken-Tuli are also gone. Those four are together, I'm sure of it. They always are. They do everything together.'

'So the other two, do you know of any way we can get to their families?'

'The last family Moses lived with were his aunt and uncle in the West End. They kicked him out about a year ago and he's been a drifting from one shack to another in Dallas ever since. Ozzy's just come out of a juvenile institution; he was living with some distant cousin right here before he was locked up, but I don't think he ever moved back with this cousin.'

They left after she directed them to where the so-called last-known relatives of the other boys could be found. She warned them not to be too optimistic because these kids had no stable base. Once again Sally-Anne had jotted down their full names on a piece of paper. Osbourne Okot and Moses Ken-Tuli, popularly referred to as Ozzy and Ken-Tuli respectively, would now join J'Alex and Koli on the missing list.

CHAPTER 13

It was a week after his brother's death, and B-man was still surviving, floating around the city centre day and night, yet somehow managing to elude the police. There was a very slight feeling that the cops were beginning to slacken their brutal offensive, but it would have been stupid to think that they were now safe. It would only take an incident as minor as a Parking-boy pissing on some constable's patrol route to renew their interest.

B-man found himself being considered something of a hero after his drunken speech. Some of the street urchins began seeking his advice on how to ride out this storm. He was always full of ideas, most of which were not worth the weed that invariably catalysed their conception. But the urchins listened anyway. They liked their secret gatherings, and B was always forced to conjure some kind of speech. Lord Kane and the real gangsters of Dallas were nowhere to be seen. Everyone believed they had all been captured; maybe that explained the slight let-up in police action. Somehow, in the middle of all this, B-man began to command a cult following.

He was sitting on yet another park bench on another bright afternoon, stoned out of his head. Eddy, another of the surviving boys, was hovering around him rambling muffled sentences with a jar of glue held against his nostrils as B-man smoked a cigarette. Eddy had apparently discovered another hideout that he swore was almost as safe as the House of Lord's.

'I come straight to you with this information because Kane's gone and now everyone's listening to you,' said Eddy. 'This joint is on the other side of the bridge. Man, I don't even know what I was doing there, but I found it. I was major stoned and I spent the whole night in there. All on my own, no one bothered me. This joint is abandoned, B-man. Completely! No one anywhere near. You can get everyone together and we can make this just like the House of Lords.'

For a while he listened to Eddy's tale about the mysterious new hideout full of scepticism. He had cigarettes, and he knew Eddy wanted one. Eddy was young, maybe eleven or twelve, but not angelic. None of these boys were, age notwithstanding. When it came to acquiring such essentials as cigarettes, these kids would be prepared to do anything, of which contriving some harmless fib would rank very low in severity. In the end he agreed to check the place out, and promised that if turned out to be any good, he would do something to get people together to discuss their options. He reluctantly offered Eddy the cigarette after all, but he made him promise to give it back if the hideout turned out to be one of his fantasies.

B-man and Eddy were setting off to the purported new hideout when a new and reasonably posh silver saloon pulled over near the taxi rank just a few yards from their bench. The young female driver who emerged from the car had her face partially wrapped in a dark blue scarf, as if it were a veil. She started walking straight towards them. The boys eyed her with suspicion, wondering whether to flee. But her sex and her age – she was probably in her early to mid-twenties – offered some reassurance; she could not possibly have been looking for trouble. The slightly oval and very light brown face behind the veil looked pleasant enough, if not a little scared. Perhaps she was lost and wanted directions; in which case she had come to the right people.

When the woman got close, B-man thought he saw her hands shaking. She was obviously terrified, and whatever it was that she wanted to say seemed stuck behind her full red lips. B-man quickly realised he could make this episode fun: a lone, rich young woman, terrified of street boys but forced to roam their streets and seek their help, was looking for something.

'Yes... can we be of assistance? Ma'am?' B-man decided to help her out with the first move, which only succeeded in making things even harder for her because this help was delivered with a quiet snicker, ill concealed behind his clenched fists. He was still under the full influence of a variety of drugs.

She looked around her for the thousandth time, and when she finally spoke it was with a sense of urgency. 'Have you got... uh... anything?' She kept fiddling with her veil to keep her hands steady. 'You know... stuff? I'm paying.'

'Pardon?' The response was from B-man.

Eddy nudged him, whispering, 'She's looking for drugs, B. We might be in luck.'

B-man had figured that out already, but he was enjoying making it difficult for her.

'Stuff...You know...?' Her voice was failing. 'Weed...anything you've got.'

The long-suppressed laugh finally escaped B-man at the way she pronounced *weed*, making it sound like *whid*. The woman almost burst into tears. B-man was thoroughly enjoying this. She started walking away and Eddy quickly stepped up to block her path.

'Hey, easy, darling! Maybe we can help.'

Eddy seemed keen to rescue the situation, but B-man butted in once more.

'So you want stuff...? What stuff do you want?' he said, mimicking her stutter. 'Speed? Coke? Or the other one you just mentioned – what was it?'

She opened her mouth to answer, and B-man was already bottling up fits of laughter, expecting her to say *whid*. And that's exactly what she said.

'Ww...whid?'

He let out a loud, exaggerated laugh, which he milked for all it was worth, doubling over in a mock bellyache before finally deciding to walk away from her, knowing he had ruined any chance of doing business. Just as well: he had no stock left on him anyway. He stepped aside to let Eddy deal with the matter seriously, and observed them chat for a few seconds, then head towards her car, presumably for the transaction.

Afterwards, Eddy was suddenly not too keen on the idea of walking all the way south of the bridge to show B-man the potential new hideout. He offered him back his cigarette and gave him some rough directions, promising he would certainly not be a disappointed, before he disappeared into the city.

*

It was after about another half hour of aimless wandering around the city centre, debating whether to make the journey south-side alone to check out Eddy's squat, that B-man spotted the silver saloon again. He would not have paid much attention to it had it not stopped by a litterbin and a hand emerged to dump a small package wrapped in brown paper. Watching closely, he saw the same young female driver behind the wheels. He also noted that the car's back windows were somewhat dark tinted; but he was sure she was alone. The strangeness of the spectacle only crossed his mind for a split second: a lone young rich woman, prowling the streets in search of drugs. But he decided not to give it much thought as he walked over to the rubbish and retrieved the package. It was full of weed, no doubt the stuff she had bought from Eddy.

He wondered why the woman had been so eager to buy the drugs only to throw it all away. On second thoughts, though, he was sure that, despite her shaking and fidgeting, this pretty young woman did not look anything like a junkie, more like a terrified little girl. But since he was not into solving puzzles he simply tucked the package into his hip-pocket with a shrug, and wandered on.

***

Once again, late in the evening at the Imperial Hotel, Inspector Limo called Sally-Anne. Maybe, she thought, they were giving this case some time after all.

'We have traced the families and most known close relatives of both J'Alex and Jon Koli, and we have put alerts with all our police units. We have also placed missing-persons announcements in major media channels. We are taking this very seriously, my dear.'

'And still nothing?'

'Nothing so far.'

She went ahead and filled him in on her and Biggy's findings for the day. She gave him the two names of the other missing boys, Osbourne Okot and Moses Ken-Tuli.

'I think wherever they are they are together,' she added. 'If you can find any one of them, you'll probably have found them all.'

'Thank you very much. I will add the two names to the list.'

The news on the political climate was now beginning to offer some hint of hope. The international community was exerting pressure on the two feuding leaders and there were signs they would be prepared to negotiate. They had begun to offer half-hearted pleas to their respective supporters to quit the violence. It was a slender hope, but better than no hope at all.

That night, before she went to bed, she turned on the radio. Inspector Limo had said the missing persons announcements would come straight after the news, and, sure enough, the announcement came. There were only the two names, and it sounded so surreal knowing it could well have been her who had placed the announcements. The announcer's voice gave some kind of ring to it: '...*J'Alex Gitonga... Jon Koli... anyone with any information, please contact...*'

*

Sally-Anne woke Biggy up with a phone call early the following morning and proceeded to run through what she wished to do that day. She did not ask if he was free or if it was OK with him. She knew he could always make himself free, and whatever Sally-Anne asked him was always OK. Biggy would make her pay it all back with interest somehow, she was sure of it. There was an unspoken deal here, and she guessed she wasn't the one on the better end of it.

She had enough time to have breakfast with the Wilsons before Biggy arrived, and she had to keep her patience in check once again when Biggy again launched into a long chat with the elderly couple. When the conversation started drifting towards football, she knew it was time to get him moving and get on their way.

They first went down to the police headquarters. This time, the inspector had brought two other members of his team to back him up. Their official stance remained: '*We are doing our best...*' The problem was that most of their investigations were relying on the media and police alerts. There was not much they could actually do on the ground in Mathary Valley, which was virtually a no-go zone for the police at the time. On the other hand, Inspector Limo was fine with Biggy and her continuing their own search in Mathary Valley, at their own risk. He even offered to loan them two junior police officers to help in their quest. But they had to agree that these two officers would not be acting in their official capacity. They would not be in uniform, and were to be considered strictly as civilian support.

'Let's just say you are touring Mathary Valley and they will be your personal bodyguards,' Limo said before introducing the pair. 'If you find anything useful, well and good. If something goes wrong, my defence will be that these two are not my officers on official duty. And the records also clearly state that I warned you about the place.'

The two backup policemen made an unusual pair: one was a lanky six-foot-seven beanpole, the other was stout and around five-eight, a dwarf in comparison. They called themselves Kip and Simi.

Sally-Anne discussed an action plan with the men. Her initial idea was the simplest conceivable plan: she wanted them to knock on every door in Mathary Valley and ask for information, promising a handsome monetary reward for information leading to a find. There would be a lot of doors to knock on, admittedly, but the hope was that some useful information would surface before they had to go too far. To avoid knocking on the same door twice, Sally-Anne suggested that they could place a mark on the doors as they proceeded. They would also place posters in strategic areas appealing for information and mentioning the reward. Someone was bound to know something.

Biggy's reaction to the idea made her feel like a stupid child. He looked at her long and hard, shaking his head as if to say: *Can you believe this girl!* – before pointing out that the shanties in Mathary Valley were myriad. There were tens of thousands of them. That would be a lot of doors to knock on.

'Why not just stick to the most obvious method?' he asked. 'You know... the kind of thing you see in all the good old detective movies. We start by talking to people who knew the boys, people who were closest to them.'

'You don't need to refer to them in past tense. They are not dead.'

'Oh, sorry.'

'And how are we going to find all these people?' she asked. 'How will we even know who these closest friends are?'

'We just need one person to begin with. The first person will lead us to the next, and so on.'

Biggy took it upon himself to delegate tasks. Even the two policemen let him take charge. Biggy was to ask most of the questions, Sally-Anne would note any significant findings in her notebook, while Kip and Simi would do the posters and attend to any other tasks that arose.

The shorter cop, Simi, was a somewhat quiet and polite gentleman who kept addressing Sally-Anne as *ma'am*, and held doors open for her. Kip, the beanpole, was a joker.

After that first day, they were driving out of the slums late in the evening with the two cops occupying the back seats when Kip wound his window halfway down, stuck his nose out as if for some fresh air, and started whistling. Then he paused, and, in a booming bass tone, said: *'Yesterdaaay...'* And resumed his whistling. Then he paused again, said the same word, in the same voice, and carried on.

This continued for well over a minute. Sally-Anne looked around in bewilderment trying to assess what the other two men thought of Kip's bizarre behaviour. They seemed totally oblivious. After about the fifth *'Yesterdaaay...'* she felt compelled to act.

'Kiiip...?' She prolonged the preliminaries deliberately, to indicate that what she was about to ask was meant in the best possible way.

'Yeees...?' he mimicked without turning his head from the window.

'What on earth are you doing?'

'I'm singing "Yesterday" by the Beatles,' he answered, swinging his head back into the vehicle excitedly. Then he cleared his throat and launched into a full rendition of the song, clicking his fingers, shaking his head and swaying his upper body right and left.

Sally-Anne regretted ever asking.

Biggy's laugh was initially bottled up, only escaping his throat in spasmodic hisses, as though he were suffering a coughing fit. Simi's was a gentle chuckle, but to save himself from this torture he raised both hands to cover his ears. Sally-Anne's was mostly influenced by Biggy's, like an infection, with the effort to suppress a giggle turning into a choking fit. Then, when she couldn't hold it any longer and exploded into loud hysterics, this in turn infected Biggy. The big man was left convulsing with laughter to such an extent that the car started swerving dangerously and he had to pull over and calm down.

'So you don't like my singing, then?' Kip asked after everyone seemed to have settled. 'I personally believe that was quite good, no?'

The faintest of hisses escaped Sally-Anne's lips. And that was enough to trigger another wave of hysterical laughter that left the whole vehicle rocking.

'I think the moral of the story is, Kip,' Sally-Anne eventually said in an effort to bring this childishness to an end, 'that you should not quit your day job.'

*

Back at the Imperial Hotel, she sat on the edge of her bed and reflected on what she considered the first properly organised day of her search. They had not as yet unearthed any significant new information. The story always seemed the same: the four appeared to be very good buddies and they had probably disappeared together. Other young boys were missing too. It was not unusual for young boys to go missing in that area. And on occasion they would reappear, richer, yet vague about where they had been. It all led towards the suspicion they were engaging in some criminal activity.

Before she went to sleep, she listened to the missing-persons announcement again. The two new names had been added to it: '...J'Alex Gitonga... Jon Koli... Osbourne Okot... Moses Ken-Tuli... anyone with any information...'

Eddy's proposed new hideout turned out to be real. But he generously ensured that it was B-man who got the credit for the discovery. After telling B-man about the potential squat, Eddy had then gone round telling everyone that B-man was working out a grand plan and would be announcing some good news soon. At seventeen, B-man was now a senior citizen in street terms. His anointment to leadership had come without his knowledge or his consent; it was just a natural progression. And with the weight of so much expectation on his shoulders, he knew he had to do something.

His first inspection of the house left him in something of a dilemma as to whether it was indeed suitable. The positive news was that this was a secluded, derelict, yet incomplete construction with nothing but woods and greenery within well over a hundred-yard radius. The problem was, it was on the wrong side of town. It was only a few miles up from the suburbs, south of the big bridge from the city centre. The building would be fairly safe and peaceful once they were indoors, but the large numbers of street children walking through the suburbs to get there would no doubt raise alarm bells.

He decided there would have to be some strict rules if they were going to use the facility, and, by word of mouth, he arranged a meeting of all interested Parking-boys the day after he checked it out. He issued clear instructions that anyone coming to the meeting would have to come alone. No walking in groups.

Everything went smoothly, and the turnout was very good.

B-man was sitting on the edge of what would have been the kitchen window of the squat, addressing the group huddled over the wildly overgrown backyard, when he yet again noticed the silver saloon, this time driving over the thick weeds, straight towards them. Everyone sensed trouble, and as they started scurrying about in panic the same young female driver got out and stood next to the car, as if expecting this to restore some calm. This probably did the trick: those who spotted her stopped on their tracks; it was only a young woman, and at a derelict building in the middle of nowhere, surrounded by a gang of street boys. If anyone was in trouble, *she* was, not they. Faces started turning towards B-man, expecting instructions.

He jumped off the window with an open-palm gesture urging calm. He then started walking slowly towards her.

'You alright, ma'am?' he started, this time with a warm and genuine smile. 'Are you following me?'

'I'd like to talk to you.'

She sounded surprisingly confident and assured; a remarkable transformation from their previous meeting.

'You want to buy more drugs?'

'No, I want to talk to you.'

'OK, go ahead. I'm listening.'

She glanced at the group of Parking-boys who were now watching curiously, and said, 'Can we talk in private? Could you get in the car?'

B-man half turned, to check with his people. He looked left at the young and pleading eyes of the intruder, then right at the inquisitive stares of his subjects who were still waiting for his deliverance speech. Then he looked left again, and the woman still looked young, harmless and lost. He had to admit she had some guts, not only turning up to a place like this, but also inviting a street boy, a complete stranger, into her car.

He was suddenly very curious. 'OK,' he said, walking round to the passenger side.

It was not until he was settled in the passenger seat, with the doors firmly shut, that he noticed the man in the back. Instinctively, he tried in vain to kick the door open as the car began speeding away from his friends, who had sensed trouble and had charged towards the vehicle. Then he turned round and found that the man was pointing a gun at him.

'Don't move, we just need to talk.'

The man sounded calm.

'We just need to talk,' the woman repeated.

B-man glanced out of the window again and knew that his friends had no way of helping. He was on his own. Without thinking, he spun round and launched himself at the man in the back, kicking the female driver in the process as he landed his full weight on the man.

The woman started screaming. 'Stop it... stop it, we just need to talk.'

The man was taken aback, but he reacted quickly. B-man was a strong and athletic young man; he was also bigger that the other man. Under normal circumstances, he could have taken this man any day, any where. But these weren't normal circumstances; he had hardly had a proper meal for more than a week. And the man had a gun.

Not a single shot was fired though.

Just when it was looking increasingly clear that B-man, despite is handicap, was overpowering the man, he somehow found the back of B-man's head with the butt of his gun.

Thus, the contest came to an abrupt end.

*

When B-man came round, he was lying on the back seat of the car, with both hands cuffed behind him. His feet were also bound. He could see it was dark outside, as a face from the driver's seat turned and smiled at him.

'How are you doing mate, all right?'

It was the young woman, the drug girl. Sitting next to her was the man who had sent him to la-la land. He had a neat, toothbrush moustache, impeccably trimmed and parted in the middle, with a close shave. He looked unrealistically smart for a man who had just been in a tussle. His white shirt was fairly clean, and the blue tie was still in place. B-man wondered if he had stopped somewhere to freshen up. He was sure he had given this man a decent fight.

'Hey, champ,' the man started. 'I said I only needed a word, for God's sake. You nearly broke my neck.'

'F-Fuck yy-you!' B-man's answer was laboured and barely audible.

The man smiled and turned to the woman. 'You know, when I was still in the service one of the easiest routines was pointing a gun at some hard crooks and ordering them to freeze. It normally does the trick. But it didn't work with this boy, did it?' He flipped the pistol over and over again on the palm of his left hand, as if admiring it, while his right hand gently stroked his moustache. 'I had a loaded automatic pointed at you at point blank range, and you still try to break my neck?'

The woman took over. 'I understand they call you B around here. Is it alright if I call you B?'

He did not reply but she carried on nonetheless.

'My name's Paula, this is Ronny,' she went on, sounding pleasant. 'I asked Ronny to help me with this, so please don't be angry with him, it's me you should be angry with. You should know we are not the police because otherwise right now you would have been in jail or dead. Sorry about that head injury, but I really needed to talk to you. Would you do that for me? Can you talk to me, B?'

'What do you want?'

'Great, that's a good start. I think maybe we need to establish some trust here. I want you to be comfortable when we are talking so we will take off the cuffs. And maybe on your part you could promise not to be violent. Can you do that?'

'What the fuck do you want from me?'

They both ignored his language as the man went ahead and untied his legs, then unlocked the handcuffs. Once free, B-man sat upright and tilted his head left and right to check that it was still functional. He quickly took in the twilit scene outside and realised they were in the car park of a big building that he recognised as the Ambassador Hotel, just outside the city centre.

He did not attack. He figured they were right: they could have killed him or put him in jail, but they had not. They wanted something, and he was curious.

'OK, I will go straight to the point, B,' the woman continued. 'I know a lot about you, I have eavesdropped on a few of your speeches to your friends in your little gatherings. I have spoken to a few of your friends... You remember me trying to act like a junkie the other day? Pathetic, wasn't it?' She smiled, revealing a set of perfect white teeth. 'Anyway, in short, I've been spying on you. We think you are a good man. You are smart, strong and you want the best for your friends. So what if I say to you now, that we can give you and your friends a home and the means to make a living. What would you say to that, B?'

His mind worked quickly. 'We are not interested in charity homes.'

'Then you will be glad to know that this has nothing to do with charity. These would be genuinely your own homes, no one to watch over you, feed you... nothing like that. We will give you the homes and regular allowances to live on. The money will be paid through you, so your friends do not have to worry about being watched over like little kids. They can do as they please in their homes. Eat, drink, smoke and sniff whatever they want.'

She waited for him to digest this and offer some kind of reaction.

'I'm listening,' he said.

'OK, here it comes. In some parts of the Rift Valley, there are homes being abandoned everyday by people fleeing the tribal clashes caused by land disputes. We want to offer you and your friends these homes, temporarily, and we will pay you to live there.'

'Are you out of you mind? You are trying to relocate a whole street population to a different province? To a place where they are going to be killed?'

'Well, just listen to me, B, we are not trying to relocate them, we are offering them an opportunity to earn money. The stay there is only temporary, maybe just a couple of weeks. You will earn very good money and still get the chance to come and spend it back in the city with your friends. It's that simple. If you had a job and a transfer was proposed, you would consider it depending on the benefits that comes with it, wouldn't you?'

'You are offering to pay us for the pleasure of seeing us killed?'

'The chances of your getting killed are very minimal.'

'Oh really? If that's right, why are these people fleeing their homes in the first place?'

'Because the other tribe are the majority, and they attack in very large gangs with big swords, arrows, machetes... all sorts of traditional weapons.'

'And you think we will not be a minority?'

'You will be very much a minority, but whereas they attack with ancient weapons–' She reached into the back and picked up a big black bag that had been lying on the floor on the passenger side. She rested the bag on her lap and unzipped it. To his amazement, she produced a big double-barrel assault riffle and waved it in the air. '– Whereas the other guys will have traditional weapons, we will provide you with some of these, and train you to use them.'

He did his best to contain his astonishment as the idea began to sink in. These were people on a recruitment drive for an army, and it was not an army looking to uphold any laws.

They were asking them to fight a war for them, and it would not be a patriotic war.

'I get the picture,' he said after another long silence. 'You do realise that we are a big group of people from a variety of backgrounds, don't you? We are, however, united and tightly bound by love for one another; and, more significantly, hate for the rest of the society. What makes you think we would be interested in fighting a tribal war?'

This time the answer came from the man with the moustache, who until then had managed to stay silent.

'Money,' he said. 'You have not asked how much money you would be earning from this.'

***

It took immense pressure from the international community, including a personal visit by the US Secretary of State, to get the two political rivals in Kenya to start negotiating. But this was now achieving the desired effect of bringing a degree of calm to the country. The atmosphere remained tense, and the resumption of normal business still appeared distant; but the news of mass demonstrations, looting, vandalism and shootings all over the country began to lessen.

The posters and announcements of the missing boys had begun attracting numerous responses, especially after the reward was added. But only a handful of them sounded credible enough to warrant the attention of Inspector Limo and his team. And as it turned out, none of these half-leads took them anywhere.

Sally-Anne was baffled. They had made it clear she was trying to find J'Alex as a friend, only to help. Yet the argument that these boys were in hiding somewhere, for some reason, still seemed prevalent among the slum folks. To her, this simply didn't make sense; the ingenuity to make themselves vanish without a trace, for a group of twelve-year-olds, seemed inconceivable; most important, though, someone was yet to tell her what crime these boys had committed to make them want to disappear in the first place. The announcements were clear: the boys were not being hunted by the police for committing a crime, so they could not possibly be hiding. They had no reason to. Why was it taking so long to find them? In addition, this was not just one missing person, these were *four* boys. Four boys who, not long before, had been very much alive, not to say notorious in Mathary Valley. Where on earth were they?

It was her third Thursday in the country, and Biggy, along with Kip and Simi, had come to pick her up. The big man was busy chatting to the Wilsons in the lobby when she asked him up to her room to help carry a pack of bottled water down to the car. It was the first time he had ever been to her room. As she was holding her door open for him, their eyes met for a second. He stopped with the pack of water in hand, and remained frozen, just staring. She felt the rays from his brown eyes piercing hers, and it sent shockwaves all the way down her legs.

'You have blue eyes,' he said.

It was an unknown zone. She didn't have a clue how to react.

'They are beautiful,' he continued.

She recoiled in a mixture of shame, horror and anxiety. Her face turned bright pink.

Was he about to attack her? Was he going to drop the pack, push the door locked and rape her? She instinctively stepped out of the room and the door began to shut with him inside. He shuffled his right foot forward to trap the door and swing it back open, then simply squeezed past her and started walking towards the lift with the pack of bottled water, leaving her rooted to the spot.

The incident was never mentioned again. And he never offered any more compliments. Their early morning pleasantries were from then on restricted to:

Good morning.

Good morning.

How was your night?

Yeah, good, thank you. You?

Yeah, great. What a lovely day today.

Yeah beautiful day.

Yeah.

Yeah...

Maybe more would be said in the course of the day, but the morning routine remained the same old mechanical formula.

*

Back in Mathary Valley, cracks started appearing in their master plan after just a few days. The people who were believed to be friends of the four missing boys were proving very difficult to get hold of. The few they found remained vague about what they knew. And it was hard to establish if they knew anything at all. A consequence of the handsome reward promised was that many who knew nothing constructed half-truths with the money in mind, and ended up wasting their precious time on wild goose chases around the valley. The few who appeared to know something seemed reluctant to talk. Knocking on doors all round the slum proved easier said than done. Some of the residents, without appearing rude, even found ways of telling them, in no uncertain terms, that they had more serious businesses to deal with. As far as they were concerned, these were just four more boys from Mathary Valley, nothing special.

The long walks through the valley in the scorching heat soon began taking their toll on the team, especially Sally-Anne. Sometimes she got so tired and frustrated at the end of the day that she would not say a single word to Biggy on their drive back to the hotel.

'We seem to be very quiet,' Biggy pointed out one evening in his best comical voice, 'could it be something I've done?'

'No, Biggy. I'm just tired.'

'Ah, OK.'

When he asked the same question the following evening she simply closed her eyes and pretended to be asleep. And the next time he attempted to inquire about her moods she was so angry tired and frustrated that she found herself blurting out.

'I don't want to talk, Biggy. I. Do. Not. Want. To. Talk!'

Somewhere amid these long, hot, arduous days, she had forgotten that she was supposed to be scared of this man.

Her frustrations did not stop with Biggy. The police, and especially Inspector Limo, got a piece of her mind, too. She did not believe they were doing enough and she was not afraid to tell them as much. The best they had come up with so far was some unconfirmed story about an incident that had occurred somewhere in Eldoret in the Rift Valley, where a lorry-load of young men had been ambushed by the Maasai and set on fire.

'That's hundreds of miles away, what has it got to do with J'Alex and his friends?' she asked him after he had told her the story.

'None of the bodies from this incident has been identified, or indeed claimed.'

'Oh, great. So four boys go missing from Mathary Valley, some unidentified people get killed in Eldoret, simply link the two and close the case. It's that simple, uh?'

'We will investigate everything, my dear. Please be patient.'

'I wake up early every morning to go and do your job for you in the slums where you should be doing your investigations. I leave you to do the easy job. And the best you can manage is some story about something that happened hundred of miles away in a totally different part of the country?'

Sally-Anne did not care what they thought of her. The decision to come to this country at such a time had been the hardest and noblest thing she had ever done in her life. One day, in the very distant future, she would love nothing more than to sit down with her grandchildren and tell this story with pride. But the tale would mean nothing if she left without seeing J'Alex's smile once again.

*

The schools' drama and dance festival was Biggy's next idea. The Mathary Valley Union Secondary School in the West End was hosting one of the heats of the nationally organised drama competitions. According to Biggy, this was a suitable place to fish for information because there would be a lot of kids gathered in one place, most of whom knew the missing boys. She thought it was an odd idea, coming from him, and for a moment she found herself wondering if Biggy intended merely to use this as a front to conduct his illegal businesses, perhaps even sell drugs to the children. Then she thought again, and admitted that maybe she was being too harsh on the big man.

She agreed because she couldn't think of anything better. Kip and Simi agreed because they always agreed with anything Biggy suggested.

Biggy had managed to get them invites as special guest of the head-teacher, and thus she found herself in the front row of the modest-sized theatre hall, just inches away from the display of gleaming trophies that the children would be competing for. Sally-Anne sat there all day sipping cold drinks and watching the young performers act, sing and dance with a level of creative talent she had never suspected possible from this part of the world.

The climax came when an all girls' school performed what they described as a *dramatised dance*. They danced out the story of a girl who grows up to become a successful lawyer before succumbing to AIDS and suffering a painful death.

It was a masterpiece!

The vigorous dancers and blasting drums had the entire hall rocking and shaking. It would be fast and furious one minute, then suddenly slow down to a sombre melody, and the dancers moved in perfect sync, as if the drummer were manipulating them on strings. They danced like women possessed; and before they were done, the whole place was dancing with them. Somewhere in the middle of it, she looked over at Biggy. She realised he had not brought her here to find J'Alex, or to ask questions, or to sell drugs. He had brought her here because he knew that this was exactly what she needed after all the long, hard, stressful and frustrating days. By the end of that piece she was madly in love with all the dancers, and wanted to marry the drummer.

She glanced out of the window at the fully costumed kids who had just come off the stage, happily intermingling with the next contestants who were preparing to go on. Their admirable camaraderie made Sally-Anne yearn to be young again. They were no different from J'Alex and the friends of his whom she had never had a chance to meet. They were just normal, happy, free-spirited children having the time of their lives; human beings with the intrinsic sense that it is wrong to kill another human being. The people who set J'Alex's family on fire, and watched them burn, had once been these kids.

When her gaze moved back to the stage, her vision was blurred by tears.

CHAPTER 15

In the end, B-man never bothered to inquire about who exactly Paula was. He did not ask who she worked for, and indeed kept away from any personal information about her. He was smart enough to know that he might never get the whole truth. The motives of a young and wealthy woman for tribal slayings was hard to fathom. Maybe her father or husband was a politician. Or maybe she was seeking personal retribution for some injustice she had suffered in the name of tribalism. It was all about race and politics, that much he knew. But young as he was, B-man was aware that they would only tell him what they wanted him to know.

He completed the deal with her the following day at the lobby of the Ambassador Hotel. After their initial encounter, Paula had given him some money and asked him to think about her offer and meet her at the hotel that evening. She instructed that she would leave a message at Reception, so all he had to do was ask for her. But she warned that it would help if he used some of the money to sort himself out and buy some decent outfits. Firstly, because the hotel would be reluctant to let him in, in his state, and, more important, they did not want him to attract any unwanted attention.

When they met at the hotel, the first thing he noted was that, as far as he could tell, Paula was unaccompanied. She met him at the bar on the ground floor and they talked over drinks. By then he had already hinted to the other boys about the prospects of earning a living as soldiers, and most of them were excited. He had sworn them to absolute secrecy.

The pair conversed, plotted and schemed, and in the end B-man felt that all his fears about the affair had been assuaged. Whoever she worked for, they had no doubt thought the plan through thoroughly. Later she invited him to dine with her at the hotel's restaurant, and that evening he experienced the most sumptuous meal of his life. Before concluding, she gave him more money and they arranged another meeting at the same place in two days. By this time, she said, the plans would be in place to ferry the boys to a secret training camp somewhere near the southern border with Tanzania.

'You don't belong in the streets. No one does,' she remarked at the end. 'I really want to help you B-man. I'm sure this arrangement will make a lot of people very happy.'

He did not agree with the idea that she was helping. As far as he was concerned, they were working together; but he didn't see the need to voice this opinion.

*

Basic training took place over the next four weeks somewhere in the Maasai Mara, near the border with Tanzania: a camp set up in the wilderness, on a clearing about the size of two football fields, with nothing but vast, raw jungle within more than a hundred miles. But the well-designed base camp was adorned with a rich array of facilities. The main accommodation was around a terrace of grass-thatched dorms set in a circle, with a green canvas shed in the middle housing all the exercise equipment. Some hundred yards from this was an outdoor shooting range comprising a series of twenty-metre lanes with a manual pulley system for varied target distancing. It was clear this was something that had taken a great deal of planning.

Paula and Ronny, the man with the moustache, dropped in every weekend during the first month of training. She grew quite fond of B-man, took him on long jeep drives through the jungle and tried to engage him in conversations about his past, without revealing anything about herself.

The four men who stayed and ran the camp were only known to them as Captain, Major, Colonel and General.

There were hard physical exercises and close combat drills conducted by Captain and Major. The intensive weapons training and target practice were run mainly by Colonel, with some help from Captain. The burly, grey-haired man known as General just strolled around, inspecting parades, smoking and talking non-stop about discipline.

They were sworn to absolute secrecy. The survival of this army would hinge on the fact that no one else would know about it.

Nights, after dinner, would be spent around a big campfire, chanting and singing, telling jokes and stories and solving riddles. The first activity at dawn would be a five-mile run through the jungle to an obscure river somewhere in the wilderness where they'd have their first bath of the day.

But they were also pampered and spoilt. At the camp, anything they required would be made available. Alcohol, nicotine, glue, weed and amphetamines were supplied in plenty for those who needed them. The endless choice of food, offered in a buffet-style service, always guaranteed a large amount of leftovers which would be dumped after every meal – something they would have killed for on the streets. More fancy stuff, including expensive clothing, video games and other digital gadgets, would come in bulk during Paula and Ronny's weekend visits.

Some of them, including B-man, were even taught to drive.

The first instalment of their allowance was paid to them in cash before the first group was dispatched to a remote village in Naivasha with adequate training and clear instructions. B-man would stay in the city and act as the link between Paula's people, the base camp in the jungle, and the soldiers, wherever they were in the country. He would travel every fortnight to see how the boys were doing, pay them their wages, and give any further instructions.

The proposed operations sounded simple enough at the outset. The troops would occupy some houses in an area which the minority tribes had fled due after the clashes. They would simply try to settle there as new residents and do nothing, just wait, fully expecting the Kikuyus to attack sooner or later. The Kikuyus' MO had always been the same: they would ambush in the middle of the night. Their weapons were likely to be the old, traditional types. So the new residents would polish and ready their guns everyday, and always keep at least three people on the lookout through the night. All they had to do was wait to be attacked. Anything they did after that would thus be self-defence.

They didn't have to wait long. Word travelled fast about the new neighbours as they strolled around the markets openly speaking the enemy's language. The Kikuyus smelled blood, but the fact that these aliens were so openly courting confrontation called for caution. Secret gatherings were held by a river deep in the forests. And on the third night the locals decided that their new neighbours were due a visit. No less than fifty Kikuyus armed themselves with *pangas*, machetes, slings and arrows, and set out for battle. They delivered the first blow at the stroke of midnight.

Only two of them survived to tell the tale of that cold, Tuesday night bloodbath.

*

By the time news of what was happening in this remote district in the Rift Valley province started filtering into the cities, the first guerilla squadron had already been shipped back to base camp in the Maasai Mara jungle. They would be allowed time off to visit friends and family, if any, and the next troop would be sent in, to a different location but with identical instructions.

During their time off visiting their old hunting grounds in Mathary Valley, the soldiers became minor celebrities. Between them they had coined the name 'The Dallas Mercenaries' (although even the name was part of their oath to secrecy, and was only to be used amongst themselves). Paula had helped B-man acquire a posh, self-contained one-bedroom flat near the city centre, but the nature of his work meant he still had to spend most of his time in hotels around Nairobi and the coast areas, pulling the strings. He was also offered a car, a second-hand but mint-condition Ford hatchback.

It was all happening for the Dallas Mercenaries.

The nature of their business remained a closely guarded secret as they walked around in expensive clothes and took expensive gifts to their friends. Everyone was in awe of them, even though none of them was sure where their money was coming from. They assumed they had got some kind of break and landed well-paying jobs in the city.

The Dallas Mercenaries killed more than a thousand Kikuyus in different parts of the country within the first month of going to war.

***

Kofi Annan, the former UN Secretary General, was the man charged with refereeing the bitter contest between the two political leaders. His mandate was straightforward: he had to get the duo to agree on something that would bring back stability and lasting peace to this country. In the diplomatic world, Kofi Annan was the best. Failure was not an option, for, if he failed, the whole world would give up on Kenya and let its people slaughter themselves into oblivion. The hopes of the nation rested squarely on Annan's shoulders.

The warriors placed their arsenal back in the armoury, and waited.

Somewhere in the midst of all this came a leak to the media: the amazing story of a young Englishwoman who had travelled all the way through this mire to find a friend. The media found it interesting enough for a leading paper to ask her for an interview. And Sally-Anne's incredible story was featured in their popular Sunday edition. In addition, on the nightly missing-persons announcements, the same four names continued to blare out: '...J'Alex Gitonga... Jon Koli... Osbourne Okot... Moses Ken-Tuli... anyone with any information...'

Within a few weeks, the four names, emphasised by the intriguing ring of the announcer's voice, began to find fame. But it was not until the film came out that the names of the four missing boys took on a life of their own...

The posters and announcements had been running for almost two weeks before the first significant response came. It was not from Mathary Valley or Nairobi; not even from a Kenyan. It came from a European couple who identified themselves as Marta and Ole Nielsen. The couple were part of a group of travelling Norwegian students who had moved to the coast of Mombasa. They had visited Mathary Valley with a charity organisation a few months back; and they had not only met all four boys, but they had also spent a significant amount of time with them. On top of this, the couple had made a habit of filming most of their travels, and in one such film they made while touring Mathary Valley, the stars were none other than J'ALEX GITONGA, JON KOLI, OSBOURNE OKOT and MOSES KEN-TULI.

It was a film that would capture a nation that was experiencing a very dark time.

The information and video were first handed to the police in the coastal province in hope that they could be useful in some way. The film was a four-minute amateur video of the four boys, somewhere in Mathary Valley, playing a game that resembled something between baseball and cricket.

Opening frame. Introductions. A close-up of each of the four boys saying their names to the camera:

J'Alex (beautiful)

Koli (very dark, prominent nose)

Ozzy (round face, like a doll)

Ken-Tuli (big ears, protruding forehead)

They all look about ten years old.

Voice of the cameraman (in the background): *So you are going to show us how to play, eh? What's the game called again?*

Jon Koli (standing nearest to the camera, holding a sort of crooked stick): *Tip-tap... it's called tip-tap.*

The camera zooms in on J'Alex's wide brown eyes. He is squatting behind Koli with a huge grin plastered all over his face.

Cameraman: *So what are you then, Koli? What's your role? The batsman?*

The four boys look at each other and giggle.

Moses Ken-Tuli: *We just play, I throw... Koli hits it... then the two of us try to catch it from the air. If Koli misses, J'Alex catches behind him.*

Both Ken-Tuli and Ozzy move closer to the camera with their arms wrapped fondly around each other's shoulders, as the former continues his attempt to explain the game.

Cameraman: *So, J'Alex, Ozzy and Ken-Tuli are all catching? How do you actually score then?*

At this point all four of them start talking excitedly into the camera, trying to explain the game, and the laughing cameraman cuts them short.

Cameraman: *OK... OK, that's enough technical information. Now just get on with the game.*

The next frame shows Koli running around and waving his stick up the air jubilantly, in apparent victory. J'Alex is still squatting in the same position, with the same wide smile, watching, as Koli breaks into a funny dance with his stick.

The other two, Ozzy and Ken-Tuli, begin a rather theatrical and comical argument over whose fault it was that Koli has won, and this leads to a pretend-fight. The pretend-fight, which is clearly staged for the benefit of the camera, breaks down when they fail to contain their laughter.

*

The video was featured on national TV and became an instant hit.

Some leaders of repute, trying to bring normality back to the country, started drawing political references from the film. The four famous names, each suggesting membership of a different tribe, were being cited as examples of the future of the country, a country that had been heading naturally towards unity before being threatened by politicians' selfish needs.

These were young friends from the most diverse of backgrounds. They were just kids who appreciated their friendship and common goals, without even being aware of their differences. And now they were caught up in this senselessness.

The four names started to become the unofficial symbol and mantra of the shameful time the country had just faced. Priests in different parts of the country mentioned the four in their prayers; poems about them were featured on radio and TV. And very soon, everyone knew of them.

Now, the whole nation was searching for J'Alex, Koli, Ozzy and Ken-Tuli.

CHAPTER 16

The central government only began considering the theory that the Dallas Mercenaries might be more than just random, armed villagers after almost two thousand Kikuyus had been killed. It was hard to investigate, though, because none of them had been captured. There was no one to interrogate.

This remained the case until, after more that ten weeks of terror, a freak road accident occurred as one platoon was being transported out of a village in Central Province after a mission. Their minibus swerved off the road and rolled through the bushes before crashing into a tree. Naturally, the locals rushed to witness the scene and try to help, but that changed when they spotted the guns. Those surviving mercenaries who were not seriously disadvantaged by their injuries were left with no choice but to shoot indiscriminately at the onlookers. They then jacked another vehicle from the high-street at gunpoint, and just about managed to load their wounded friends into it before they heard sirens. Four of the soldiers in the accident vehicle were presumed dead, and when the police started closing in, the mercenaries decided not to risk the lives of the survivors for their dead comrades.

The only problem was that their presumption had been wrong. The four were all still alive when the police arrived on the scene, although one of them died before they got him to hospital.

*

One week later, en route to the camp, a few minutes after 10 pm., B-man parked his newly acquired black Ford hatchback outside a small café off Mombasa Road on the outskirts of Nairobi. He needed some takeaway coffee for the six-hour night journey. When he came out five minutes later, balancing two styrofoam cups in his left hand and sipping from another with his right, a spectacular scene awaited him. The still night of the deserted fringes of the city was suddenly alive from one end of the strip to another with bursts of bright red and blue lights glimmering, bobbing and weaving. The lights were the flashing beacons of otherwise quiet police vehicles with their sirens off. They were set in a neat row across the strip, adequately covering the entrance of the café and the adjacent shops. B-man counted at least a dozen uniformed police officers standing at various vantage points with their guns pointed directly at him.

*

Later, they all formed a convoy around the Land Rover into which B-man had been bundled after being handcuffed. The man who sat next to him in the back had very thick lips, smoked a thick, foul-smelling cigar, and constantly blew the smoke in B-man's face, as if aiming to incite a reaction.

'You smoke, son?' he asked, revealing that his speech was slightly impeded by his thick lips.

B-man had had his moments with smoking, but he had never really been a smoker. He answered by shaking his head. The man chuckled, the thick lips widening into a rueful smile to imply that he was only kidding. He was not really about to offer him a cigar. A beep on Mr. Thick Lips' radio, followed by a crackling voice, took his attention momentarily. He spoke to whoever it was for about a minute, then he switched off his radio and produced a mobile phone from his hip pocket.

'Are we taking him straight in?' he asked on the phone. No pleasantries.

B-man could just about make out that the voice on the other end was male. Thick Lips listened attentively before saying, 'OK, so we check him in at Central the usual way, then take him in?'

His colleague must have said yes, because he then said his thanks and started dialling another number.

'Ever heard of the SR2, son?' he asked in the midst of dialling.

B-man elected to remain silent, to show that he was not scared and that he was not going to cooperate with these people at any point. But yet again Thick Lips had the last laugh, because he had already begun speaking on the phone without taking the slightest notice of B-man's attempted display of defiance. The question had obviously been rhetorical.

B gathered from Thick Lips' brief chats that they were probably taking him to this place known as the SR2: after returning the phone to his pocket, Thick Lips asked again, 'Ever heard of the SR2?' And just as before, the policeman made it clear that he was not expecting an answer because he proceeded on almost immediately, 'They don't punish bad boys, they don't punish law breakers, they don't punish criminals,' he said, puffing another cloud of smoke in B-man's face, 'they punish sinners.'

***

The peace negotiation brokered by Kofi Annan was beginning to make some significant progress. The country was slowly regaining relative stability as a lasting peace deal began to look more and more promising. This was particularly helpful in reassuring Sally-Anne's dad, who was now a devout follower of Kenyan news, from the comfort of his leather settee in London.

Sally-Anne was by now fairly conversant with Nairobi city in general. And as far as the routes from the Imperial Hotel to the slums went, she had become an expert. They had used three different routes to get to the slums so far, and she knew them all by name, down to every small dirt road. Mathary Valley was north of the city centre. Two of the roads started off at right angles to their destination, heading west and east, and then meandered through the suburbs, estates and the other slums before eventually getting to the big slum. The westbound way, Biggy's preferred route, was fairly comfortable, but sometimes slowed by heavy traffic. The eastbound road covered about the same distance with considerably less traffic, but guaranteed at least three police checkpoints; this was Biggy's least favoured. The most direct avenue went straight through the city centre; it was busy, bumpy and crawling with traffic lights every few hundred yards. It was a route they only used when they left the slums very late in the evening.

Sally-Anne had given up on the media. These streets were her only means of assessing any hint of progress. She looked out for every small sign: an extra couple of vehicles queuing up at the lights, open windows on skyscrapers inching a floor higher, one less armed policeman, one more tentative vendor... they all added up. The nation was turning a corner towards the right path. Everlasting peace was still a dream, but there was hope in the meantime that these people could get back to their normal lives.

However, there was still no sign of J'Alex, Koli, Ozzy or Ken-Tuli.

It was another mild morning and the search team of four were all in their usual places in the Land Rover, heading for another day in the slums.

'So, how's your wife, Kip?' Sally-Anne initiated her customary courtesy chitchat with the two policemen in the back, an act she had devised to ease the apparent awkwardness between Biggy and herself.

'Yeah, she's fine. Still getting bigger by the day.'

Sally-Anne chuckled at this. She was aware that Kip's wife was pregnant.

'Are you excited about the baby?'

'Well, not extremely: it's a boy. We already have three boys.'

'Oh, have you? I didn't know that. What are their names?'

'The eldest is Matthew, then Mark and Luke.'

'Ha! No prizes for guessing the new arrival's name then?'

He smiled. 'Yeah, we do have a name in mind. We'll call him William.'

'No way!' she turned round to look at him. 'You can't be serious!'

'Why not? It's a good name, lots of variations: Will, Bill, Liam, Willy, Billy...'

Sally-Anne could not contain her shock. 'You name your first three boys Mathew, Mark and Luke,' she was shaking her head in disbelief, 'and you want to name the fourth *William*?'

'Yeah, what's wrong with that?'

'The Gospels, Kip. The first four books of the New Testament. Isn't that what you were thinking of when you named the first three?'

'I have no idea what you are talking about,' he said, folding his arms over his chest and turning his face to the widow. 'We just did what we normally do, put a bunch of boys' names in a hat and picked one. We picked Mathew the first time, then Mark, then Luke, and now William's come out of the hat.'

'Oh my God, what are the chances of that? It would be a travesty if you didn't complete the Gospels now, Kip. It has to be Mathew, Mark, Luke and–'

She suddenly noticed the giggles doing the rounds, from Biggy in the driver's seat to the normally reserved Simi at the back, and she realised Kip had got her yet again. She smiled. Then she picked up from the dashboard a long cardboard packaging tube they were using to store the missing-persons posters and jabbed it playfully at the beanpole cop.

'You cheeky, cheeky, cheeky man, you almost had me then. Now, tell me the *real* name of your unborn son. I want to hear you say it, you cheeky man.'

'OK, OK, I was just checking that you know your bible, young lady,' he said, turning round to reveal that he too had been stifling a giggle. 'It *is* John. We would still have called it John if it was a girl.'

The two cops had turned out to be an essential part of this mission, mainly because, even after nearly eight weeks of seeing nothing but his smug face from dusk till dawn, Sally-Anne could still not find one thing to like about Biggy. But after what for them was just under a month, even the two nice cops began to crack with disillusion. She could see it in their eyes, their waning belief in this search. And them, she could forgive, for theirs was understandable. The bulk of her frustrations and resentment lay with Biggy. The big man appeared to have lost even his initial desire to impress the beautiful young English girl.

One evening, as he was dropping her off, Biggy complained of a mild toothache and said he would not be able to help the following day because he wanted to get it checked. Sally-Anne did not believe the toothache story, but she was fine with a day's break, she needed one too.

The next morning, she went downstairs to the restaurant, where she expected the Wilsons to be having breakfast in their usual spot. When she noticed that they were not there, she ordered a coffee and waited a few minutes with the local newspaper for company. It soon became clear that the old couple would not be coming down for their breakfast, and she walked back to her room a little disappointed. She surfed the internet aimlessly for a while; then, just after midday, she decided to call the Wilsons' room to see if they were up for lunch. But there was no answer, so she grabbed a light sandwich and some fruit and went over to the gym. Around mid-afternoon she walked over to the Wilsons' room and knocked on the door.

There was no answer.

The Wilsons had not been seen by anyone at the hotel since the previous night.

She knew it would be stupid to panic, but she felt a twinge anyway. She checked a few more times, and just before seven o'clock in the evening she asked to see the hotel manager and expressed her concerns. The manager made a few internal phone calls, and, for about half an hour, shuffled up and down the lifts of the massive hotel to speak to different people with Sally-Anne in tow. Then he decided there was reasonable concern, and instigated a full-blown internal search.

To avoid unnecessary fuss, the manager wanted to make a thorough internal search before involving the police. The first breakthrough came when the search party went back to the security office for a third time. The new security team had just arrived to sign on for the night shift, and one of them revealed that he had in fact let the Wilsons out of the gates in the very early hours of the morning. The old couple had apparently been riding in the back of a grey Land Rover driven by the same big man they had seen pick Sally-Anne up from the hotel on many occasions.

The Wilsons had gone off with Biggy.

A few members of staff were gathered round the security station next to the gates listening to the guard's account and wondering what to make of it. The guards had not felt there was anything suspicious about the old couple leaving in the wee hours of the morning with a man who was not entirely a stranger. But these people did not know Biggy. The scheming, ruthless gangster had used Sally-Anne to get closer to the helpless old couple. The odds were that he had robbed them by now of all their possessions, or was holding them captive for some kind of ransom; probably both.

The hotel manager looked inquisitively at Sally-Anne. 'You know the couple better than all of us. And you also know the man who took them. What do you suggest I do?'

'I... I don't really know...' she started, but couldn't continue.

The whole group had turned to stare at her; some heads were shaking in a castigating manner. The manager was still waiting for further instructions.

Then, just as she thought she was going to cry, they all heard, then saw, the grey Land Rover roar up and come to a standstill outside the gates, right in front of them.

Biggy was slouched in the driver's seat, calmly tapping along on the steering wheel to a tune that was playing on the stereo, waiting for the gates to open. In the back seat Mr.

Wilson was leaning awkwardly on his wife's shoulder, seemingly in a deep sleep. Mrs. Wilson caught sight of Sally-Anne and shifted closer to the window to wave to her, and this woke her husband up.

In the front, Biggy turned round and said something to his passengers. Then, without waiting for the gates to open, he leapt off the driver's seat and walked round to help the old couple out of the car. Mr. Wilson was first, and, once out, he held on to Biggy's hand in the longest handshake Sally-Anne had ever witnessed. When Mrs. Wilson's turn came, she pulled the big man towards her chest, wrapped her arms around him and held on tight. She released him momentarily, only to look into his eyes whilst still holding his hands. Then she hugged him again.

They seemed oblivious to the group watching in bewilderment from the other side of the locked gates, and Sally-Anne had to wait till dinner time for all this to begin making sense.

During their previous chats with Biggy, the Wilsons had talked about their mission here in Kenya and the flamingos of Lake Nakuru. They had continued drumming in the subject to Biggy so much that, at the crack of dawn that morning, when he was supposed to be getting ready to see a dentist, Biggy gathered a few of his friends with connections in the Rift Valley, and together they went ahead to give the old couple their flamingos. The elderly couple had just spent the entire day touring Lake Nakuru in an open-top jeep, watching and listening to the amazing pink birds.

The Wilsons still had no idea what Biggy did for a living, but the mafia king had just made a dream that had dogged an eighty-year-old man for most of his life, come true. The Wilsons were going back home to England tomorrow with the sense of a long and fulfilled life.

The words Mrs. Wilson used to describe Biggy were: '*Heaven-sent, the man's a true angel!*'

*

Sally-Anne called Biggy the day after the Wilsons had flown back to England.

'How's your tooth now, Biggy?'

'My tooth is fine for now, Sally-Anne.'

If he had detected any hint of sarcasm in Sally-Anne's question, he was obviously willing to let it slide. Of course his tooth was fine. She didn't know if she was supposed to admire him or be angry with him for taking such a big risk with an elderly couple's lives. Biggy was without doubt expecting her to be impressed, so she decided she was simply going to ignore the incident altogether.

'Would you be OK to carry on from where we left off in Mathary Valley?' she asked.

'Yeah, I'm fine now, I don't see why not.'

'Would tomorrow be alright?'

'Well, it is late afternoon now. I'll probably need some time to round up Kip and Simi. Why don't we say the day after tomorrow?'

That left her with the following day free, and minus the Wilsons. Seeking alternative company therefore, she drew her curtains and stared outside. The Bell-Bottom was there as usual, with a good proportion of its windows now open, showing signs of life rekindled. In the foreground of Bell-Bottom's scrotum, Tom Mboya Street was also now slightly busier.

She watched the vehicles climb the curve of the street, disappear into the scrotum and reappear on the other side, and suddenly decided that her earlier theory about the size of this scrotum was seriously flawed. She had not factored in the curve of the street. The cars were taking slightly longer travelling from one side of the building to the other than they would have taken on a straight path. If she considered this curved road to be an arc on a circle, what she had calculated before would then have been its circumference. The actual size of the building's base should have been the diameter, and thus significantly smaller than her original estimate. She didn't even need to get her notebook out this time: she took the seventy-one-metre figure she had calculated before to be exactly half the circumference of a perfect circle. To get its diameter, she simply doubled this number and divided it by pi on her mobile phone's calculator. Within seconds, she had chopped twenty-six meters off the size of her loyal companion's scrotum.

And it was all Biggy's fault.

She looked at the figure on the calculator and smiled. Then she tossed the mobile phone on to the bed, picked up the hotel's landline and dialled Inspector Limo's direct line.

As expected, the inspector still had no news, or clues, or leads, or even a credible action-plan. His tone was gradually descending into that of resignation; and it seemed that the police were somewhat lazily trying to link the case to the so-called 'lorry incident' in Eldoret, just as an easy way out. She could feel everyone now wishing Sally-Anne Symmonds would go home like the Wilsons and leave them all alone.

The following morning, though, Biggy and the two cops arrived at her hotel as planned. Just as she was making herself comfortable in the car, the big man strayed from their usual routine of morning greetings, and started some small talk. Maybe in the short break Biggy had forgotten the limits of their conversations.

'Ever had a toothache, Sally-Anne? Jesus... that was the mother of all toothaches the other day. And the night-time is the worst: there is not a lot you can do about it then. Ooh... my... God.'

When he looked over at her and realised that his attempted theatrics were not having the desired effect, he shrugged his broad shoulders. 'Well, anyway,' he said, 'the tooth is all good now.'

It was unexpected. Before the break and the Wilsons incident, they had almost stopped talking altogether. She did not like him. And she knew he was aware of it. Each had found a way of using the two police officers to avoid having to talk to each other directly unless it was absolutely necessary. But now he was asking her if she'd ever had a toothache. What the hell was he up to? She was tempted to answer him, just out of curiosity, to see where he was heading with this. But she decided not to. She simply stared at the road ahead in silence.

When they got to Mathary Valley, just before she stepped out of the car she said, 'Have you got a problem with all this, Biggy?'

'What?'

'You know exactly what. Are you getting tired of bringing me down here? You know... driving me around and everything. Is that becoming a problem now?'

'No, not at all, why would you think that?'

'Well, if you are trying to say you've got a toothache, or indeed if you have a toothache, and you think it is not convenient for you to bring me here, just say it. No need to beat around the bush. I don't need you!'

'Jesus. What is wrong with you? I was just talking, trying to make conversation. What is the matter with you?'

'Conversation? Ha! Don't make me laugh, Biggy.'

The day was a disaster. Biggy went out of his way to make it clear to her that he was getting fed up. He followed them around like a zombie, saying nothing, leaving Kip and Simi to take care of translation and all other tasks that required a local. Biggy was having none of it. He carried on shamelessly collecting money from poor residents and conducting his illegal deals without even pretending to care. He stayed with the group, but it was clear he was now serving only his own interests and, in the process, acting like a spoilt and petulant child.

They were questioning a middle-aged couple in their dingy living room, sipping on some very hot strong tea, which Biggy had rudely declined, when he suddenly removed a black pistol from one of his hip pockets, and a dark brown handkerchief from the other. Everyone, including the two policemen, gasped in horror as Biggy wiped the pistol slowly and methodically with the handkerchief, before shoving it nonchalantly back into his pocket, as if it were nothing but a cigarette-lighter. Then he slouched back and propped his feet up on the couple's stool like he owned the place.

It was a gesture most probably aimed at her, Sally-Anne guessed. He was clearly unhappy with the way she had spoken to him that morning. He was worried he was losing his street-credibility, and this was the best he could come up with? Sally-Anne even managed a smile after the initial shock. It might have been an act designed to remind them all that he was a mafia lord; but it was at precisely that moment that Sally-Anne decided she was not scared of this man anymore.

*

Later in the evening, with the two policemen gone, they were about halfway back to the hotel when Biggy finally decided to speak again.

'How old are you anyway?'

She stared at him suspiciously. Even though she was not intending to answer him after his antics earlier in the day, she still found the question interesting. All this time, and he did not know how old she was. This was the only set of circumstances that could possibly excuse one for knowing so little about someone with whom they had spent so much time. Lost in thought, she found herself drifting off to sleep in her seat, without venturing to answer the question.

When Biggy stopped at the hotel, she snapped awake and stormed from the car without saying a word, only to realise, after barely a few yards, that she had forgotten her handbag. She turned round, and as she picked up her bag from the back seat she managed to steal a glimpse of his face: it was a perfect picture of perplexity.

She hesitated. Then she looked up at him again, this time straight in the eye. 'Twenty-three,' she said.

'What?'

She smiled. 'I'm twenty-three years old.'

'Oh... OK... Thanks,' he said.

'You?'

'Twenty-nine.' He smiled.

CHAPTER 17

B-man thought being blindfolded was strange, but it was not important. He had been caught, he was in trouble. There were a number of things he imagined his captors might do to him, but being blindfolded was just strange.

B-man had never expected to get away with what he was doing forever, but he was disappointed that his comeuppance had come so soon. He had respected the trust bestowed upon him by his peers; he had tried his best to be a good leader. He had given a new lease of life to a group of hopeless people who had been waiting to drop dead. He was saddened that the Dallas Mercenaries would probably disintegrate. He hoped they had not completely unravelled the organisation, and that maybe Paula was still in the clear. Whatever happened to him, Parking-boys would always be there, and with Paula there was a good chance that the Dallas Mercenaries would not be completely extinguished. He hoped they would let him talk to Paula once he was in the cells.

When the blindfold was removed and he was dragged into the room by the three men, he couldn't work out whether it was the strangeness of the cell or the nasty smell that worried him more. The room was dark, sooty and smelly, but spacious. Narrow transparent strips below the soot-covered ceiling formed the closest thing to a window. The place was virtually a cave. Even with the poor lighting, he could make out silhouettes of what he assumed were other men, three of them, lying at the far end of the cave.

'I'll need to make a phone call,' B-man started. 'I'll need to speak to my lawyer.'

The men looked at him as if he'd just spoken a language foreign to them.

'I know my rights, and I have a lawyer. If you even consider denying me any of my rights, I will make a lot of trouble.'

The short, stocky cop who had acted like their leader all along, had a bald and strangely-shaped head, sharply pointed at the crest. He spoke first. And when he did, an ugly network of veins protruded at the sides of his head. The dark space first drowned his speech, and then turned it into a series of echoes.

'My friend, I don't know what you've done, but you won't need any lawyers. I think we have gone past that stage. We don't bring many people here, but when we do, we make absolutely certain that they are very bad people.'

Other than his short and heavy-set frame, his ugly pointed head, and the bulging veins on his neck, B-man also noticed his thick, prominent Adam's apple sway up and down his neck as he spoke.

For some unknown reason, a chill started creeping up his spine.

'I don't know the offences any one of you has committed, and I'll never ask. We are just law enforcers... we love enforcing law! We are doing God's work. God punishes all wrongdoers, and sometimes the written law of the land is not enough. So we have to find other ways of doing God's work.'

Echoes were criss-crossing the room, making it sound like a ghost speech.

'He promised hell for wrongdoers, and the least we can do is give the part of hell we can provide to the wrongdoers for him.'

The cop delivered every word with the passion of a great politician.

'Today you will learn my friends... you will learn.'

To add emphasis, he used deliberately placed pauses after each point.

'I don't know what you have done, but you will learn the value of life... you will learn to fear the Lord... you will learn to respect your country... to respect authority... to respect your people... your freedoms and liberties... you will learn, my dear friends. You will learn.'

He paused to give each of the four a stern look, as if he wanted them to remember his ugly face later, and then he concluded.

'My friends, we are fair people; firm but fair. And being fair means only very few criminals get to see the inside of the

SR2. The very few that do, never survive. But in the very unlikely event that you survive the SR2, you will never forget it. Welcome to the SR2!'

With that he charged out and the other three officers took that as a signal to shut the huge metallic doors with a loud bang that left echoes haunting the cave for what seemed an eternity.

B-man gave his companions a closer look. Two of them were limping painfully towards the dark corners. He could not make out their features clearly in the dark, but from their laboured movements he could tell they were tired and emaciated. They made the cave even creepier. The third man seemed to have some life. He looked B-man up and down from head to toe, and smiled.

'They brought me in this morning,' he started. Then, indicating the two frail men, he continued, 'Those two... they don't talk. And me, I... I feel like touching you this very moment... you ever had a man? Fucking hell... fucking hell... I am one fucked up motherfucker.'

He was looking up at the roof, swinging his hips left and right: most definitely a lunatic.

'If only this room didn't stink so much... if only I wasn't this hungry... fucking hell...'

He suddenly stopped and stretched his hands to outline B-man's face. His heart sank. Out of shock, he simply stood still.

'I could have made love to you... right here, right now... I'm not a psycho, I'm only a perv–'

B-man slapped off his hands and took a step back. In any other place his automatic reaction would have been to hit the man hard in the face, but the creepy state of this cave had taken something out of him. He made a mental note to spit on this sick man's face before he got out of this cave.

Of course they would let him out sooner or later. He had connections now. People would enquire about his whereabouts. Paula and her higher contacts were probably still in the clear. They would surely do something to help him. Maybe they would turn up flanked by the best lawyers, get him out of here and make sure he received a fair trial. He was sorry for the other two men, but he knew he wouldn't be sticking around long enough to protect them against this sick man.

Upon his retreat from the pervert, he trod on the legs of one of the other men, who was now lying curled up near the wall. The man raised his head painfully and whispered to him: 'If I w-were you –' his painful stutters got B-man's attention '– if I had k-k-killed someone, I'd c-confess so I d-didn't have to come h-here,'

'What's this all about? Who told you I killed someone?'

He opened his mouth to answer, and then closed it again.

The pervert explained from a safe distance.

'People come here only for extreme crimes. People are brought here when a top-cop hates you. I'm here for giving a five-year-old boy some pleasure. I didn't kill him, just showed him a good time. But it happens that the chief superintendent's seven-year-old daughter was done by a killer paedophile, and then murdered, five years ago. So when the judge said I should go down for ten years, someone thought it wasn't enough. As a result they say I'll be brought in here for two nights every month of my sentence, they say that's the slowest most painful death one can ever die, I'd be lucky to do a year.'

He explained as though he were talking about someone else.

'Sometimes they also bring people here before court if they can't find evidence and they want a confession. That's why he's asking you to confess. It's only his second day here and look at him.' He nodded towards the crumbled creature. 'He knows what he's talking about. If all they want is a confession, you'd be better off giving it before you have to go through this.'

'Two days?' B-man could not believe he was now speaking to a paedophile, but he suddenly felt an urgent need to know what they had got him into. Wasn't this a cell? And did people look like this after only two days?

'Are you saying they've only been here two days? Holy Jesus... What have they done to them!'

This time the tired figure himself answered.

'Yes, son. I'm a political prisoner... the more they hurt me, the more the people out there grow bolder and empowered. So I have a good reason to endure this... have you?'

Political prisoner! That rang a bell, although not once since he began leading the Dallas Mercenaries had he thought of it as politics. He was just a seventeen-year-old former Parking-Boy trying to earn a living. For him and his people, the war was the best – the *only* thing available. For some unfathomable reason, he started thinking of Poppa. So far, he had managed to push any thoughts of his fallen brother aside. That was probably what had made him such a good leader. Poppa would certainly not have approved of what they had turned into. But he wasn't working for Poppa; he was working for *the people*.

The other creature, who as yet had not spoken a word, did so for the first time.

'They bake us... they freeze us... they whip us... and they–'

He did not know what the man meant but he did not like the sound of the whip bit. He began to edge slowly away from the three; they had suddenly turned very scary.

He was attempting to turn, when the back of his head banged painfully on the massive metal structure that was the door. It was a heavy blow and he felt his head begin to spin. Disorientated, with both hands rubbing the wound, he turned once again to face the threesome.

A huge, squealing bat flew over their heads. He saw the figure now speaking writhe on the floor in pain. He twisted into impossible positions like a contortionist, and B-man watched the ripples on his dry skin in horror as he did this. Then another bat flew past.

The political prisoner spoke again.

'You a-alright, son –'

As soon as the words left his mouth, B-man knew the voice belonged to someone else. It was Poppa. Poppa was talking to him through this creature!

And, as if to emphasise, the echoes followed:

'*A-aalright sson... sssson... ssssson...*'

He heard the sounds of bats getting louder as he examined the horrifying, wrinkled ripples on the emaciated men's skins. Then their red eyes, set deeply inside the skull. And he suddenly realised he had been speaking to ghosts.

One of the skinny creatures spoke again. 'They s-say the two of us'll go out t-t-tomorrow, b-but we w-wont b-be human–
'

B-man ran to the furthest corner of the cave. The cold that had been crawling along his spine got even chillier, as he felt his brain desert him. His heartbeat was on the rampage...

The cave was getting warm!

The injured spot on his head was throbbing with pain, but his situation was unmistakable: the ugly cop with that terrifying network of veins on his head; the bony skeletons that he had assumed were starved human beings; the creepy cave... He could not even remember dying, yet he was in hell.

No! Oh my God, no! he thought; then he realised he had said the words aloud.

A skeleton spoke, straining for audibility on account of B-man's new position at the furthest corner.

'They haven't even s-started, y-you poor boy.'

He barely heard the statement, but the echoes got him.

'*Poooor booooy...oooor booy....booooy....ooooy...ooy...*'

The cave was getting hot. The skeleton mumbled again, but this time he only got the echoes:

'*Feeeeeel hheeeat...eeeeel hheeeat...hheeeat...heeat...*'

The cave was getting hotter, so he loosened the buttons of his shirt, but it did not help much. He ripped the whole shirt off and wiped the sweat off his head. Something one of the skeletons had said earlier sneaked back into his mind: '*They bake us... they freeze us... they whip us...*'

The four of them were burning in hell.

***

The power-sharing deal between the two political parties was announced in spectacular fashion on the steps of the Kenya International Conference Centre. They had worked out a plan that would allow both parties to share equally in the leadership of the country. Not many people understood exactly how it would work, but that didn't matter because the protagonists seemed happy. The two fierce rivals shook hands and hugged in front a huge crowd of national and international journalists, diplomats, observers and members of the public. It was a huge occasion with all the jazz: flags, songs, several heartfelt renditions of the national anthem, and even white doves being released to symbolise peace and the country's return to normality. Again people took to the streets, but this time in utter jubilation. Finally, they had peace.

But there was still no J'Alex, or Koli, or Ozzy, or Ken-Tuli.

Most of the reports that came in about them were based on rumours and theories that could not be substantiated. There was the obvious school of thought that these were just four of the many people that had been killed by the police in the skirmishes. But the twist in this case was that, due to the unprecedented rise to fame of these four little boys, the government was forced to cover its back and hide the evidence. It was not good for politics. Being the notorious bad-boys they were in Mathary Valley, there was also the other theory that they had been involved in some secret criminal activity and that they were alive and well and hiding in the slums. Some seriously far-fetched tales even went as far as claiming they had been seen crossing the border into neighbouring Tanzania.

But the person who ultimately summed up the mystery best was Bolo, the sugar-cane vendor they had spoken to under his shaded stall in Dallas. Biggy had spotted the shady tree in the background of the video footage, and, because he recognised the tree, they decided to follow it up. It was well known that men of all ages gathered on the benches under Bolo's tree mainly to discuss politics, and maybe also enjoy the sugar-canes. The four boys, apparently, had become regular attendees of the arguments of this local assembly.

'They liked playing around here, all four of them. They seemed like very close friends to me,' said Bolo. 'But there's nothing more I can tell you. You see those chickens over there?' He tilted his head to indicate the flock of birds rummaging through the waste sugar-cane peel. 'There's this goat that comes to graze out here with them: scrawny little brownish thing. I haven't seen that goat in about a week now, and that is not unusual, it happens. Maybe it'll come back next week. Maybe I won't ever see it again. Or maybe next week someone will show up asking if I have seen a brown goat around here lately. Only then will it strike me how strange it is that I have never known where that goat came from, how it got here everyday and why it chose to graze here amongst chickens.

'I wish I had spoken a few more words than casual greetings to those boys. I wish I could tell you something about them now that would help you in some way. But I knew nothing at all about them, and that was because I was so familiar with them.'

The police, on the other hand, were slowly but surely narrowing everything down to the Eldoret 'lorry incident'. For them, it was the easy way out. As long as the boys were never found – as long as at least four of the bodies from the burnt lorry remained unidentifiable – then the police could make an argument that would tie the loose ends together, and close the case.

By now the entire nation knew about the famous four. A TV station had managed to work some technological and creative magic on the four-minute amateur video footage, and added a moving soundtrack song to create a tear-jerking film that left not one dry eye in this African country. The soundtrack song was immediately adopted as the official memorial song to all those who lost their lives in the massacres. The sales of its newly rereleased version sky-rocketed, as one or other radio station seemed to be playing it day and night. It was a well-known gospel piece with a simple two-line refrain:

... Shine, Jesus shine,
Glory be to the father...

The song was cleverly infused within the slow-motion pictures of the four young best friends playing *tip-tap*, smiling and laughing happily, with Koli jumping and dancing around in jubilation while waving his homemade baseball bat. It added up to a movie that Sally-Anne could not bear to watch. She cried like a baby throughout the entire film when it was featured in a special programme after the prime-time news.

The boys became the Kenyan roses.

In this country, replica jerseys of famous football teams were commonplace with kids running around in playgrounds. Most of these jerseys were soon bearing the names J'Alex, Koli, Ozzy or Ken-Tuli on the back. Everyone had their favourite, but Koli seemed to be slightly more popular. His victory dance had captured imagination. Some professional soccer players adopted the 'Koli dance' goal celebration. A well-known bus company decided to name its entire fleet after the famous four. T-shirts, bearing pictures of one or other of the four in various poses from the film, were big business for clothing manufacturers.

And the more famous they got, the clearer it dawned on Sally-Anne, and the entire nation, that the boys were probably not alive. They were now heroes even in the smallest, remotest corners of the country. They could not possibly have been hiding somewhere, leaving it to other people to cash in on their fame.

It was early evening, and relatively cold by Kenyan standards, when Sally-Anne and Biggy wound up back at the central police station and spent about half an hour listening to Inspector Limo and his colleagues trying to justify the Eldoret 'lorry tragedy theory'. Their strongest link yet was that the lorry had been identified as one that had been car-jacked in Nairobi, somewhere near Mathary Valley.

'But what would the boys have been doing in Eldoret?' Sally-Anne inquired.

'We don't know. And nor do we know why a lorry that was jacked in Nairobi was packed with men and driven to Eldoret. There are things we just may never be able to explain, my dear.'

'I don't get it, someone would have seen something and said something, even if they are dead.' She was calm, they were discussing this; there was no point appearing to berate their efforts. 'What if they are actually hiding somewhere? They have done something bad and they don't want to be found. Wouldn't that still be a possibility?'

'With all the exposure they have had, that would be nigh on impossible now. There wouldn't be a corner of the country they could hide in, without someone recognising them.'

It was dusk by the time they left the police headquarters and got back to the Land Rover in utter despair. Somehow, in the back of her mind, the idea that she might never again see J'Alex alive had always lurked; but what really hurt was the lack of answers, of credible explanations: closure! Only now was she beginning to understand what families who had lost their loved ones meant when they spoke of the need for closure. Some part of her brain had almost agreed on the compromise that her whimsical trip and subsequent ten weeks of hard work would not be all in vain if she could only get to see J'Alex's dead body. As the inspector had once put it, she could then go home and grieve for her friend in peace.

As her wild thoughts continued to collide in Sally-Anne's mind, she suddenly noticed something strange happening in the vehicle. It was nothing extraordinary, and she was sure it had probably occurred a few times before. But this was the first time it caught her attention. Biggy lifted his left hand from the gear stick to his face and started caressing his cheeks gently. Then she saw his tongue sliding inside his mouth and settling somewhere at the corner of his jaw, roughly where his left wisdom tooth would have been. His face made a movement, a slight twist, a grimace maybe. A painful wince that that lasted no more than a couple of seconds. She barely saw it. Then it was gone.

'You should see a dentist,' she said quietly, trying not to look directly at him, 'about the tooth.'

His shock was more visible than his agony. As if this white woman speaking to him had been mute all her life.

'I will,' he said. 'Been planning to, but, it's nothing major, you know... this pain...' he shrugged, '...it comes and goes.'

Somewhere amidst this exchange, and nearly three months after the strangely drawling voice arrived at her hotel and declared, '*They call me Biggy*', a human being had finally made an entrance.

The man had always been there, she was sure of it. But she had never truly seen him. Her instant dislike for Biggy had formed a barrier that had kept the man concealed from her; and the barrier only strengthened when her dislike turned to hate and then fear, when she realised he was a gangster. Then, when she felt ready to transcend her fear, the issue of Biggy's position in the politics of the war arose. And, convincing herself that she just didn't want to know this man's opinion, she left him right where he'd always been, lurking but obscured behind some dark and faraway cloud. Now, though, with one quick and barely noticeable facial expression, the cloud had cleared. And the big man was here.

The suddenness of his appearance stunned her, like he had just fallen from the skies and landed with a thump on the driver's seat. For the first time, after more than ten weeks of riding in this vehicle, she noticed the almost spiral scratch on the black dashboard, about three inches in diameter. She heard the soft whistling sound somewhere near the rear offside wheel that interrupted the smooth hum of the Land Rover's engine every thirty seconds. She could even smell the exhaust fumes.

'Do you want to fuck me, Biggy?' She did not know where the words came from; her mouth just opened, and they slipped out. But she was not shocked either. She did not even turn to see his reaction.

'What?'

'I said: Do. You. Want. To. Fuck. Me?'

Biggy said nothing. And if he was shocked, he didn't show it.

Sally-Anne lowered her tone, as if explaining a very important point to a clueless child. 'You are a Mafia lord, right? A big-time gangster. So why the hell have you been driving me around and following my orders like a poodle since I arrived?' Her voice began to rise. 'What the fuck do you want from me, Biggy?'

'I think you should calm down.'

'What the fuck do you want from me! Do you wanna fuck me? Do you want me take you to England? Do you want money? Just what the hell do you want?'

He did not have to look across to know that she was crying.

'You... you have never asked me for anything, Biggy,' she stuttered between hysterical sobs. 'You haven't asked, Biggy... *Why*?'

'I think you should calm down.'

'Don't... don't try to be nice to me.' Her voice was still teetering.

'I think you miss home. You've seen enough of the slums.'

Gradually, she simmered down, and halted the shaking and sobbing. She produced some tissues from her handbag and used them to dab the tear-tracks that had formed down her cheeks.

'He was just a kid, Biggy. He had no one. I really wanted to help him...'

She broke down afresh.

He stopped the car in a side-road and sat there watching her cry. When she had finished and calmed down again, he opened his mouth to say something that seemed to escape his lips before he was ready. The result was a weird sound somewhere between a moan and a prolonged grunt. He stopped, took a deep breath, then attempted to open his mouth again, and to his surprise Sally-Anne laughed. A short, snorted laugh, but a laugh nonetheless.

'You are not very good at this, are you?' She was smiling now.

'Uh... huh.' He arched his eyebrows and looked hard at the steering wheel, as if for inspiration.

'A grown woman goes crazy and cries like a baby in your car...' She was still wiping her cheeks even though they were now dry. 'And you have no idea what to do.'

'I was thinking of offering you a drink or something. But I realised that you are probably not crying because you are thirsty.'

She chuckled.

He added, 'And I haven't got a drink anyway.'

She laughed again, and a tear dropped from the corner of her left eye.

CHAPTER 18

At first B-man thought it was his fear that had led him to imagine the increasing temperature. But the truth slowly dawned on him. There were miniature heat pumps over the roof, pumping in hot air in gradual measures. The temperature of the cell was being deliberately increased very slowly, painfully slowly, by fractions of a degree. It was part of the torture.

He could remember being arrested. He remembered the thick-lipped policeman. He could recall going to the central police station and completing all the necessary processes of his arrest – or so he had assumed. Because he still was not sure it was normal for someone to be blindfolded as he was led to the cells.

Now he was beginning to understand what the ugly cop had meant when he said that most criminals who saw the SR2 never survived. The sweat flowing down his face and neck were making him feel like a tiny slice had been cut around his throat to let in the painful salty sweat. All three of the other men had removed their shirts, and one of them, lying facing the sooty ceiling like a dead man, opened his mouth to let out a continuous moan.

He had absolutely no sense of time, but after what must have been very many hours he looked up and observed the paedophile, who had earlier loosened the buttons on his trousers, begin to slide the sweat-soaked trousers down further to reveal tight-fitting blue underwear. He remembered that this was a person who had raped a five-year-old boy, and looked away. He wanted to scream at him, but when he opened his mouth he could not make a sound; instead he inhaled a whiff of the horrible smell.

He feared that if this carried on a few more hours, then *he* might be forced remove his trousers as well, in front of a sick, twisted pervert. He tried to move as far away as possible from the threesome, leaving a trail of sweat. The floor was scorching, and so were the walls. He heard one of the weary old creatures crying to the pervert to help him out of his dirty pants, which he could not summon the energy to remove by himself. The thought of a pervert helping someone to remove their pants made him sick. He kept his face away.

The cell grew hotter. The shirt he had been using to wipe his sweat had become useless. It was virtually drenched. All positions were uncomfortable. The room stank, and he thought he was going to get drunk on the salty liquid that was flowing into his mouth. Soon even his trousers could not soak up all the sweat, and they felt sickeningly uncomfortable. He knew he was going to have to take them off, and by the time he finally did, the cell, filled with the pained moans of big men, was spinning before his bleary eyes. B-man had never known a man could hold such greats amounts of sweat.

The four were also suffocating. B-man's huffing and puffing in an effort to gasp the dwindling oxygen made his jaws ache. He did not know a lot about the capabilities of the human body, but a few more minutes of this and he would be watching someone dying, if he himself did not go first.

The pervert suggested amidst spasms of pain that they find a way of breaking the narrow windows near the ceiling to let in some air; the only problem was they were too high. He offered to let B-man climb on his shoulders, since they were the only two in the cave left with a bit of life in them.

In a million years B-man would never have knowingly got within miles of a half-naked pervert who had raped a five-year-old boy. But his survival instincts kicked in, the instincts that helped him outlive his father and grandfather on a farm that had yielded nothing but misery and despair. The very instincts that had helped him survive Jude and Titto 'K9'. His instinct to stay alive made him climb onto a sick pervert's shoulders. But this proved fruitless: the windows turned out to be a few inches higher that they had anticipated. He could not quite reach. The weakening man crumbled under him, and they both fell in a heap.

The next time he looked at the pervert through eyes blurred by sweat, he saw him gently slide down his underwear.

Right in front of his eyes, a paedophile was bearing his sick body; as naked as he had been when he came out of his mother's womb. He turned his eyes away and found himself retching up a meal he could not remember having, adding it to the pool of sweat on the floor. Even worse was that after a while everyone in the cave, himself included, had followed suit and removed the last soaked item on their body.

He lay naked, helpless and breathless on the scorching floor and waited for death.

***

Biggy waited in silence for a few minutes after Sally-Anne had stopped crying, before he restarted the car.

'What happened to them, Biggy?' she asked calmly as they got back on the road. 'I just want to know what happened to them.'

Biggy did not answer for a while. And she did not expect an answer, so she simply closed her eyes and meditated, listening to the smooth hum of the Land Rover's engine as darkness began to swallow the city.

Then, as if from a distance, she heard Biggy's voice.

'They are dead, Sally-Anne. They were in that lorry in Eldoret.'

'But you don't know that, Biggy. Nobody knows that for sure,' she said sleepily, her eyes still closed.

Then there was silence in the car.

As if on cue, the now-famous gospel track came on the stereo, and the pair left it to the spiritual female voice to fill the void.

Towards the end of the song, Sally-Anne opened her eyes and thought she noticed the trace of a tear rolling down Biggy's cheek. She closed her eyes again and considered that maybe she was imagining things. This, after all, was Biggy – '*They call me Biggy*' – the big man, the mafia king, the undisputed leader of the million-plus population of Mathary Valley. Surely he could not be crying.

She slowly opened her eyes again, this time a little wider, although careful not to startle him. And there was the confirmation: Biggy was still intent on the road ahead, both hands firmly on the wheel, but the occasional snivel and the path etched on his brown cheek by a rolling teardrop gave him away. All of Sally-Anne's senses were suddenly jolted back to life. She was now fully awake, her mind buzzing with all sorts of thoughts. But she kept her eyes shut and stayed still. She did not want to disturb him. Whatever was wrong did not matter.

She let the big man cry in peace.

*

As they continued to cruise through the deserted Nairobi highways, the darkness that had gulped down the city swiftly opened its belly to reveal wavy bands of dazzling bright lights. Glowing beacons seemed to have replaced the might of a single yellow sun in the time it took for Sally-Anne to blink. The attempt by man to defy nature and stay eternally awake was universal. And this was Nairobi city's contribution to that global course.

Sally-Anne Symmonds's eyes remained closed to the spectacular display. But she was not asleep. She needed to focus. She needed to stay still and not move – not even breathe. Because the faint sound of what she believed to be this big black man's sobs was threatening to fade away before she could grasp it. She froze everything in her vision and her mind. Her entire life as she had known it froze, and then gradually began to dissolve into a colourless horizon, till there was only her and the soft sounds of this stranger's sobs. The moment swept over her with a tingling chill that left her awash with such comfort that she had never before imagined. Hanging somewhere within the tranquillizing calm of the night breeze were beautifully crafted poetic lyrics. The silence was talking. The silence was singing:

> ...time to rest, o thy guardian angels,
> time to sleep, all thy earthly custodians.
> You have toiled...
> you have guided me...
> to this moment.
> And this moment, is where I want to be.
> This moment, is my home...

In fact the moment only lasted seconds, and Sally-Anne opened her eyes. At first the eyelids parted a crack, just enough to sneak another glance. But that was enough to let the waves of reality come flooding back, the first of which came in the form of some blue flashing lights that she noticed reflecting off the Land Rover's mirrors. She was forced to blow her cover and fully open her eyes to establish that the lights were coming from a police car close behind. Biggy noticed her staring, and turned himself to look in the rear-view mirror. He quickly jolted to attention, and incredibly managed to conceal all the signs that he had just been crying.

'I think they want us to stop,' Sally-Anne said, jabbing her right thumb backwards to indicate the approaching police car.

'I know,' he was already slowing down. 'I want you to hide while I go out and talk to them. Push your chair back and sit on the floor.'

'Why, is anything wrong?'

'I can't explain now. Just sit down on the floor so they can't see you.'

She stayed still.

'Just do it please, quick!' he said, reaching for the lever between her legs and yanking her chair back. 'This could be trouble. Go down, now!'

She saw the panic on his face and started crouching, a little hesitantly. He reached out and shoved her all the way down to the floor as the police car stopped on the road, side by side with the Land Rover. She tried her best to squeeze herself into the small space, keeping her head down as she heard Biggy open the Land Rover's doors and begin to step out.

The next thing she heard was a loud bang.

Then she felt a body crash back against the driver's seat.

The impact caused a loud squeak from the car's suspension system, leaving it rocking momentarily. The second bang flung the body up and back squarely onto the seat. And the third sent it sprawling across to the passenger's side, landing on top of the curled and horrified figure of Sally-Anne.

She did not hear any more, of anything, for what seemed a long time.

Then she heard a soft, laboured whisper above her.

'I tried to bring him back, Sally-Anne... I wanted to help too...'

Then everything was dead quiet again save for the continuous echoing ringing in her head of the bang she had just heard. She wondered if she had indeed been deafened by the bang, and whether the whispering voice above her had been a delusion.

She could not even feel the heavy, lifeless body squashing her to the floor, or the stream of blood channelling through her to form a pool in the cramped space within which she had curled into a tiny, foetal ball.

When she regained her hearing, the only sound was of a woman's voice from Biggy's stereo, soulfully belting out:

'...shine, Jesus shine,
Glory be to the father...'

CHAPTER 19

As they continued to burn in the cave-like cell, it once again occurred to B-man that this could be just a nightmare. He was still not fully conscious. The cave and the creatures seemed to be swaying before his eyes. His skin had gone pale with the burns, and seemed ready to peel away from his flesh. The other men in the room were still moaning with pain – or maybe one or even two of them were already dead, B-man didn't know. He closed his eyes once again and knew he might never open them.

He did open them again. And this was because he thought he had heard a continuous, loud crackling sound around the top of the cave. He forced his heavy eyelids open wide enough to catch a glimpse of the high, narrow windows sliding open.

The windows they had been so desperate to get to were now simply winding down and opening by themselves!

He closed his eyes again.

Hours later his eyes we still shut and he still could not move, but the room was not burning anymore. In fact the temperature seemed almost back to normal. The awful truth had well and truly settled: this was not just simply happening; they were doing it. They had deliberately taken them on a long journey to the jaws of death, only to bring them back, or maybe just to prove they could bring them back.

Now the thick, metallic doors cracked open and B-man battled to shake a slight movement off his stiffened neck, trying to jar himself back to focus. His pounding head felt heavy, as though his neck were lifting a chunk of lead, but he managed to raise it enough to see that it was the same ugly man and his gang in the doorway. They were still in police uniforms, and he wondered if they were the same clothes they had had on before, looking for any clue as to exactly how long he had been in the cave.

The uniformed men's eyes nearly popped out at the sight of four men lying stark naked on the floor. B-man was not in a position to care. Maybe they did not know what had happened. He did not want to think about anything apart from the fact that there was a chance he could get out of this alive. He was consumed by anger, even in his pain. And after enduring so much, not only here, but throughout his life, he thought it would only be right that he survive this. He was not ready to die.

The ugly man shouted: 'What on earth is going on here?' He looked in horror at each of them, lying naked on the floor. 'Are you having an orgy here? Someone told you could go ahead and have one big orgy in my cell, uh?'

He picked one of the frail men up off the floor with ease and crushed him against the wall. 'Answer me, big boy!'

When the policeman let go, the fragile man crumpled to the floor. Then the ugly man turned towards B-man. B felt the huge soles of steel-capped military boots on his ribcage and knew that a rib or two was now broken. The gang produced whips from nowhere, and laid in to their prisoners' naked bodies mercilessly.

'I am talking to you, you goddamn devil-worshippers, and I need an answer,' continued the ugly cop above the sound of the whips and the screaming of the men. 'Were you having an orgy in my cell?'

The pervert answered first, in tears. 'No sir... the room was burning... that's why we took our clothes off–'

His reward for his answer was another kick in the head.

'The room was burning? Are you fucking with me? Where the fuck is the fire, where is the smoke?' A whip came down on him hard. 'Show me the fire, motherfucker, don't mess with me. Show me the smoke!'

'I meant it was hot, they made it very hot in here and–'

The sound of another pair of military boots on another person's head resonated violently through B-man's guts as though it were his own head. Another effort to puke only resulted into painful knots tightening across his stomach.

'They made it hot? Don't you like warm rooms? Hang on a minute, I'm the bad man here for providing some heating in my cell?' He sounded so sincere that B-man was sure he had nothing to do with the heat-treatment. 'You ungrateful products of cheap whores! I just tried to give you a little bit of heat, and now I'm the bad man, eh?'

Although the whip was still descending with some might on his naked body, B-man managed to hear the pervert whisper an answer. 'It was too hot sir... too hot... too hot,' he kept repeating in spasms of pain.

The ugly cop was enraged. 'I gave you heat!' he shouted.

The cave echoed: '*I gave you heat... you heat... heat... heat... eat.*' And the whipping and kicking intensified.

'You don't want heat? Fine! No more heat for you.'

'*... no more heat for you... heat for you... you... you... you...*'

The echoes never stopped ringing in B-man's head: *I gave you heat, no more heat for you... I gave you heat, no more heat for you... I gave you heat, no more heat for you....*

The next *real* thing he heard was the ugly man suddenly ordering his men to stop whipping. Then, in a very dramatic change of tone, he said: 'Come to think of it, my friends, I believe this cell really *is* burning.' B-man assumed he had meant to say *was* burning: he did not quite catch the sarcasm. 'Boys, I think we have got a fire to put out, let's go.'

Next thing B-man knew, the policemen were dragging some huge long rubber pipes into the cell. He found himself facing the heavy rusty metallic nozzle of a massive water cannon, and realised that these boys had no intention of fighting fire. He tried to drag himself off the ground to escape the first thundering jet, but it caught him squarely on the head, sending him flying back to the ground.

The water was freezing cold.

It hit them, battered them, again and again and again. And they screamed like babies.

***

The new peace accord seemed to invigorate the country. Suddenly it was like a new state. Proud citizens resumed their everyday business with enthusiasm. Patriotism had been rediscovered. The national flag was now the must-have fashion item, flying gracefully over vehicle roofs and high-rise buildings everywhere.

Kenya is back to business as usual... was the mantra everywhere.

However, some areas of the country's so-called 'business' were still struggling to recover from the aftermath of the war. One such area was its health services. The hospitals were inundated with victims of the conflicts. There were neither enough hospital beds nor sufficient doctors and nurses to go round.

The state of the Nairobi General Hospital was dire, but by comparison it was one of the better institutions in the country at the time. One of the first state-run hospitals in Kenya,

Nairobi General had been around since colonial times. It had grown and expanded, with new wings and state-of-the-art technology introduced; but all its original buildings were also still in use. The mortuary was one such department, located within these relics. The ICU was in the most modern wing, but the victims of the election violence had exhausted it resources.

However, for a certain young English lady who had absolutely nothing wrong with her medically, the hospital had somehow managed to find a spare bed in its ICU. The bed was squeezed into a small ward that already had another patient in it.

She was there because of the other patient.

Sally-Anne Symmonds had absolutely and categorically refused to leave the critically wounded patient, even for a second. She waited night and day next to a body whose only link to the living world was a series of tubes and a life-support machine. The doctors had said he had a very slim chance, but they left the machine on anyway, and waited for him to make the next move. It was all up to him; there was nothing more they could do.

If he failed to come out of the coma after a while, they would declare him clinically dead. And, they would want their hospital beds back – both of them.

*

Sally-Anne was there when the patient made his first move.

It was the slightest of movements, a frail flick of his index finger that she could so easily have missed. When he flicked it again, she stormed out of the room to find the doctor, screaming, 'He moved! He moved!'

The surgeon who had attended to him was a bearded and bespectacled gentleman known as Dr. Oloo. He followed her to the room, towing two nurses with him, and all four formed a ring round the lifeless body. And with a mixture of shock and jubilation, they all witnessed Biggy's eyes slowly come to life. Sally-Anne thought she even saw a hint of a smile but she wasn't sure.

'He's back,' the doctor said, as if to himself; then he turned to her with a smile and said, 'I don't know how he managed it, but your friend will be alright.'

Later he would word that statement more colourfully: *They shot him once in the neck and twice in the head... The boy is fucking Superman, that's the only reason he's alive!'*

CHAPTER 20

As their naked bodies continued to be battered by the freezing water of the cannon, B-man once again lost all his senses to pain. The water shot with such force that it could virtually push a helpless body across the length of the cell.

The ugly man continued to shout: '*I gave you heat...no more heat for you!*'

They continued firing the water till none of the prisoners could cry any more. Then one of the men in uniform started marching up and down the cell, avoiding the pools of water as he collected the prisoners' discarded clothes. When he came across one of the lifeless men he stopped, bent down and informed the ugly cop, 'I think this one's dead.'

'Take him out,' replied the ugly cop nonchalantly. 'He is no good in here if he can't feel the pain.'

Then they all walked out, taking the body and their clothes with them. Before the heavy, metal door slammed, the ugly man roared, 'You complained about the heat. Fine, now let's see how you like it cold!'

Three naked, battered bodies were left shivering in the cold. They could utter no more sounds, no painful moans; their lips could only shake, and their teeth rattled as they did so. B-man put his hands around his shoulders and left them there for along time. He could see the other two crawling to a small, dryish patch of floor in the far corner. Then they just lay there huddled against the walls.

The cops were playing with the room temperature again. This time they were lowering it; as slowly as they had raised it. The next minute was a fraction colder than the previous. Soon, thinking became impossible, the cold was virtually penetrating the skin and his nerves were freezing. He kept his hands tightly around his shoulders as his teeth rattled wildly.

B-man looked at the other two again and saw them attempting to crawl towards each other. This took some significant effort. Then he saw them cuddle up together in a last attempt to stay alive. He wanted to join them in that small dry patch in the corner; it seemed his only hope of survival. He could not imagine embracing a paedophile pervert, but he needed to be in that corner. But when he tried to release his arms from around his shoulders to begin crawling in that general direction, they were tugged back by some invisible might, as if he was in the chilling eye of a tornado. He was a captive of his own body, unable to effect even the slightest movement. He was freezing in this position.

He finally summoned enough energy to roll towards them. When he got there, he tried to lodge himself somewhere between the pair, who were locked in tight embrace, and the walls. He used what force he could muster to shift them away from the corner, and still they did not break their tightly locked embrace. They were frozen too. Their corner was dryer and maybe just slightly warmer, but his hope kept ebbing by the second.

Every part of his anatomy was numb; very soon his brain would follow, and then: death from hypothermia. After putting them through all this torture, the cops were killing them after all.

***

Like Dr. Oloo had said, Biggy turned out to be super-human indeed. First, they said he would not survive, and he lived; then they said one of the bullets had grazed a part of his brain and would paralyse him, and he most probably would never walk again – but he did. Speech remained the most difficult faculty to regain. One of the bullets had gone right through his neck and damaged part of his voice-box.

He continued to improve tremendously, to the stage where he could smile and manage simple facial expressions and basic communication using hand-gestures. He even accomplished the process of getting himself from bed to the wheelchair unaided.

After his extraordinary recovery, Sally-Anne knew that his voice was no major worry. It would just be a matter of time before he began talking.

And again, she was there when he uttered his first sound.

Sally-Anne was standing over his bed, along with a nurse and the doctor, when he began muttering something while keeping her in a fixed stare. He was neither audible nor coherent; but they were words, he was speaking, and that was the most important thing. The doctor was impressed, but urged patience, because the attempt to speak appeared to be agonising. He was trying too hard to do too much too soon, was the doctor's opinion.

The following day his speech had improved. He spoke in barely audible whispers, but he seemed coherent, and he kept looking at Sally-Anne as he spoke. The onlookers had a little fun debating what he was trying to say. Biggy would lift his arms each time, in a gesture indicating a wrong guess, and then repeat his words.

It was Sister Mary, the nurse, who finally got it right. 'He is trying to say "I am sorry",' she guessed.

The hand-gesture confirmed she was right.

'It's OK,' was Sally-Anne's reply. 'Don't worry, there's nothing to be sorry for. You need to rest.'

Two days later he managed to communicate to them that he wished to say something important. He wanted to write something in the form of a statement which Sally-Anne assumed would be for the police. Dr. Oloo insisted that he was still too weak, and attempting to write would not do him any good.

'Are we still updating the police on his progress?' Sally-Anne asked the nurse. 'Maybe he wants to say something that will help the police figure this out.'

He lifted his hands to indicate that that was not the case. 'No... no police,' he said with difficulty.

So far, the only thing the police could say with confidence was that the vehicle that stopped them was not a real police car. They could account for all their patrol vehicles at that particular time. Sally-Anne had given her version of what happened as best she could, and they had asked to be kept informed of Biggy's condition. Now that he was talking, they would no doubt want his statement, but Biggy seemed to be implying he wanted to give the statement his own way, without a police presence.

'OK, I will not get the police involved, if that's what you want,' the doctor conceded. 'We will help you write a statement, but not just yet. Now, rest.'

It took a lot to convince Sally-Anne that Biggy would be safe at the hospital and that she could go back to her hotel. She needed to sort herself out and catch up with her life. She could always pop back in to see Biggy any time.

That evening, back at the Imperial, she took the time to call everyone she had dealt with in her time in Kenya and thanked them for their assistance. She spoke to Inspector Limo and told him she would be leaving imminently, but she still wished to be informed of any developments. She did not mind calling regularly. The inspector took all her contacts details and promised they would get in touch if anything significant came up.

She called her dad last.

'If you are not here by the weekend, I am coming up to Kenya, Sal,' he threatened.

Howard Symmonds had got himself worried sick during the time Sally-Anne had insisted on spending at Biggy's bedside. The occasional text message insisting that she was fine was all her dad had received, and it had only taken an expired passport to stop him making the journey.

'Don't worry, Dad, I will be home by the weekend. Just tying up a few loose ends,' she assured him.

She was back at the Nairobi General very early the next morning. Dr. Oloo was standing by the reception chatting candidly to two young female nurses. When she waved at him he stopped, gestured for her to wait, and walked over to give her an update on her friend's condition.

Biggy was OK, he said; and he added that he had been slightly worried about her absence the previous night. 'He asked where you were maybe ten times,' the doctor said with a smile. 'Like a kid who's lost his mother in a supermarket, his eyes kept darting round the room, and then he'd ask, "Where's Sally-Anne?"'

In his attempt to impersonate Biggy's deep, stuttering voice, the doctor was clearly trying to create a light-hearted moment, so Sally-Anne responded with a smile.

'He seems edgy and worried, and his speech is not too good,' Oloo proceeded on a more serious note. 'Otherwise he is fine. He's spent quite a bit of time with Sister Mary, trying to do that statement he's been so keen to make. They won't be putting it in writing now; they've decided to record it instead. But his voice is very poor. So they have come up with a system whereby sister Mary listens carefully to what he is whispering, then repeats it to the recorder. So it's all in sister Mary's voice. Very clever.'

On the bench outside Biggy's ward, Sister Mary was sitting with her head resting on her palms.

'You seem tired,' Sally-Anne told the nurse. 'Just finishing your shift?'

The nurse nodded.

'How has he been?' She asked, pointing towards Biggy's ward.

A sigh escaped through the nurse's nose as she turned her face away from Sally-Anne. She stayed still, facing away, for a while. Then she removed a handkerchief from her pocket and wiped her face.

When she looked back at her visitor, Sally-Anne realised she was crying.

'Oh my God. What's happened... is he alright?'

'Yeah, he's fine. I'm sorry... he's fine. It's just that thing we were recording... the statement is actually for you, not the police. And I think it's got to me a bit. Sorry... just go in.'

CHAPTER 21

The next time B-man woke up he was floating in a sea of whiteness. His eyes opened for a split second and all he saw was white. The flash was so bright that he felt blinded, first his eyes and then his senses, and he felt himself slipping back to a peaceful, unknown place. He saw a few more of these flashes before he got sufficiently used to them to stay awake.

His entire body was heavily bandaged and there was a bottle hanging above him dripping clear liquid through a tube that was connected to some part of his arm. Even in his condition, he soon figured out he was in a hospital.

Mr. Thick Lips was standing over him.

'You are awake, son.' Mr. Thick Lips was smiling. 'We saved your life.'

The words were still ringing like echoes, but this time the echoes simply lulled him back to sleep.

The next time he opened his eyes, a man and a woman, both in blue overcoats, were standing over him. 'Can you hear me?' the woman was asking.

He tried to nod, but the pain was unbearable. He opened his mouth and a sound emerged. The couple must have taken this as a positive thing, because the man smiled and said, 'Good. Very good. You will be alright now.'

He was informed that he was at the Nairobi General Hospital, and that he had been there four days. It took two more days before he could lift his own weight off the bed, and a further three to walk unaided.

That's when Mr. Thick Lips reappeared. He walked in just as the doctor was leaving after checking on him.

'Hey, look who is back in the land of the living,' he started, as if he was addressing an old friend.

B-man wondered for a moment if he had enough strength to fling himself off his bed onto this animal, and rip his mouth apart by his thick lips.

'Listen, I'm very sorry about what happened to you,' he went on. 'But I got you out of there just in time to save your life. And I'm here to make sure it does not happen again.'

Thick Lips waited for some form of response from B-man. He got none.

'I strongly advise that you corporate, son, I'm sure you don't want to go back in there. Are you listening to me?'

Still there was no answer.

'Would you rather be tortured to death?'

'If you don't kill me... I will kill you,' B-man said coldly, and even managed a mocking smile at Mr. Thick Lips' shock on hearing the clear and threatening tone of a seventeen-year-old that had just arrived back from the jaws of death.

'Good. A bit rude, but at least I know you are listening.' Thick Lips stayed calm. 'I will not waste any more time trying to be nice to you, I know how you feel. But here's the deal. I am offering you a chance to survive and carry on with your life. You can take the offer and still continue hating me, I do not care.' He lowered his voice and continued. 'All you need to do is round up your boys, tell them you are fine and that you are all going back to business as usual. You are to carry on killing, and you will still get paid; this time even better.'

B-man said nothing.

'I'm only asking you to do something you were already doing. It's either that or you go back to the cell.'

It only took B-man a few seconds to understand what this cop was implying, but he took his time coming up with a response.

'Why don't you do it yourself? You are the government, you've got the forces, you've got the weapons, why would you need us to fight a war for you?'

'I was hoping you would ask me that. Yes, we are the government, and yes we have our armed forces. We are more that capable of dealing with our enemies, sometimes ruthlessly, as you will no doubt be able to testify. But you see... this does not give us a very good image in the outside world. There are always investigators and smartass journalists trying to work out who is killing who. When we kill, it is the government doing the killing. This might lead to something stupid like international forces being deployed in my country, and we don't want that. If you were to do it for us on the other hand, it would simply be seen as a good old duel between two feuding races, maybe a tribe avenging the killing of their people. The international community understands this. They would understand that this was a matter for us to deal with internally, and may even offer us some assistance in terms of funds.'

B-man shifted on his bed, closed his eyes, and lay there for a while before saying his next words.

'You want us to keep on fighting.'

'Yes. Only this time, we want you to kill the *other* guys.'

***

Sally-Anne walked into Biggy's ward and once again breathed the air of sheer relief that came with the sight of the figure on the bed. He was now completely free of all the gadgets and tubes that had previously sustained him. The last of the disconnected IV drips was hanging redundant at the foot of his bed, like a labourer waiting for his bus home after a hard day's work. Biggy's body was covered with a white sheet; his head and neck were still heavily bandaged. She could see that he was peacefully asleep. His soft, regular breathing added to the air of calm and relief in the room.

At the top of the bed she spotted an electronic gadget that she recognised as the recorder. It was small, the size of a

Walkman. She inched closer and inspected it. She could tell it was fairly simple to operate, and the temptation to turn it on was only suppressed by her fear of waking him up. It was only now that she was beginning to realise just how little rest this man had had in the months she'd known him. She sat down quietly at his bedside and watched the big man sleep, feeling good, knowing he was going to be alright.

After a few minutes, though, she found herself back at the top of the bed and fiddling with the recorder. She turned it on and wound it back to the beginning. She kept the volume low and began listening without taking her eyes off the sleeping man. It sounded awkward initially, Biggy's words coming out in the high-pitched voice of Sister Mary; a voice that was helping to convert into words the thoughts of a man who could not speak for himself:

Hi, Sally-Anne. This is me, Biggy.

Short pause.

You will have to forgive me for communicating with you in this way instead of waiting to talk face to face, but I've been worrying a lot lately. Sometimes I close my eyes and I think I may never open them again. I don't know why I'm writing this to you. But you have come a long way, and you have done so much. Maybe this will give you some peace of mind. Or maybe, being from the free world, you could use it to bring some kind of justice.

Pause.

Sally-Anne, as far as I know, J'Alex and his friends are dead. They were in that lorry in Eldoret. I know this might not sound like the boy you knew, but J'Alex and his friends were part of a secret army that was in Eldoret to fight a war. The existing chaos in the country provided a perfect smokescreen. And these boys were sent there armed and trained to pose as civilians, with specific orders to kill the Nandis and the Maasai.

Pause.

Now, I guess you want to know who sent them there, who ordered them to do this. That person Sally-Anne, the person who sent these innocent young boys to their deaths, was me.

Pause.

For many years I have recruited poor young boys into a secret army. I was seventeen when I started. I was a homeless street boy; we were what they call the Parking-boys, the scum of the city. We had nothing to live for. Our friends were dropping dead on the streets everyday like flies under police gunfire, and nobody even broke stride in their normal life to pay any attention. Those who escaped the gunfire would die of drug overdose or hunger, or in prison, or from the harsh weather... you name it. Not many lived to see the age of twenty. And they all knew it. They all knew they would die sooner rather than later. So with the knowledge that there was nothing to lose, we ran riot in anger, committing all sorts of crimes and atrocities. It was a difficult time for all of us. But I was a big talker, always positive, always keeping the mood optimistic with false hopes. And they began looking up to me as leader. They respected me and listened to me, expecting me to come up with some sort of magical survival plan.

Then one day someone came to me with a proposition. They offered us guns, training, and even to pay us, to perpetrate the same crimes that we were already committing for fun. They picked me because they knew that all the Parking-boys trusted me. And I did not fail them. I turned them all into soldiers within a month. And believe it or not, the boys considered this the best thing that had ever happened to them. They loved me for it, they respected me, they worshipped me; I had offered them a new lease of life. They didn't know who they were killing or why. They killed for one reason only: they were paid to do it. I was their leader, and even I did not understand the war we were fighting, until a few months later, when I was captured.

Pause.

The police captured me, Sally-Anne. They incarcerated me and tortured me beyond human fathom. But they did not put me to trial or break up my army. Someone high up gave an order that I could be released to go and continue the killing. They even offered us more money to do what we had been doing before. The only difference was that we would be doing it for them.

Pause.

We are the army that does their dirty work when they don't want it to look like the government's hand is involved. It is better that way, politically. Every time there are scuffles between neighbouring tribes, and one tribe inexplicably appears to have greater numbers and better weapons than the other, I am responsible. My contact with them is a thick-lipped officer who calls himself Superintendent George Komarock. I am fairly sure it was they who tried to kill me, to silence me. And there is a distinct possibility that they will be back. But that's a small matter. The most important thing is that someone knows the truth. So, there you have it, Sally-Anne Symmonds. I don't know how useful this will be to you, but that is the truth.

Pause.

I did try to bring J'Alex back to you though. When you arrived with your story, I was moved. I spoke to them about it. But by that time there were so many young boys involved, and so many who had already been dispatched to remote corners of the country, that even they completely lost track. It had slipped out of my control, so all I could do was ask them nicely to bring this one boy back. They promised to track J'Alex down and do so. I just had to keep you occupied and avert any suspicion till he arrived. Then, when the Eldoret incident happened, they said J'Alex and his friends were all in that lorry. They could have lied. There's a chance that they don't know where they sent these boys or what happened to them. They may well have died in some other way that we will never know about. Or maybe they just didn't want you to have him. But again, we may never know that. This story will probably never ever reach the people that need to hear it. Nobody will go to court. I could be dead before even you hear this. But I hope you do get to hear it: it would mean a lot to me.

Pause.

Now that you know, you probably wonder what I feel about my part in all this... I'm ashamed? I'm sorry? Do I feel any remorse?

Long pause.

I buried my last remaining relative, alone, with my bare hands, when I was twelve years old. I had grown tired of rounding up villagers to help me mourn. So I dug a shallow grave and laid my grandfather to rest, then I took off for the city in which no one would even bear the sight of me. The person who first spoke to me in this city was a good kid, the kindest person I ever met in my life on the streets. He became a very good friend, and then he became my brother and my only family.

Pause.

I only knew him as Poppa, but I knew his thoughts, his hopes and his dreams. He could mend shoes. His dream was to be a cobbler, live a normal life and belong to society. He hoped that one day someone would shed a tear for him when he died. He told me that all he wished for when his time came was 'just one person to shed one tear'. That, to him, would have been enough to validate his time on this earth. And guess what, Sally-Anne? A few weeks after telling me this, he drops dead. And not one person out there even knew his real name. I watched Poppa drop dead from a gunshot and I couldn't even cry. He didn't ask for much: just one tear, one drop, and I could not even give him that.

For more than twelve years I refused to grant Poppa his one simple wish, Sally-Anne. That was until that night in the car, just before I was shot. I was just driving along, while you were sleeping peacefully. Must have been that song on the radio, I don't know, but suddenly I notice a tear rolling down my cheek. I'm sitting there in shock, wondering what is happening to me, and the tear just keeps rolling. Then somehow Poppa appears in my head, and suddenly it feels good... I tell myself 'That is for Poppa,' and it feels good. Then, all of a sudden, I'm seeing my father, my grandfather, their sickly livestock and arid farms that took away their hopes and eventually their lives... I'm seeing everyone, even my mother, who died giving birth to me. And the tears are rolling down relentlessly... and it feels good.

Pause. Sister Mary's voice begins to break with soft hissing and sobbing.

One tear drops, and I'm seeing the sweet smile on the face of innocent, wide-eyed J'Alex... Another stream, and I can see young Ozzy and Ken-Tuli happily laughing in their wrestling games... Another drop, and there's jubilant Koli running around dancing and waving his stick in the air... And I am sobbing like a little baby...

Pause, with some crackling noise from the tape, and sounds of Sister Mary snivelling and blowing her nose as her weeping intensifies. She sniffs out a soft '*Oh my God,*' which clearly isn't from Biggy.

I am so sorry, Sally-Anne... they were just kids...

Sister Mary's voice breaks down into spasmodic sobs. There is another click, then nothing but crackling and hissing.

*

Sally-Anne found herself unable to move any part of her body. Her breathing came with difficulty as she waited with bated breath for the story to go on. But there was nothing more. The hissing had turned into a distant, flowing river over which the bandaged face above the white sheet was now floating before her dampening eyes. She was biting her lower lip again, unaware that she was crying, and almost enjoying the warmth of the saline liquid rolling down her cheeks. Even the movement of her shaking left hand towards the lifeless body was totally uncontrolled; it wandered and hovered just above his face, wanting to touch but afraid to wake him up.

Then he woke up. There was no other movement apart from his eyes suddenly coming to life, and she slowly withdrew her hand. She saw that he wanted to smile at her, and a lump appeared in her throat.

'What is your name?' Another bubble rolled down the side of her nose before she finished asking.

She waited.

He looked at her, the faint attempt at a smile still noticeable.

'I just want to know your name... that's all.' The last part of her sentence almost stuck inside her throat.

He began to open his mouth. She edged closer and strained to read his lips through her tears. She couldn't.

But then she heard his voice. It was a soft faint whisper.

'They call me Biggy.'

Then he smiled, seeing that she got the joke.

'They used to call me a lot of different things, none of them good. But after a while a whole generation disappeared and there was no one left who knew any of my old names.'

He smiled, again, fully aware that she was still waiting.

'I was born Jack Jakoyo Janabi.'

She repeated after him. 'Jack... Jakoyo... Janabi.'

Then she softly traced the outline of the bandage across his forehead with her fingers and cried again.

'All I know about you, Jack, is what I saw in your eyes every morning when you woke up early to pick me up and when you dropped me off after dark. You did everything... you guided me, you protected me, you cared for me. Every day, you were the first face I saw at dawn and the last at dusk... And I saw only kindness in your eyes, Jack. I looked at your imposing figure and your rough way of life to find something I could hate, but I couldn't. I looked at your defects, and found not one wrong. You did me no wrong, Jack. Yet I failed to treat you like a human being! Not once... not once did I say, "Thank you, Jack." Not one time did I treat you like a human being, when all this time you were just trying to be good... to be a person... to be my friend.'

She wiped her eyes with the back of her hands and took a long breath before continuing. 'We may never know what happened to J'Alex or Koli or Ozzy or Ken-Tuli... but I've shed a tear for them, Jack... I have shed a tear for them.' Here, she broke down again. 'I don't want to be sitting somewhere in England, one day, years from now, wondering what ever happened to Jack Jakoyo Janabi.'

She looked into his eyes and fumbled under the sheet to find his hand. She held it and gave it a gentle squeeze.

'I am staying right here, by your side. When they let you out of this hospital, I will hold your hand. If you want to pack and run away to England with me, I will help you. If they come for you here, I will be here, and I will do whatever I can. I'm not leaving your side, even if I can't protect you. I will do whatever I can... I will do whatever I can, Jack Jakoyo Janabi... even if it is simply to shed just one tear...'

EPILOGUE

This poem was written by a fifteen-year-old wheelchair-bound paraplegic girl from an orphanage in the lakeside town of Kisumu:

> To our guests, you showed a game,
> of our leaders, you exposed shame.
> To you, was pure youth,
> what to humanity, is bitter truth.
> That no war, can yield a *win*,
> only a *settlement*, of utter ruin.
> But a game of *tip-tap*, you win,
> for you live, to play again.
> Arise, Jonathan Paul Atai Koli,
> today, my brother, you win.

If you liked this book, don't miss the author's next offering:

DUDLHAM SINGS

Visit www.michaeloren.co.uk for more information

ACKNOWLEDGMENTS

I am massively indebted to the many friends who read this book in its early draft stages and contributed immensely to its development. Ladies and gentlemen, you know yourselves and I will take time to thank you again personally. If I attempt to list individual names I'm bound to forget someone, and that wouldn't be cool. My most heartfelt thanks, however, has to go to everyone who purchased and read this book in its present form; it's because of you that I might one day be able to call myself a writer.